Sometimes They Fall

Light in the Darkest Hour

Book One

Pamela Gail

and

Denise Samples

Summary: The Oliver boys know how to hide, lie, and steal
to get what they want. The ties that bind even the closest of
families isn't always enough to keep a family whole.

ISBN: 978-1-7335521-0-3

Due to graphic content, this book is intended for readers 18
and older.

Carey

"Get the fuck off my property unless you want me to break something else! I don't ever want to see you again! Stay the hell away from me and my family!" I yell at my best friend; well former best friend now, I guess.

"Carey, please let me…"

"GO!" I yell, raising a fist. He takes a few steps back, then turns and runs.

As I watch him retreat with a bloody, broken nose, my anger boils over, and all I want to do is follow through on my threat of breaking something else. Did I do something to provoke him? I can't begin to wrap my head around what just happened. The only thing I know for certain is I just lost my best friend. I replay the past thirty minutes, trying to figure out what the hell went wrong.

Seth and I are shooting hoops in my yard even though it's almost 100 degrees. That's the great thing about living on the beach. When we get too hot, we just walk down to the water and cool off. I'm breathing heavy as I go for a layup and miss.

"Shit!" I yell. My game is off today. I know why, but I'm trying to ignore the shit storm that is my life.

"We can quit if you can't handle it," Seth teases. He knows I hate to lose.

"There is no way I am letting you win," I retort, trying to steal the ball. He spins away from me and scores again before I can stop him.

"Dude, you're down eight points. You don't stand a chance," he laughs, throwing the ball to me.

"Shut the hell up, Seth."

I dribble around him, and he almost steals the ball. This time I make the basket. I am determined, and there's no way I'm going to let him get the best of me. I'm sweating like crazy and out of breath. Maybe I should lay off the smokes. I need a water break, but I refuse to stop. Seth misses his next shot, and I get the rebound. I score another two points and close the gap a little more. The game is back and forth for a while. We both make a few shots, but miss some, too. We're playing to 30. Right now it's 22-18, and Seth's still ahead. I know I have to do something fast if I am going to win this. Seth has the ball again, and he's going for a layup. I have to take him out before he widens his lead. I run up beside him and shove him as he's jumping. It was a cheap shot, but I don't play nice when I'm losing. He hits the ground hard. At the same time, I lose my balance and land on top of him.

"Shit, Carey," he chokes out, shoving me off of him while coughing and trying to catch his breath.

"Sorry, man. Are you okay?" I ask, laughing as I start to get up. I just wanted him to miss the shot. I didn't really want to hurt him.

"Yeah, but you're not," he says, grabbing my leg and pulling me to the ground. He's on top of me and has me pinned face down before I have a chance to react. Damn him and his wrestling moves.

"Alright, I give up," I relent. He's got my arm pulled behind my back, and it hurts like hell. I'm pissed because he's winning the game, and now he just pinned me. When the hell did he get so strong? Looks like I need to start working out. Seth let's go and shoves me once more as I try to get up. Now he's just poking the bear on purpose. He should know better. I grab his arm when he offers to help me up and pull him back to the ground. We lie there for a few minutes trying to catch our breath. Finally, I get up, and offer a hand to Seth.

"Are you okay, man? I would say that I wasn't trying to hurt you, but we both know I'd be lying," I joke, pulling him to his feet.

"Well, I know what an asshole you are when you lose. That's why I usually let you win," Seth teases.

"Fuck off," I laugh, pushing him. He stumbles a little, but grabs my arm to steady himself and pulls me closer in the process. We're inches apart for an awkward moment. I start to turn away because I don't know what the hell is going on, but he pulls me toward him. At the same time, he leans in and our lips barely touch before I step back and shove him away.

"What the fuck, Seth?" I yell, punching him in the face as hard as I can, sending him to the ground. He curses and covers his nose with his hands, but I can see blood seeping through his fingers. I'm sure I broke his nose, and I think I broke my hand. I shake it trying to ease the pain and keep yelling not giving Seth a chance to respond.

After going through everything that just occurred, I know for certain that I didn't do anything to provoke Seth. I'm in a daze as I walk to my front porch and sit on the swing. There are a hundred questions running through my head, and my hand is throbbing. I just can't understand why he did that. Is he gay? How could he keep this from me? No, I know Seth isn't gay. He has been going through a lot lately, but I don't care. He can stay the hell away from me. Who needs friends anyway? Especially, ones who try to kiss you.

Seth has been my best friend my whole life. All 15 years of it. We grew up on the same street. The only thing separating our houses from the beach is two sets of dunes. Our mothers became friends when my parents bought the house three doors down from Mr. and Mrs. Kelley. That was when my mom was pregnant with my oldest brother, Jason. About four years later, Seth and I were born nine months apart. Seth is the oldest in his family with a younger sister. I'm the third of four boys.

Seth is a little taller than me, and we both have dark, brown hair. He keeps his cut short, but mine falls just past my chin. My eyes are brown where his are green. We've been mistaken for brothers more than once. It's been years since we even bothered correcting people. Sometimes, I feel like he is more of a brother than my own. We were friends from the beginning, being forced to play while our mothers spent time together. After my mother left, Seth's mom, Melody, started helping my dad with us boys. Between their house and the diner Mrs. Kelley owns, we spent as much time with the Kelley's as we did at our own home.

My dad is a detective for the county. Melody would often watch us when he had to work late on a case. Even as we got older and my brothers made other friends, Seth and I remained close. His mom is the closest thing to a mother I have ever known. Mrs. Kelley is a truly wonderful person and has always been an important part of my life. She's kind and caring and continues to be one of the few constants I can always count on. Plus, her pie is to die for!

Growing up, Seth and I spent most of our weekends hanging out, playing football or basketball, surfing, watching sports on TV, or playing video games. To be honest, I had other things that I would rather do. Don't get me wrong, I'm good at sports, and I like spending time with my brothers and friends, but I have passions that I can never reveal to any of them. It doesn't matter how close we are, they would never understand or even want to know the real me and the things that get me excited about the future. I've never felt like Seth or my brothers would appreciate my love for writing, or music. So I've always hid my interest to protect myself.

Today was one of those rare Saturdays when it was just the two of us. Usually, at least one of my brothers is around. Sometimes his sister, Rachel, will tag along when his mom needs a sitter. She's a couple of years younger, really annoying, and I hate having her around. Rachel and I have never really gotten along because she's nothing but a brat. She's always trying to get me in trouble by being a tattle tale. She thinks she knows more than anyone else and doesn't mind telling me. I try to be nice to her for Seth, but sometimes it's just impossible.

I'm still reeling when a car door catches my attention. I look up to see my younger brother, Sean, being dropped off at the end of the driveway. I quickly make my way inside and head upstairs to take a shower. I need to get myself together before I speak to Sean. He'll know something's up, and I don't want to share this with him. I start the shower and find some ibuprofen in the cabinet. The steaming, hot water feels great, and I wish I could wash away everything that has happened in the past hour.

Hell, in the past three years.

I've been so lost in my own thoughts, I didn't realize the water had turned cold until a knock on the door brings me back to the present.

"You okay, Care?" Sean calls from the other side.

"Yeah," my voice breaks as I choke back tears. I don't need Sean realizing that something is up. He picks up on things quicker than any of us. Sean and I have always been close. He's only eleven months younger, and we've shared a room since he was born. I clear my throat and try again.

"I'll be right out, man," I call, turning off the ice cold shower. I dry off and pull on the gym shorts I grabbed from the bedroom. My hand really hurts. It's swollen and starting to bruise. I probably need to see a doctor, but I'm not up for explaining how I injured it. When I open the door, Sean is nowhere in sight. He must have accepted that I'm fine and gone back downstairs. I head into the bedroom and walk past Sean's spotless side of the room to search the clothes tossed everywhere on my side. Sean is always organized. Everything has a place and nothing is ever left where it doesn't belong. It grates on my nerves.

I finally find my favorite Black Sails shirt, and give it the old sniff test. It's clean enough so I pull it on. Black Sails is the best metal band out there. I would give anything to see them in concert.

I pick up my phone and see three texts from Seth.

I delete them without reading them, and send one to him.

Stay away from me or you'll be sorry.

I hope that's the last contact I ever have with him, but I know that's wishful thinking. We live on the same street and school will be starting back soon. I have no idea what he was thinking, but I'm more than willing to give up fifteen years of friendship. No explanation needed. That might make me the biggest asshole alive, but I don't care. It's his own fault for trying to kiss me. He should have at least told me he has the hots for me. Honestly, it may have kept him from getting a broken nose. I've got enough shit in my life. I don't need this from him.

I head downstairs trying to ignore the pain in my hand, but it's excruciating. I join Sean on the couch to watch the rest of the Braves game. I would rather watch football or basketball, but since it's July, we have to settle for baseball. Sean watches baseball, but he actually prefers to skip the sports. He keeps quiet about it always being on TV because it keeps us from picking on him.

Sean definitely looks different from the rest of us. He's got these long bangs that hang in his eyes and are dyed green. The rest of his hair is short and brown. It looks stupid, and my older brothers and I have no problem telling him that on a regular basis.

Still, Sean is the baby, and we would do anything to protect him from other people. None of us will ever let other kids say the things we say to him. He likes manga and anime and is even in some ridiculous club where they play these fantasy, role playing, card games. I don't understand how my baby brother became such a weirdo. I tried watching one of those anime shows with him, but it's nothing more than a cartoon. Why can't he just be like the rest of the family? I know I sound hypocritical since I'm not into sports like our older brothers or Dad. The difference is I am smart enough to pretend so they don't have ammunition against me.

He seems to be into the game so I refrain from making any derogatory comments at the moment. There will be plenty of time for that later. We watch in silence for a while. Then at the bottom of the ninth inning with the Braves down two runs with guys on first and second, their rookie hits a home-run to win the game. You don't have to care about the game to know it was an awesome play. We start cheering and yelling. I high-five Sean without thinking about my hand.

"Shit!" I yell, attempting to shake the pain away.

"Dude, you okay?" Sean asks with concern.

"Yeah, I'm fine," I lie.

"What's up with your hand? I'm guessing it wasn't a freak high-fiving accident."

"No, dip shit. It wasn't a 'freak high-fiving accident,'" I roll my eyes.

"So, are you going to tell me what happened?"

"No, I'm not!" I snap. "I'm fine," I say, sinking back into the leather couch and turning up the volume on the TV He is quiet for a few minutes, and I hope he is going drop it.

"Call Riley," he says, picking my phone up from the coffee table and handing it to me.

"Hell no! I said I'm fine," I say, standing to leave. I don't need this on top of my shitty day. I hate my uncle. He is the last person I want to call. Granted he is an ER doctor, and I probably should go see him. My hand is throbbing.

"It looks like it really hurts, Carey. You need to call." I know Sean won't drop this.

"Fine," I concede, taking the phone from him. It rings several times, and I am about to hang up when Riley finally answers.

"Dr. Oliver," he sounds winded. He is probably really busy.

"Uncle Riley. It's Carey."

"What do you want, Carey? I'm at work." Why does he always have to be such a dick?

"Um...," I hesitate.

"What?" he clips clearly annoyed.

"I think I broke my hand playing basketball."

"Well, what do you want me to do about it?" he asks exasperated.

"Really? I need an x-ray or something. I don't know, Riley. You're the damn doctor." Why does he always have to be such a jackass?

"Watch your mouth, boy," He scolds. "Meet me at the ER in an hour. Can your little, pansy ass wait that long?"

"Sure," is all I manage. I hang up before I say something that will get me in trouble. I sit down on the couch with a sigh. Riley is always a jerk to me, and I'm not looking forward to seeing that asshole.

"He said to meet him at the ER in an hour," I tell Sean.

"Call Nick. He'll come home and drive you." Nick is two years older than me with short, dark, blonde hair. He's a dumb jock and doesn't think about much other than playing defense for our high school football team. At seventeen, he's already 6'1" and built like a brick shit house.

"I'll drive myself. Jason's car is here," I say, hoping Sean will go along with it, but knowing he won't. Jason is the oldest at nineteen with dark, brown, shoulder length hair. It's a little longer than mine, but my hair is wavy while his is straight. All of my brothers have blue eyes, but mine are brown. Jason says it's because I'm full of shit. He might be right.

"You're fifteen. You don't even have a learner's permit. Besides, Jason will kill you if you touch his baby. He probably even knows the mileage and how much gas is in it." Sean has a point. Jason treats his car better than any girl he has ever been with, and he's been with plenty of girls.

Jason and Nick both think they're car guys.

Dumbasses. Jason knows a little, but they always call me when it is anything major because I know more about modifying and fixing them. All Nick knows is how to race cars. He races out on Route 1 at the dirt track on the back side of the Curtis farm where guys have been going to race since our grandparents were teenagers.

"It'll be fine. Jason will never know," I say, standing up.

"No way. I'm not going along with this," Sean says, getting in my face like he thinks he can stop me. We are almost the exact same size. He is about an inch shorter than me, but he is skinny and weak. I doubt he has a muscle anywhere on him. He pulls his phone out, no doubt to call Nick for me.

"I said I would get myself there!" I yell, grabbing his phone out of his hand and throwing it across the room.

"What the hell, Carey?"

"Stay out of this!" I yell, shoving past him, grabbing the extra set of keys from the hook, and slamming the door behind me.

"Carey, CAREY!" I hear him yell as I close the car door. I almost hit a parked car when I screech out of the driveway and speed down the road. I have no idea why I'm taking this out on Sean. I guess because he was the only one there. I hope I didn't break his phone. I don't have the money to replace it, and there is no way Dad will pay for it when he finds out that I threw it on purpose.

Sean

"Carey, CAREY!" I call after my brother. What the hell is he thinking driving Jason's car? Jason LOVES his car. He will kick Carey's ass if he finds out. I watch Carey almost hit a car as he races out of the driveway. Once he is out of sight, I go back inside to see what kind of damage he did when he threw my phone. It's in three pieces. After I put the battery back in and snap the back on, I realize the screen is cracked. It powers on when I press the button on the side. I breathe a sigh of relief. At least it still works. I take care of my stuff, and now I have to deal with a cracked screen because Carey can't control his temper. I am so frustrated with him. I try calling him several times as I pace the living room, but of course he doesn't pick up. I need to get my mind on something else, so I grab my newest manga from my room and head out to the front porch swing.

What is wrong with him? He's always been a hot-head, but lately something else is going on and he won't tell me. He's become more and more angry and keeps pushing me away.

Even though we share a room, we're becoming strangers. I feel like he's hiding things from me, but when I try to talk to him, he just gets furious. There was a time when we told each other everything. My mind can't focus on the book and keeps wandering back to my brother.

I know I should call my dad and tell him that Carey took the car, but it's hell on everyone when Carey is angry, and I don't want to give him another reason to be pissed off at me. I would rather cover for him than deal with his wrath. Brothers can be jerks, but lately Carey has been down right mean.

Even more than the way he treats me, it kills me knowing that he is going through something that he doesn't feel like he can share with me. I can't stand to see him hurting. He's not the only one keeping secrets. I have secrets, too. I know he is doing drugs. I saw him smoking pot at a party a couple of months ago. When I asked him about it, he said it was a one time thing, which I know was an outright lie. Claimed it was the first time he had tried it; another lie.

The next week, his bottom desk drawer was left unlocked, which never happens. I took the liberty to look inside. It appeared to just have some notebooks and pens, but as I moved those aside something caught my eye. It looked like the wood in one area was a slightly different color. I pushed on it in several different places until it finally popped loose revealing another compartment. I knew he must be hiding something significant if there was a false bottom in his drawer. I found some pills, a couple of packs of cigarettes, several hundred dollars, and a bag of weed with rolling papers. I've never told anyone what I found.

I don't know if the changes in him are because he's using or if he's using because there are things going on I don't know about. Either way, I am scared for him, and I don't know how to help him.

I try to read a few more pages as I continue waiting on the front porch swing. It takes forever for Carey to get back from the hospital. I'm freaking out that someone is going to come home. I can't cover for him if the car is missing. It's been close to three hours when I finally hear the car coming down the street. He screeches back into the driveway almost taking out the mailbox. Wow, he really sucks at driving. He looks irate as soon as he spots me.

Carey

Well, shit. Jason is going to kill me if he finds out that I used his car. My dad will ground me for the rest of my life. Sean is right, I just turned fifteen a few weeks ago and don't even have my learner's permit. Not that having a learner's would make this okay. My cell keeps ringing in the cup holder, but I ignore it. Good, his phone must be working. I know it's Sean, and I don't feel like listening to him lecture me right now. He is such a little, goody two-shoes; always doing the right thing and following the rules. I pull into the parking lot at the hospital and walk into the lobby of the emergency room.

"I'm here to see Dr. Oliver," I tell the nurse at the desk.

"Name?"

"Carey Oliver."

"Fill out these papers."

"I don't think I can fill those out. I broke my hand," I tell her, refusing to take the clipboard.

She looks at my right hand and sees that it is swollen and bruised. It hurt like hell trying to drive the car. I didn't really think the whole broken hand thing through before hopping into a car with a manual transmission.

"How old are you?" She looks at me skeptically.

"Fifteen."

"Have your parent fill it out for you," she says with finality, pushing the clipboard my way.

"I came alone," I deadpan, pushing it back towards her.

"I can't check you in without a parent or legal guardian."

"Dr. Oliver is my uncle. He's expecting me." She eyes me with uncertainty before she finally gives up.

"Fine. Have a seat, and I'll let him know you're here."

I sit down, wishing he would just hurry up and give me something for the pain. I should have rummaged through the house and found something stronger than ibuprofen. With a house full of boys, there have been plenty of injuries and broken bones over the years. Surely, I could have found some pain pills, but maybe not since I usually borrow a few from every prescription someone gets.

"Carey Oliver." When my name is called, I make my way toward the door leading to the back.

"I'm Carey," I say, approaching the nurse.

"Hi, Carey. I'm Macy," the nurse says with a smile.

She's really pretty with with long, black hair and beautiful green eyes. Seth is the only other person I have ever met with that combination. Stop it Carey! I refuse to ever think about him again!

"You can sit in here. Dr. Oliver will be right with you," Macy pats the table.

"Thanks," I mumble, getting more pissed at myself.

"Are you related to him?" she asks, smiling at me again.

"Yep. Someone has to be," I clip sharper than I should. I don't look at her, and finally she gets annoyed and leaves with a sigh. I wasn't trying to be an ass, but thinking about Seth has me pissed off all over again. Plus, I just don't want to be here facing Riley. It seems to take forever for him to arrive. Sitting here waiting gives me time to think. I start to worry that Dad or Jason will get home before me and find the car is gone. It's not the first time I borrowed a car without asking. Hell, I've even borrowed a few cars that didn't belong to family members. I hate having no control over how long this will take. I'm getting more and more antsy to get back home with the car.

"Hello again, Carey. I'm going to take your vitals. Dr. Oliver will be in soon." The same nurse who walked me back comes into the room and proceeds to check my temperature, listen to my heart, check oxygen levels, and all the other crap you have to go through. As she's finishing up, Riley walks in. He asks Macy about my vitals, thanks her, and then she leaves.

"Let me see the hand," he says.

"What? No 'how are you' or 'good to see you?'" I ask sarcastically. He just gives me an annoyed look, and then proceeds to lift my arm and poke around my hand.

"Shit, Riley, that hurts!" I pull my hand away. "I already told you it's broken. Why are you making it worse?" He rolls his eyes and sighs with exasperation.

"I'll order an x-ray to see how bad the break is, and then we'll go from there. Where's your dad?"

"He wasn't home so I got a ride with a friend," I lie. It wouldn't go over well if he knew I drove myself. "I'll call when I'm done, and he can come get me." I hope Riley is too busy to follow up.

"Radiology will be in soon to take you to x-ray," he says and closes the door behind him. Always so pleasant to be around Riley. I know why he hates me so much and the feeling is mutual, but I have to act normal around my brothers. It would kill them to know the truth.

It took longer than I expected at the hospital. My hand is broken in two places. I'll have the cast for several weeks, but at least I managed to score some good pain meds. I thanked Macy since Riley never came back to see me. He did sign off on the papers to release me, so I head for the car.

My hand is throbbing even though the nurse gave me two pain pills about an hour ago. She told me to take two every four hours as needed for pain. Wait, maybe it was four every two hours. Doesn't matter. I'm in pain so it's probably best to take a couple more now. I pop two more in my mouth, wash them down with the energy drink I bought from the vending machine on my way out, and head home. If I thought it was hard to drive the car here, man was I wrong. Driving a manual transmission with a cast on your right hand is impossible. I hope I don't get pulled over. I'm praying the whole way that I'll make it back without wrecking the car or getting stopped and that

Sean is still the only one home. That's a lot of praying for someone who has never been to church.

Dad is on a case and will hopefully be late. Nick is with some friends or on a date. Who really knows? Jason is out on the boat with his friend, Brody, probably banging another nameless chick or two, so there is no way to know when he will get back. As I pull into the driveway, I'm relieved to see no one but Sean is home. Maybe my luck is changing after all.

Jason

I love the weekends; no school, no work, just me and a bunch of chicks. Who am I kidding? I don't actually go to school anymore. My dad insisted that I go to college even though I knew it was a bad idea. I managed to pass five classes my freshman year. Three the first semester and two the second semester. Granted most of those were D's. After I earned a 0.8 GPA the first semester, I was put on academic probation. I was invited not to return after I rocked the 0.6 GPA the second semester. I proved my point; I'm not college material. My dad was pissed and decided that I had to get a job if I'm not going to be in school.

I've been home for about six weeks and already have experience working in fast food, landscaping, and retail. I got fired from my fourth job yesterday. *Apparently*, you can't tell a lady that her ass does in fact look fat in her outfit. She didn't ask, and I was working at a gift shop, but damn her ass was huge, and she was being a total bitch. I haven't told my dad yet. Those jobs were stupid anyway.

I need a job where I can party and have fun with hot chicks. I have a vision and have been working on it for a few months. I've been scoping out some properties and researching what I'll need to make this happen. I'll either have to get a partner or I'll have to wait until I turn 21 to get the liquor license. That isn't for another eighteen months. I'm not sure how my dad will react when I tell him, but I am absolutely going to open a strip club. This town has plenty of hot girls and no strip club. It's a win win for me.

Today, I'm heading out on the boat with a group of friends. Okay, one friend and a group of girls. Brody and I don't have friends who are girls. We have girls we bang and girls we don't. There are very few in the don't category. Neither of us really cares what she looks like or her size as long as she's willing to spread her legs. We've had this contest going since we were thirteen, and Brody found out that I lost my virginity to a high school chick. He was jealous and found some girl to bag the next weekend. Since then, we've kept a running tab to see who can get laid 250 times first. I am up to 198. Brody isn't far behind with 193. Today, we have six girls on the boat with us. I know we will both be getting laid by at least a couple of them. I've already had two of them, but who cares. I have no problem with chicks coming back for seconds. It only proves that I am as awesome as I know I am. Maybe we can talk at least one of them into letting us share. I have no interest in guys, but it's hot as hell when a girl will let us go at her from both ends. Brody and I have done that several times over the years. It's sort of our specialty.

We head out toward one of the barrier islands where we can anchor a little off shore. We'll be able to dinghy onto the beach or swim off the side of the boat. This way if Brody or I need some privacy, the others still have somewhere to go. By the time Brody drops the anchor, I already have Brittany in my lap. She is smoking hot, but makes a box of rocks look like a Mensa party. Her hand is down my bathing suit and if she doesn't let up soon, I'm not going to last. By the laugh I hear from Brody as he steps onto the stern, he must know what she's doing. He quickly loads the cooler onto the dinghy.

"Why don't I head to shore with the other girls? Text me when you're done, and I'll come back for you two," he winks.

"Thanks," is all I can manage. He knows I would do the same for him. As soon as they pull away, her lips are on mine. I pull her hand out so I can have a minute to get myself together. I don't spend long kissing her lips. It's a little too intimate for me, plus I would rather have my mouth in other places. I push her to her feet and take off the sheer bathing suit cover from her body. Then, I make quick work of removing the red, string bikini. As soon as I have her naked, I stand up and park her in the chair. I am well aware that any boat passing by can see us, but neither of us care. I push her legs open, then toward her chest. She is resting on the edge of the chair completely open to me.

I kneel in front of her and run my tongue along her folds. Her soft moans spur me on. She tastes so damn good. I lick her for a while and then push my tongue inside her sweet opening. She cries out in pleasure. Now she is at my mercy. I rub the pad of my thumb over her clit, and she begins to move against my face. I rub her harder as I fuck her with my tongue. It doesn't take long before her orgasm surfaces. I need to hurry if I'm going to take what I really want before she comes down from her orgasmic high. I slowly lick down and start to rim her hole before she can stop me. I'll give attention to her sweet ass for as long as she'll let me. Some girls make me stop when their brains catch up, but Brittany doesn't stop me even as her breathing slows.

"That feels so good," she moans. As soon as the words leave her lips, I push my tongue into her back hole. If she'll let me toss her salad, she'll probably let me do anything I want.

"Jason," she starts, but I reach up and cover her mouth. I don't want to hear her say my name. I rarely remember the girl's name, and I prefer that goes both ways. Sometimes, I don't even ask them their name. My hand doesn't stay on her mouth long. As I continue to tongue her ass, I push two fingers into her soaked pussy while rubbing my thumb over her clit again. My other hand finds her small tits and begins massaging one and then the other. My cock is painfully hard, and if I don't get inside of her soon, I am going to blow my load in my bathing suit.

I can feel her second orgasm building, so I pinch her nipple harder than necessary. Her scream is a mix of pain and pleasure as her juices coat my hand. I suck her sweet nectar from my fingers. While she gets herself under control for the second time, I remove my bathing suit and slip on a condom.

"Stand up and turn around," I tell her as I pull her to her feet. I place her hands on the arms of the chair.

"Hold on, babe," I whisper in her ear. I push into her soaked pussy and rock back and forth several times coating my cock. Then, I slowly push into her ass. I know her juices aren't much in the way of lube, but it's all I have. She cries out a little when my tip pushes in. I wait a minute for her to adjust, but not long enough for her to change her mind. Then, I push myself all the way into her tight ass. When I am balls deep, I stop. She needs time to adjust to my thickness, and I need a second or I'm going to blow. I start moving. Slowly at first, pulling myself almost all the way out and then slamming into her. My thrusts quickly become faster and harder as my need for release takes over. She is moaning and crying out in pleasure, or pain, I don't care which. Damn, this girl's a good fuck. She is too fucking tight around my cock. Before I am ready, I explode into the condom.

"199!"

"What?" She asks.

"Nothing." I pull out, tie the end of the condom, and put it in the trash. I hand Brittany her towel without saying anything before I hit the head to clean myself up. It may be a dick move to leave her naked on the stern while I go inside, but she's just a lay. I don't give a shit about her feelings. By the time I'm done, she's dressed, and I can see Brody approaching in the dinghy. I texted him while I was below deck.

"That was amazing, Jason," she smiles wrapping her arms around me. I hate it when a girl smiles like that. She better not get all clingy because I don't plan for her to be the only girl I bang today. I remove her hands from my waist and step back.

"I'm always amazing. Just ask your friend," I say, referring to the girl who invited her. There is a flash of hurt in her eyes, as if she thought she was special. Recovering quickly, she fakes a laugh, and then looks away.

Nick

Saturday afternoon on the beach is the best. We won't have weekend team meetings or workouts until football season starts so I'm able to relax after my morning run. My buddies and I drink, surf, and pick up chicks. Life doesn't get much better. Several guys from the team and I are hanging at our usual spot on the pier when we spot a few of the losers from school and make our way over. I love the power trip I get from fucking with losers. This is Sean's crowd, and I'm glad to see he isn't with them. I try to back off some when he's around. I can't understand why he hangs out with these kids. How my baby brother became such a freak is beyond me because I know I taught him better than that. He should be into sports and partying like the rest of the family, but instead he has green hair and watches cartoons. He's just as much of a weirdo as these kids.

"Hey dumbasses," I start. They try to walk away, but we block their path. I knock a drink out of some nerd's hand and shove him hard.

"Leave me alone," he says quietly.

"What?" I yell, holding my hand to my ear. "I can't hear you, jizz breath."

"I said leave me alone," he says a little louder, but it is still a whisper.

"Don't tell me what to do, you fucktard," I say, pushing him against the railing.

"What are you going to do about it, loser?" I taunt. The laughs coming from my friends spur me on.

"Come on, just let us go," he begs.

"Fuck, no," I say, shoving him again. "You're mine, bitch."

"Back off!" Sam tells me. I hate him the most. He thinks he can stand up to us, but he's wrong. He and Sean are becoming good friends, and I blame him for dragging my brother down.

"Did I give you permission to speak to me, butt monkey?" I ask, turning on him. He flinches and looks like he might cry, but stands his ground.

"I don't need your permission to speak."

"See, that's where you're wrong, dickhead," I say, grabbing him by the front of his shirt. "We own this town. No one messes with us. In case you haven't noticed, people do what we say, when I say to." My friends continue to block the stairs so Sam and his cocksuckers can't get past us.

"You and your little loser friends need to stay off my pier. You don't belong here. Next time I find one of you shitheads disobeying me, I won't be so nice," I tell him, then snap my fingers at one of my friends. He takes the red slushie from another loser and hands it to me. I pour it over Sam's head. Then shove him toward the steps.

"Get the fuck off my pier. NOW!" The group scrambles, getting out of there as fast as possible. It's fucking hilarious.

"That was awesome!" Truck says, clapping me on the back. He's the biggest guy on our team and the best defensive player we have. We call him Truck because he can stop just about anyone in their tracks.

Our adrenaline is pumping now. We'll be bragging about this for days as we ride the high from getting the best of those losers. It's one of the few reasons I enjoy going to school. Damn, that was almost as fun as football.

Carey

When I get back, Sean is waiting on the front porch, and he is pissed.

"Thanks for waiting up, Dad," I say sarcastically.

"What the hell were you thinking? You can't drive."

"Technically, I can drive."

"Technically, you suck at driving," he bites back.

"At least that's the only thing I suck." Guilt eats at me when I see a flash of hurt in Sean's eyes. I don't know why I said that. I've heard the rumors about Sean and Sam being gay. Nick makes asinine comments all the time. I know the rumors aren't true, but pride won't let me apologize.

"Dad is going to kick your ass," Sean recovers and turns the conversation back to me.

"No, he isn't. He isn't going to find out, baby brother," I say pointedly, poking a finger into his chest.

"Don't call me that," he whispers, focusing on the ground. He hates being called baby brother. I roll my eyes and head for the door.

"You better be glad that no one came home. I've been freaking out for three hours."

I walk inside while he's talking, and close the door in his face. It will just get him angrier, but knowing Sean he won't say anything. He usually keeps his thoughts and opinions to himself, and we all take advantage of him. We treat him like a baby, even though he's entering high school in a few weeks. We always boss him around, and he usually listens without argument. I am definitely the worst about it and have talked him into to a lot of things that could have gotten him in trouble or hurt. It's selfish, but what can I say, I'm a dick.

As expected, Sean doesn't follow me inside. He retreats to the porch swing to mope. I'm glad because I'm feeling light headed from all of the pain meds and don't need him to see me sway like a drunk. I slowly make my way upstairs hoping to get to my bed before I fall over. I run into the wall a few times, but make it to my room. I just need to sleep off the pills. It's not the first time I've taken something like this. Nothing too heavy, just some painkillers and pot. I also drink, but so do all of my brothers. My dad even buys it for us. He would go ballistic on me though if he knew I was using drugs. He only allows us to drink when we're at home and not planning to go anywhere. However, none of us adhere to that rule when he isn't around. Being a cop for years and now a detective, he has seen some bad stuff go down over drugs. He's always lectured us on staying away from them at all cost, but he doesn't think drinking is a big deal and will even sit and have a beer with us when he's home. It's kind of cool.

The next thing I know, it's after seven, and I'm groggy from my afternoon nap. Dad must still be at work, otherwise he would have woken me and made me come down for dinner. He's so weird about us all eating together when he's home.

My hand is killing me, I have a massive headache, and my stomach is in knots. Probably wasn't a good idea to take all those pills on an empty stomach. I haven't eaten since breakfast, and that was just coffee and a protein bar almost twelve hours ago. I reach for the pills on my nightstand and pour two out. Picking them up with my good hand, I head to the bathroom for some water. Leaning down, I drink directly from the faucet, and swallow the pills. I'll run out quickly at this rate. I rummage through the medicine cabinet in the bathroom that Sean and I share and find some pain pills from last year when he inexplicably cracked a rib. He said he fell down the stairs, but I don't believe him. Sean isn't that clumsy.

Score! The bottle is almost full. Sean will notice if it's missing, so I pour the contents into my bottle and fill his with aspirin that are similar in shape and size. I put it back the exact way I found it to keep from raising his suspicion, then sneak down the hall to the bathroom that Nick and Jason share. I don't make a sound and try to listen for anyone else. Nick's door is open, and I see that he isn't inside. Jason's door is closed, but that could mean anything. He never leaves the door open even when he's out.

He could still be on the boat or he could be in his room with a girl. After all, he's been sneaking girls into his room for years. No one is around so I slip inside.

Silently, I search their medicine cabinet. There are two bottles on one of the shelves, both from times when Jason got hurt playing football in high school. One bottle only has about five pills left, but the other one is over half full. I pocket the half full bottle quickly, but leave the other one behind for later.

The bathroom window faces the front of the house. Dad's car isn't outside so that means he's still at work. I quickly make my way to the other end of the hall and enter his bedroom. I look in his bathroom as well, but find nothing. I take the stash back to my room. This should get me by for awhile. By the time I'm out, it should be realistic for me to get a refill, I just have to act like I'm still in pain. I faked a pulled muscle a few months ago and Riley prescribed so good shit for me with no problem.

I have a contact who I usually buy from, but he's getting too expensive. I wish I had been smart enough to check for a stash at my mom's house after she died. At the time, I was only twelve, and it didn't occur to me. I hide all of the pills in my desk drawer where I built a false bottom a while back to hide pot and cigarettes. My drawer holds a nice collection of painkillers. It's good to have variety.

I head downstairs for some food. Man, I'm starving. Nick and Sean are on the couch watching a movie, but Jason is nowhere in sight.

"What's for dinner?" I ask. Sean doesn't respond. He doesn't even glance my way.

Great! If he keeps acting like that Nick will know something is up and get all nosy. Sean will usually keep his mouth shut unless Nick starts asking questions. Then, Sean will get all weird and nervous and spill his guts. I am officially screwed if he doesn't get over himself.

"There's pizza on the counter," Nick says.

"Sweet!" I respond, making a beeline for the kitchen. Thankful my dad keeps the fridge stocked, I grab the box with the whole pepperoni pizza still inside and two beers then head back to the living room to join my brothers. I eat several slices of pizza, then down half of the first beer. Sean better keep his shit together.

"Where's Seth?" Nick asks. Crap. I should have known he would ask. It's unusual for Seth not to be here when I'm home. I steel myself and try not to sound angry when I speak.

"He had a date," I say, hoping I sound convincing.

"Yeah? Good for him. Who's the girl?"

"I don't know, Nick," I snap.

"Okay, sorry I asked," he says, rolling his eyes. "Jealous much?"

"I am not jealous of him!" I yell.

He laughs. "Dude, I'm just kidding. Calm down."

Stupid, stupid, stupid. Could I be any more obvious that something is up? I finish off the pizza and the second beer without another word. I shouldn't have gotten so angry. Nick has no idea that I hate Seth, and I have no intention of telling anyone, ever.

I'm getting a buzz a lot quicker than I should. Probably not the best idea to drink right after taking those pills. I finish watching the movie with my brothers. Jason comes home about the time it ends and him and Nick disappear upstairs. The tension is thick with just Sean and me. Finally, he gets up and goes to the kitchen, probably to clean up and avoid me. Like the asshole that I am, I follow him in there. I just can't leave well enough alone.

"Aw, look, the good son is cleaning up so Daddy will be proud," I say in my most condescending voice.

"Fuck off, Carey."

"Language," I scold, acting horrified. "Look, we need to talk abo…"

"Don't worry, I'm not going to tell on you. There's nothing to talk about. You're a dumbass for using Jason's car, but you'll dig yourself into a hole you can't get out of eventually. I just hope it's before you end up in jail or dead."

He walks away and slams the back door when he leaves. I stand there a little surprised at first. Sean rarely cusses and isn't usually that vocal with his opinions. It kind of pisses me off, but makes me proud at the same time. He acts like I am some kind of criminal or something. I don't do anything that bad or harmful.

Screw this! I grab two more beers from the fridge and head to my room. It's only been a couple of hours since I took the last two pills, but I need more to wash away my anger for a couple of hours. I'm angry at Sean for being such a jerk to me, angry at Seth for trying to kiss me, angry that I broke my hand, and still angry at my mom. Angry tears start filling my eyes as I make my way up the stairs. I blink them away. I'm not going there tonight. I need to put everything out of my mind, just for a little while. Sitting on my bed, I put my earbuds in and start my favorite playlist. I wash down a couple more pills with the beers. The playlist starts slow with a couple of ballads from two of my favorite metal bands. My taste in music is nothing like my brothers'. The heavier, the better; none of that cookie cutter, pop crap for me. As the songs get heavier and angrier, I begin to feel calmer and more relaxed. I don't know if it's the music, beers, or drugs. I don't care as long as it pushes away the pain.

Nick

I follow Jason upstairs leaving Carey and Sean alone. They must have had a fight. I could feel the tension in the room, and they are both clearly pissed off. I'm staying out of their little boy drama. They're probably fighting over something stupid like who gets the last grape popsicle. I have a race tonight and need to get my mind on that and off the babies in the living room.

"How was the boat?" I ask, closing Jason's door behind me.

"Exhausting," he winks.

"Damn, you know you could pass some of that my way," I say, shaking my head. Jason can get any girl to spread her legs for him. I don't know how he does it.

"Like you have a problem getting laid," he says.

"Not usually," I agree even though it isn't true. Jason thinks I get laid as much as him, but I don't. Believe it or not there are actually girls who have turned me down. Girls are complicated. I prefer to be on the football field where I know I can always make the play.

"You ready for the race? Who are you up against?"

"I'm ready. I've got Gator in the first race. After I beat him, I'll be taking Skin in the second race."

"Shit, Skin's tough to beat." Jason rubs the back of his neck. "I think he's adding some kind of boost to his car. It's wicked fast."

"I can take him. It won't be the first time I've beaten him. Never doubt me, brother."

"I don't doubt you. I'm just saying his car is fast, and he doesn't always race fair."

"Neither do I." It's true. If needed, I'm not afraid to play dirty, and Skin's an asshole. Jason's probably right. I've always suspected Skin uses something illegal in his car. Not that there are any real rules at The Pond. Just some unspoken guidelines that most of us follow.

"Be careful. I don't want to explain to Dad why you and your car need to be fished out of the pond," he laughs.

The Curtis farm is over 1,000 acres of land that was once a working farm. Now, it's just acre after acre of overgrown land with a small farmhouse that sits at the front of the property. Mr. Curtis still lives there. A hidden dirt road leads to the backside of the property where a pond sits, surrounded by a grove of trees. We race on the track that circles the pond and more than once cars have ended up in the water. Dad would kill me if he knew. When he agreed to buy Jason the '69 Pontiac GTO and me a '68 Mustang GT Fastback, there were endless lectures on safe driving and no racing. Of course, Jason and I agreed with no problem. However, that didn't stop me from racing out there almost every weekend. I'm quickly making a name for myself as one of the best in town.

We drive down the hidden dirt road and pass the line of trees dotted with cars. There's no light out here so everyone parks just inside the treeline facing the water so the headlights light up the track. As we pull up to the clearing around the water, my car is immediately surrounded by groupies. This shit never gets old.

The first race starts at ten-thirty. Usually just some newbies trying to act tough. The real competition starts at eleven. There are two groups before me so my races will start closer to midnight. Since I have the last two runs of the night, I watch the first race. The two idiots wreck before they make it a quarter of the way around the track. Clearly, neither one knows what he's doing. Gator keeps his distance as the next race starts. I think he's scared of me. Pussy.

"Hey, Nick," some girls from school call dreamily as they pass. I give them a slight nod. I can't deal with them right now. I need to stay focused on my race.

"Ladies," Jason winks. The girls giggle at his attention, and I swear one of them licks her lips knowingly.

"Ready to lose, Oliver?" Skin walks up behind me. Jason and I turn to face him as the races continue in the background.

"That's not fucking happening, and you know it," I counter.

"Dream on. Tonight's my night. Guaranteed," Skin pops off confidently.

"You'll never beat my brother," Jason steps up to Skin. Jason has several inches and about fifty pounds of muscle on Skin. Skin takes a visible step back. "Nick's proven that more than once."

"He got lucky those times."

"Luck?" I question. "Try skill, asshole."

"You have no skills, Oliver. Trust me. I've seen you on the football field." He's pissing me off on purpose. I take a step toward him ready to solve this problem with my fist, but Jason steps between us. He looks at me while speaking to Skin.

"Walk away, Skin. I won't let my brother do something stupid." Skin starts to walk away but turns back after only a few feet. Jason must have heard him stop.

"I said I wouldn't let Nick be stupid, but I won't hesitate to rearrange your face. I have nothing to lose." Jason's right. I can't afford an assault charge. There are scouts looking at me this season. Skin must take Jason's words to heart because he grabs his girl's hand and storms back to his car.

"You cool?" Jason asks as soon as Skin is out of earshot.

"Yeah. I'm good."

The other races go by quickly. I am getting excited and the adrenaline is pumping. I love this!

Gator and I are announced as I pull my car up to the starting line. The crowd is much bigger now than it was an hour ago. I always draw a big crowd. My fans erupt when they hear my name, and I can't help but smile. Hearing my name cheered always gives me a thrill, whether it's here at the track or on the football field. Gator pulls up beside me and we both rev our engines. You can practically smell the testosterone in the air. I'm sure there are plenty of girls already wet and hoping for a chance with the winner. Let's be honest, football and racing get me laid. Without them, I might actually be a virgin. I shudder at the horrifying thought. I shake those thoughts away and focus on the girl with her scarf raised. She drops her arms, and dirt flies as I pull away from the starting line. I'm in the lead going around the first turn, but as soon as the track straightens, Gator is gaining on me. I drop a gear, gun it as I come out of the second turn, and I'm quickly in the lead again. By the time I take the third turn, Gator is several car lengths behind me. It's clear as I take the final turn and head for the finish line, there is nothing he can do to catch me. The crowd goes nuts as I cross the finish line and my friends surround my car before I come to a complete stop.

There isn't much time for congratulations before my race with Skin. I get some water while Jason and Brody check my car over and make sure it is ready for the next race. Jason is just finishing gassing it up when I return.

"You're good to go," Jason says, clapping me on the back. "Skin's going to be harder to beat. Be careful. He's already been talking shit. Brody thinks he has something up his sleeve."

"Skin always has something up his sleeve, and it's never legal or safe. I'll be fine. I've beaten Skin several times before."

"Which is why he's out for blood, Nick. Don't do anything stupid."

"Stop worrying, Jase," I tell him, getting in the car and pulling up next to Skin. He looks over and flips me off. Wow, how mature. I roll my eyes and return the gesture. More of the same from the crowd when we are announced except Skin's group is much louder than Gator's. We both rev our engines and wait for the hot brunette in the skin tight pants to drop her scarf. Skin takes the lead early. I shift the gears twice before the first turn, but I'm still behind. I start gaining on him when we hit the straight away. He only has a few inches on me going into the second turn. I slowly start to inch past Skin as we approach the third turn. I'm finally in the lead as the track straightens. I shift and gun it hoping to put some distance between us, but Skin does the same thing. As the front of his car nears the back of mine, he jerks toward me, hitting my back bumper. I gain control before I spin out, but it gives Skin the chance to take the lead.

Fuck that. I am not going out like this. We are neck and neck coming out of the final turn and heading toward the finish line. I see Skin out of the corner of my eye, and I can tell he is about to jerk his car toward me again. I shift gears and push the pedal to the floor in an effort to pass him before we crash. I only have time to gain a few inches on him. He hits the back right side of my car as I cross the finish line. This time I don't have as much control and the car does two 360s. I get slammed into the door a few times before I finally come to a stop. I'm breathing heavy, but I'm not seriously injured. My left side is going to be sore as hell tomorrow, and my car is going to be fucked. How the hell am I going to explain two dents to my dad? I'm out of the car and on Skin before he sees me coming.

"What the fuck was that, shithead?" I yell, shoving his back hard. He jerks forward, but uses his hands and car to stop himself from falling. I am so focused on yelling at him about damaging my car that I don't see his fist until it's to late. He knocks the shit out of me, and Jason has to stop me from hitting the ground. Damn, that's going to leave a mark. I fight against Jason's hold as he pulls me away from Skin.

"Get the fuck out of here," I hear Brody tell him.

"Tell that little Oliver shit that I want a rematch," Skin yells back.

"Why? It's obvious you can't beat him," Brody counters.

"Rematch, Oliver!" Skin says before getting in his car and tearing down the dirt road.

"Let go of me," I shove Jason off me as soon as Skin is in his car. "I could have beaten the shit out of that asshole. Why did you stop me?"

"Because I don't need you getting arrested. You know if shit gets crazy out here, the cops are going to show." Jason's right. I need to check on my car and get out of here. It isn't unusual for the cops to show up when it gets this late. It's already close to one in the morning.

"Shit." I say, looking over my car. The dent in the bumper isn't bad and Dad might not even notice it. However, the side has a huge dent that covers most of the right quarter panel. That is going to cost a shitload to fix.

"Do you think Carey can fix that?" I ask Jason.

"Yeah, if he can stay sober long enough," Brody snorts out. Jason and I both give him a death glare. We all know Carey uses drugs, but I'm not gonna let my friends get away with talking shit about him.

"Sorry," Brody mumbles, taking a step back as Jason takes a step toward him.

"Watch it. Don't ever disrespect my family," he says, grabbing the front of Brody's shirt.

"Okay, sorry, man." Jason shoves Brody away and turns back to me.

"I think Carey and I can fix it. Park it as close to the hedge on the side of the house as possible. We'll look at it in the light when Dad isn't around."

"Thanks," I tell him. Brody gets in his car, and Jason and I head home.

Carey

I don't know how long I've been out, but when I wake, it's dark. Sean is in his bed, and my head is pounding. I blink a few times to bring the clock into focus. It's after two. The music has stopped so I pull my earbuds out. I need to pee so I sit up. Bad idea. Suddenly, I need to get to the bathroom and not just to piss. I wait for my stomach to settle down, but as soon as I stand, the nausea comes back with a vengeance and the room starts spinning. I attempt to get to the bathroom without waking Sean, but I trip over a shoe or something; maybe just air.

"Shit!" I mumble as I run into the door jamb. Sean asks if I'm okay as I reach the bathroom, but I can't respond. I hurl, barely making it to the toilet. When I finish, I put my head on the cool bathroom tiles, hoping for relief or death. At this point, either would be welcome. Something besides the constant pounding and spinning in my head. Through the fog, I hear Sean's distorted voice.

"You okay?" he asks. Why does he sound so weird and far away? Yeah. I say. Or at least that's what I planned to say.

"Carey. Carey! Are you okay?"

Why is Sean yelling? I just wish he would go away, and let me sleep. Shut up! I try to scream, but the words seem unable to make it to my lips.

"Answer me, Carey! Carey!" he yells again, shaking me this time.

I moan and open my eyes a little. He looks terrified as he leans over me. I must have passed out.

"Carey," he says with a crack in his voice. "What's wrong?" he sounds like he is about to cry. I didn't mean to scare him.

"I'm okay," I manage. "Help me up," I continue, reaching for his hand. As he helps me to my feet, I notice that my shorts and the bath mat are wet.

"Shit," I mutter, realizing that I pissed myself in the process of losing my dinner and passing out. Sean closes the toilet seat and helps me sit down. Without a word, he starts the shower.

"What's going on?" Nick asks, entering the bathroom that is barely big enough for one of us much less three.

"Carey isn't feeling well. Go get a plastic bag for his cast so he can take a shower." Nick looks questioningly at me, but then disappears to do what Sean said.

I must really be losing it. Is Sean actually giving orders? Is Nick actually listening to him?

It doesn't take long for Nick to return. Sean covers my cast with the bag and tells Nick to go back to bed.

"Get in the shower and clean yourself up," Sean clips with disgust. Then, sighs and continues a little more gently. "Leave your clothes on the mat, and I'll take them to the washing machine. Here's a towel. I'll bring you some clean clothes." He leaves so I can get undressed. I can't believe that Sean just sent Nick back to bed so he can cover for me. Sean knows I'm not sick. I'm sure that he saw the empty beer bottles and the pills on my bedside table. I'm thankful that he is taking care of me and keeping everyone else out of the loop. The hot water helps me feel a little more human. I hear him come back in to leave some dry clothes and gather the stuff I soiled. It isn't easy to bathe one handed while the room is spinning, but I do the best I can. By the time, I turn the water off Sean has cleaned the floor. I towel off and put on the clothes he left.

Nick

I don't know what the hell is going on with Carey, but I know Sean is covering for him. Sean always covers for Carey, and it only gets him in trouble. Just like last year when he took the fall for the joint that was in my car. When will Sean ever learn? He better not follow in Carey's footsteps. That's why I try so hard to push him away from Sam. Jocks are way better.

I walk away from the bathroom so Sean can handle our brother, but I'm not going back to bed like he said. This looks a little more serious than a drunken night. I worry about Carey more than I will ever admit to him or any of my brothers. He's been in a downward spiral for a while, and I have no idea what to do. We all see it, but nothing we say or do seems to help. He just gets more and more angry. He's the brother that we need to take care of and protect. We all act like it's Sean since he's the youngest, but the reality is Carey has problems. Even though I want to help him, I'm so angry at the choices he's made that it's getting difficult. The more he pushes us away, the more I let him.

Now he's acting weird about Seth. Seth is his best friend and a jock, but Carey got all defensive when I said something about him tonight. He needs Seth's influence. Finally, the shower starts, and Sean comes out of the bathroom.

"What the hell is going on in there?" I ask from the doorway of my room.

"I told you to go to bed. He puked. No big deal. Probably something he ate," Sean explains, entering his room and trying to close the door in my face. I stop the door before it hits me and push it open.

"Why are you lying for him?" I ask. Sean comes back out of his room with some clean clothes and pushes past me without answering. He enters the bathroom, but quickly comes back out with the dirty clothes and bath mat.

"Sean, I'm serious. What the hell is wrong with him? Did he take too many pills?" I follow him down the stairs.

"I told you. It's probably just food poisoning," Sean insists, but I can tell by the tone of his voice he doesn't believe it either.

"What happened to his hand?" I ask not believing the story he gave earlier.

"Drop it, Nick. He already told us that he broke it playing basketball."

"You believe that?" I ask.

"Yes," he says.

"You don't sound convinced."

"Nick, I don't know what's going on with him. He said he broke it playing basketball. He's been a dick all day, drank a few beers, took his pain meds, and woke up puking. That's all I know." Sean sounds overwhelmed and emotional. That bothers me because when Sean shows his true feelings, you pay attention.

"I'm worried about him," I admit, hoping to get more out of Sean.

"Me too," he whispers without looking at me. Sean starts the washing machine and heads upstairs.

"What are we going to do?" I ask, following him.

"I don't know," he admits sadly. "Right now, I'm going to try to get some sleep. Let's just see how tomorrow goes," he says, entering his room.

"Sean," I stop him. "If he tells you anything, let me know." He nods once, but I continue. "Seriously, Sean. I need to know." Sean nods again before closing his door.

I'm still standing in the hall staring after Sean when the shower stops. I go to my room, but leave the door cracked enough to see Carey when he comes out of the bathroom. He's clean and dressed and looks better than he did a few minutes ago. He goes into the room he shares with Sean.

"Thanks," I hear Carey say.

"You're clothes are washing. Don't forget to put them in the dryer," Sean replies coldly.

"Sean, can we talk?" Carey asks.

"Here are your *precious* dog tags. I cleaned the vomit off of them." Sean snaps. Then I see something fly out of their room and hit the wall near the bathroom. Carey angrily walks back into the hallway again. He closes the door a little louder than necessary, and I worry he's going to wake Dad.

"I'm not up for dealing with this shit right now," Carey mumbles to himself. He grabs what looks like a necklace, and pulls it over his head as he passes my door.

When he reaches the steps, I follow quietly so I can spy without being seen. He pours a glass of water, and goes to the couch. I watch him for a while as he scrolls through some channels then gets up to put the clothes in the dryer.

Carey is slipping away from us. I tried not to let Sean know my true thoughts, but watching Carey tonight scared me. He needs help, but I can't help him. I wouldn't even know where to start. Most of the time, I try to stay clear of him because the last thing I need is him dragging me down. If Carey does something stupid and I'm with him, I could lose my chance at a football scholarship. You know, guilt by association and all. I just don't understand why he chooses to use drugs. He just needs to stop so I can have the old Carey back. His shit is getting old and it's starting to affect me, on and off the field. I had some skinny ass, motherfucker break my tackle Friday night. Nobody gets past Nick! And after the game, I could only go about 4 minutes with Ashley before I blew my load. The Nickster can usually get in a solid 7.

I stay on the steps out of sight watching Carey until he finally falls asleep. Then, I return to my room to get a few hours myself.

Reid

Last night, I worked late and then went out. I know I should tell the boys I'm dating, but I try to keep that part of my life away from them. Sarah and I were separated for years before I finally filed for divorce. I didn't feel it was right to see other women while we were technically still married. After that, I was so busy working and being a single parent, there wasn't time for a social life. In the year since I started dating, I haven't met anyone who I want to introduce to the boys. Actually, I haven't found anything that lasted past the first few dates.

I thought this lady might be different. I mean, we seemed to be having a great time. She's about ten years younger than me, very career oriented, and has never been married. Things were going so well, I decided to tell her I have four teenage boys. Suddenly, she remembered an early morning appointment. I offered to walk her to her car, but she said she was fine going alone. She exited before I could even pay for dinner. Maybe I shouldn't try to date until the boys are grown. After another train wreck of a date, I met Riley for a couple of drinks.

It was after midnight when I got home. Sean and Carey were in their beds. Nick and Jason weren't home yet; I guess they had dates. They were safe and sound this morning when I peeked in their rooms. I'm up early even though I don't have to be back at the station today.

Carey is asleep on the couch when I come downstairs a little after seven. I thought I heard someone up during the night. I wonder what happened. It couldn't have been too bad or they would've gotten me up. Carey and Sean must have had a disagreement. Pausing on the steps, I watch him for a few minutes. Carey looks so young and innocent sleeping on the couch with his mass of brown hair in his face. That boy loves his hair and so do all of the girls. That's going to get him in trouble one day. I smile at the thought because I would love nothing more than to see him happy.

Looking at him as he sleeps, I wish I could go back in time and fix whatever is going on with him. I shake my head and walk toward the kitchen. I need coffee before I try to deal with Carey. He barely talks to me anymore. He started pulling away from all of us after Sarah died. He took it harder than his brothers, but it's more than that.

I start the coffee pot and take my favorite mug out of the dishwasher thankful that someone, probably Sean, cleaned the kitchen.

Since Carey entered high school, he's become more distant and withdrawn. He is angry all the time, and it's put a strain on his relationships with his brothers and with me. My biggest fear is that he's on drugs. I went so far as to search his room a few weeks ago, but I didn't find anything. Either I'm wrong or he has a great hiding spot. I hope I'm wrong, but I have a sickening feeling I'm not. The thought forces a heaviness into my chest. I'm not paying attention and inadvertently add more cream and sugar than is necessary to my coffee.

Carey has so much potential, and he's just throwing it all away. He barely passed his freshman year, and I'm willing to bet that he won't do much better this coming year. He's the smartest of all of my sons, and school has always come easy to him, but he's no longer interested in doing the work. He fights with his brothers all of the time and is usually the instigator with them and me. I love this boy so much, but I feel completely helpless. The other boys talk to me about things that are important. Not Carey. He's never been one to let any of us get too close, but none of us ever had a strained relationship. When they were kids, he was closer to Sean and Nick, but I haven't seen him speak to either of them recently without anger or an attitude.

I need to try to talk to him before his brothers wake. I don't understand why he didn't call me yesterday when he broke his hand. I finish my cup of coffee and head for the living room.

Carey

Sleep doesn't last long enough. I wake to my dad in the kitchen brewing coffee. God, could he be any louder? I try to ignore the noise, but when it gets quiet, I can feel his presence.

"What?" I ask, not opening my eyes.

"Sit up, Carey," he says.

"I'm tired, Dad," I reply, not moving.

"Sit up, now," he says with a little more authority.

"Leave me the hell alone," I snap.

"Ow!" I yell, finally opening my eyes when he smacks me with the rolled up newspaper. "What the fuck?" There he goes, hitting me again. I am so sick of his abuse. I wish he cared about me like he does my brothers. I've never seen him beat them like dogs.

"Watch your mouth, son!" he says firmly. He takes a deep breath. "Sit. Up. Now," he continues. Crap, this isn't going to be good. I wonder if he knows about the car or about what happened during the night. I do as I am told because I know I don't have another choice. I don't want to be smacked again like some kind of animal.

"You want to explain the cast?" he asks.

"Did you talk to Riley?"

"Yes."

"What did he say?"

"You need tell me what happened."

"I broke it playing basketball. I went to see Riley in the ER and got a cast." I try to keep it simple, hoping he won't ask how I managed to get to the hospital.

"It didn't occur to you that I might want to know my son was in the emergency room?" he questions.

"You were at work," I shrug "You don't like to be interrupted when you're on a case."

"You went to the hospital, Carey. You're more important. My job can wait."

"It's not a big deal. It isn't the first time I've broken something," I say matter of factly. "Dad, can we not do this now? I'm really tired."

He sighs, running his fingers through his hair.

"Carey, we care about you. Don't shut us out. What is going on with you?"

"Nothing. I'm fine." Where the hell is this coming from, and why do we need to talk at this ungodly hour?

"You most definitely are not fine. You have not been yourself lately. Your grades were in the toilet last year, you're always giving Sean shit, you're an ass to everyone. This isn't you, Carey. I am..."

"Like you know anything about me!" I yell, standing up. "This is bullshit, Dad. Go to work." I head for the stairs. It is too early for his crap this morning.

"It's Sunday. I'm not going to work," he calls after me. "Carey stop. We need to talk about this."

"No, we don't," I say, rushing up the stairs to my room. I slam the door behind me startling Sean out of his sleep.

"I can't go anywhere in my own damn house without being around someone I can't stand to look at!" I yell even though I don't mean it. Guilt eats at me when I see the hurt in Sean's eyes. Great! I've hurt Sean's feelings twice in less than twenty-four hours. I ignore it and change into a pair of jeans and a band t-shirt, then toss my wallet, phone, a pack of cigarettes, and a bottle of pills into the backpack that has my notebook in it. I am not dealing with this today. Sean just watches. I guess he knows to keep his mouth shut. He hates covering for me, but if he was going to spill, he would have done it by now. I slam the bedroom door again as I leave. My dad is waiting when I hit the bottom step.

"Carey, wait," he says as I push past him without speaking. "You are not leaving this house!" He grabs my arm to stop me.

"Let go of me!" I yell, trying to shove him away. He tightens his grip. "I said let go of me. You're always fucking hurting me, asshole!" I yell louder while pushing harder. He let's go this time as I slam his back against the wall. He looks completely destroyed. Right now, I don't even care if my words and actions hurt him.

Before I turn away, I see my three brothers at the bottom of the stairs watching us, disbelief etched on their faces.

I head out the back door and over the dunes to the beach. I can't stand to be in that house any longer. I walk north just past the lighthouse. I know where I'll end up without even thinking about it. The only place I ever feel completely myself is at The Reading Corner. It's closed on Sundays, but even if they were open no one would look for me here. I walk up the steps to the secluded, outdoor reading area that overlooks the ocean. This is my favorite spot on the island and the place I always run to when I need to get away. I've never told anyone about it, not even Seth. I take a joint out of the cigarette box, light it, and sit back on the old swing to read a book and get high. I love coming here to read and write.

There is so much my family doesn't know about me. I've been writing for years; songs, stories, poems. I keep a notebook and write in it all the time. I'm working on a novel, and my plan is to get it published as soon as it's complete. I know it would only sound ridiculous to my brothers. There's no being different in this family.

I have some songs that I would love to sell, but they probably suck. There's no alarm on the local high school, so I've been sneaking in for years and using the music rooms. I've taught myself to play the piano, guitar, and drums by watching online videos. I'm not great at playing any of them, but the escape I get when playing is almost as good as getting high. Growing up my dad happily drove us to sporting events and practices, but never asked if any of us wanted to take music lessons. I would have jumped at the opportunity. I guess I could have asked, but I'm sure he would have told me no since music isn't a sport.

I wish I could tell my brothers, but I know they won't understand. We don't really have anything in common. I just pretend that I like the stuff they like because I don't need to give them a reason to hate me anymore than they already do. They all think I'm just the family screw up; always in trouble at school, crappy grades, bad attitude, smoking pot, drinking. Not that my brothers are angels, but I seem to be the one always getting my ass handed to me for it. My dad and I don't get along, and he's always picking on me about something. He doesn't care about me the way he cares about my brothers.

No one knows the secrets that I keep. I can't tell anyone the truth. They wouldn't believe me anyway.

I spend hours on the Watson's back porch reading and writing. It's late afternoon, and I'm starting to get hungry when I finally decide to make my way back home. I can't escape my dad's lecture so I might as well get it over with now.

Reid

"Carey," I call, starting toward the door he just slammed. I can't believe he shoved me into the wall. Things are beginning to escalate with him. He's been different lately, but not violent. He's hurt all of us with his words and actions, but never physically.

"Let him go, Dad," Jason's words stop me, "We've been through this before. He'll be back and in the meantime we can have a few hours of peace." Carey is a master at hiding. He runs when he doesn't like the way things are going. Jason is right, though, Carey always comes home.

"You three. Sit. Now!" I bark at my sons. They all scramble to the couch.

"Start talking!" I'm angry at Carey and shouldn't take it out on them, but I need answers. Jason just stares at me. Nick and Sean look everywhere else. They are both clearly hiding something.

"Talk!" Sean and Nick both jump when I yell. It takes a lot to get me angry. They aren't used to hearing me raise my voice.

"What do you want us to say, Dad? You know how he is," Jason says.

"I want to know what the hell is going on with that boy."

"Nothing," Nick says. "Jason's right. This is just how he acts."

"Bullshit! It's more than that, and I'm sick of you three covering for him," I tell them.

"Sean, why was he on the couch this morning?" I ask hoping Sean will break. I may never get anywhere with Jason and Nick, but I can usually wear Sean down.

"How should I know?" he counters.

"What happened in the middle of the night? I heard someone up." Nick and Sean share a look, telling me they both know something.

"Carey wasn't feeling well. I guess he ate something that made him sick," Sean offers.

"Are you sure it was something he ate and not something he took?"

"I didn't *see* Carey use drugs if that's what you're asking," Sean tells me.

"Please, boys. It is not going to help if you continue to cover for your brother," I try a different approach. "You have no idea how worried I am about him."

"I think we do," Nick comments and immediately his eyes go wide. He clearly didn't mean to say that out loud. Jason and Sean both glare at him. Nick's shoulders sag, and he looks like a scared little boy instead of a high school senior.

"I'm worried about him, too. He was puking in the middle of the night, but I think it was more than something he ate. Sean wouldn't tell me anything. He made me go back to my room while he helped Carey," Nick explains. As far as I know, it's the first time one of these boys has betrayed another one. Sean and Jason both stare daggers at their brother.

"Sorry, Seany. I'm not trying to get you in trouble, but that shit last night scared me."

"It scared me, too," Sean whispers. "I don't know what's going on with him. I'm not lying. I didn't see Carey take anything, but that doesn't mean he didn't," Sean relents. I am shocked that these boys are giving me this kind of information. It scares me shitless. If they're willing to rat Carey out, this is bigger than I thought.

"I don't know what to do, boys. We're losing him." I admit. "Nothing I do works."

"We've all tried, Dad. It doesn't do any good. The more we try to help, the more he pushes us away. It's not your fault we're losing him," Jason echoes my words. If self-absorbed Jason is voicing his concerns, then I should be overwrought.

"We have to do something, boys."

"Like what, Dad? Unless you have some brilliant plan, I'm going back to bed," Nick gets up from the couch.

"Please sit down, Nick."

"Tell me your plan," Nick stands his ground.

"I don't have a plan," I admit, "But surely the four of us can come up with something." It's crazy to ask parenting advice from a bunch of teenage boys, but I am desperate.

"I agree with Nick. Since you don't have a plan, I'm going to watch the back of my eyelids," Jason is up the stairs before I have a chance to respond.

"Sean, you spend the most time with Carey. You must know something."

"I told you that I don't know what's going on with him," Sean stands up, "I have to get started on my summer reading."

"Sean, please," I beg as he walks away.

"Sorry, Dad," he doesn't look at me. He takes the stairs two at a time, obviously not able to get out of here fast enough.

"Where are you going?" I ask Nick as he walks toward the kitchen.

"First, I'm going to get some food. Then, I'm going back to bed."

"What happened to your face?" I ask, forcing myself to speak in a calmer tone. "Piss off some girl?" I tease, hoping to lighten the mood a little. This morning did not go as I had hoped. I struck out with the other three boys. Maybe some light hearted humor can salvage this time with Nick.

"It's nothing, Dad. Wrong place, wrong time."

"Want to explain?"

"Nope," Nick says with finality. I follow him into the kitchen. He pours himself a bowl of cereal and fills it with milk while I pour myself another cup of coffee.

"Nick, I need you to tell me what happened to you."

66

"What you need is to figure out how to handle Carey. I *said* it's nothing. Wall got in my way."

"Were you drunk?"

"Does it matter to you? Carey is rarely sober and you never confront him."

"Were you?" I slam my fist on the counter. Nick knows how to push every one of my buttons.

"No! Jesus, Dad, just drop it," Nick walks away, leaving his untouched bowl of cereal on the counter next to the open box and milk jug.

"Clean up your mess, Nick," I call after him.

"Clean it the fuck up yourself," he snaps, reaching the top of the stairs.

"Nick! Nicholas!" I shout just before his door slams.

"Dammit!" I shake my head. "Strike four! Way to go Reid. If this was baseball, you'd already be sitting the bench," I yell to the empty kitchen.

Jason

"C, Wake up," I try to rouse my brother; he sleeps like the dead.

"Go away. It's too early to be awake," he shoves me back.

"Come on, C. Nick's car got messed up in the race on Saturday. I need you to help me fix it." I hope today goes better than yesterday. Carey stayed away most of the day and went ballistic when we confronted him last night.

The mention of pending car repairs gets Carey on his feet immediately. He loves working on cars. I know a lot about them, but I will never be as good as Carey. It just comes so naturally to him, like he's some kind of weird genius. He's definitely smarter than the rest of us. If he put any effort into it, he could easily graduate at the top of his class. I hate seeing him throw his life away.

He pulls on a pair of jeans and a band t-shirt. Does he own anything else? He must have fifty band t-shirts. He loves heavy metal, but I don't understand it. Whatever. To each his own. He wouldn't be caught dead listening to that country crap Sean listens to or the club and techno stuff Nick and I like.

"What's wrong with it?"

"That asshole, Skin, hit him twice. Once in the rear bumper, and then on the right side.

Screwed up the whole right quarter panel and the passenger side door," I explain.

"Damn. That's going to suck to fix. Where is the car now?"

"Nick parked it on the side of the house. Dad just left for work, so we should have a good twelve hours."

"Good. We're gonna need it."

Carey spends about twenty minutes looking over the damage and making some notes. Then, he hands me a list of stuff to get from the garage, and Nick a list of stuff to go buy in town.

"Here you go," I hand him our box of tools.

"Thanks," he says, getting to work. Carey works silently, and it's making me antsy. With one hand in a cast, I know he needs me. I want to help, but I don't know what to do when it comes to body work. I pick up a hammer and start trying to work out the dent in the bumper.

"What the fuck are you doing?" Carey yells.

"What? I'm just trying to help."

"Well don't. You're going to cause more damage. You don't use a hammer to do that." He grabs the tool out of my hand and tosses it on the ground. "Using the wrong tool only makes it worse."

"Why are you being such an ass? I'm out here to help you!" I don't need his shit.

"I'll do it right myself in a minute," he bites out, "If you want to help, go get me some water."

"Fucking asshole," I mumble as I walk away. The last thing I want to do is take orders from my little brother, but I get the water anyway. Mainly because it gives me a chance to cool off before I say something that I'll regret. We need Carey to fix this before Dad finds out.

"Here," I toss the bottle of water at him. He catches it, but his glare tells me he knows I meant for it to hit him.

"Use this and start taking the tire off." I do as I'm told because I really do want to help and spend some time with Carey. I get the tire off and turn around to ask what's next.

"What's ne...what the fuck are you doing? Did you just take something?" I yell, watching him shove the pill bottle back in his pocket.

"No," he lies and turns back to the car.

"Bullshit, Carey! I saw you! I'm not blind! I can't believe you are lying to my face."

"Fuck you, Jason! Riley gave them to me for my hand. Why don't you mind your own business, so I can get Nick's car fixed before Dad gets home?" Carey turns back to the car like the conversation is over.

"We are not done here." I bite out as I grab his arm and turn him toward me.

"I am *done* with this conversation, and I suggest you drop it or you'll be on your own with this car." Carey yells, shoving me away from him.

"I'm worried about you, C. We all are. We don't want to see you make any more bad choices."

I try to calm down and be honest with him, but my tone is still too harsh.

"Like you make good choices. You're balls deep in a different whore every night. That's your drug of choice, asshole!"

"I guess we all have vices, but drugs will kill you, Carey,"

"So will AIDS, dickhead!" Carey screams at me and turns to the car.

"Fuck you!" I yell not able to control my anger any longer. I'm done. I tried talking to him and all he wants to do is turn it around and tell me how I'm the screw up.

"No, Jason, fuck you!" he throws the wrench at me and barely misses my head. Good thing I have fast reflexes.

"Good luck with the car, asshole. My hand hurts anyway," he storms off toward the house.

"Carey, come on. Carey. CAREY!" He doesn't respond as he slams the door. Well, shit, now I have to figure this out by myself. I spend the next hour waiting for Nick and looking at Youtube videos on body work, but damn if I can understand half of what I'm watching.

Nick

Carey didn't react well when he came home last week to the four of us waiting on him. After we all got some rest and calmed down, we decided it would be a good idea to confront him. We were so wrong. Ambushing him like that was a bad idea. He was more pissed than I have ever seen him. He blew up as soon as he walked in and wouldn't listen to any of us.

That was only the beginning of hell week. Since then, Carey has been more of an ass than normal to all of us. He got into it that night with Dad, and I thought it was going to come to blows. I have never seen my dad that angry. Growing up our dad would spank us if we got into any major trouble, but that was rare. We've all experienced his belt on our ass a time or two, but nothing that left a mark or that we didn't deserve. My dad has never punched any of us, but I really thought he was going to hit Carey that night. Then on Monday, he flipped out at Jason over car repairs.

Things only got worse as the week went on. I can't sit in this house anymore with Carey here, so I walk to the pier to meet up with my friends.

"'Sup, guys," I say, greeting Tim and Truck. They each have a chick on their knee. Truck and Taylor have been dating for awhile, but I can't remember the girl's name who is sitting on Tim's lap. She's been hanging out with Taylor all summer, but she's just going to be a freshman this year. Tim better be careful with that little girl. He's already eighteen.

"Hey, babe," I say, joining my friends and pulling Ashley into my lap. I don't do girlfriends, but Ashley is the closest I've come to having one. We've been friends since middle school and have been on several dates. She's head cheerleader, and she's my go-to girl for things like Homecoming and Prom. We look cute together in pictures. Plus, she's willing to screw whenever I call with no strings attached.

"You look damn sexy in that purple bikini," I whisper.

"Maybe I'll let you take it off of me later," she responds in a sexy whisper that has me instantly hard.

"You will. You know I'm working on my stamina for football." She shudders slightly at my words. I know how to get her going, but I need to wait. I'm still worked up from all of Carey's shit, and I'm afraid I'll hurt her if I fuck her now. Hopefully, I can find a way to get rid of some of this aggression soon.

"You guys ready for the season?" Taylor asks. We go back to school in a couple of weeks and our first game will be the Friday after we start.

"Hell, yeah. We're going all the way to state again this year," Tim says. We've won the state championship in our division for the past three years and none of us are giving up on making it four in a row. We plan to be the first to have that honor.

What a way to go out! Truck and I have been starters since we were freshman; the only two freshman to start in the history of our school.

"No doubt, boys," Ashley agrees; always the cheerleader.

The sun begins to set, so we head to the south end where Truck parked. He always has a cooler of beer in there. Tim and I start a fire on the beach while Truck grabs the cooler and the girls set out some blankets. We spend the next few hours on the beach, talking, drinking, and making out with our dates.

"Umm...Ashley," Tim's girl says as it nears eleven, "Sorry, but I have a curfew."

"Of course," Ashley says, "We'll go."

"Don't go, Ashley. Let Tim drive her home," I say. Tim kicks me from the other side of the blanket.

"Ow, what the..."

"It's okay," she saves him. "Daddy won't be happy if a boy brings me home. I'm not allowed to date yet," she explains. Well, then maybe she shouldn't have been screwing Tim a few minutes ago. I'm not that stupid. They just came back from the other side of the fire. Even though they were under a blanket, it was obvious what they were doing. Tim is a dumbass because that girl can't be more than fourteen. He better pray her *daddy* doesn't find out.

"Are you sure you have to go?" I whisper, pulling Ashley away from the group. I can't stop thinking about how much I want to take that bikini off of her.

"Lose your friends and meet me near the rocks in an hour. I'll take her home and make an appearance at my house. As soon as my mom thinks I'm in for the night, I'll sneak out."

"Wear the bikini," I wink and slap her ass as she walks away. Tim is putting the fire out, and Truck is gathering up the empty beer cans. Taylor picks up the blankets and takes them to her car. Truck follows, and the two of them leave.

"You better be careful with that little girl," I warn Tim.

"Her *name* is Honor, and I like her. What does it matter to you?"

"First of all, you like that she puts out. Second of all, she's jailbait. We need you on the field, not in jail."

"Well, *Dad*, I think I can handle it," he bites out sarcastically.

"Don't say I didn't warn you."

"Drop it, Nick," he says, knocking my shoulder as he walks past. I want to punch the shit out of him, but I know it will just make things worse. You don't do that to a teammate.

I stay silent on the beach until Tim is out of sight. Then, I start to make my way toward the rocks. It'll take a little while to walk there since they are on the south end of the beach.

As I pass the pier, I see that faggot, Sam, walking down the sidewalk across the street.

He must be heading home from our house where he and Sean were hanging out when I left. Without thinking, I cross the street. I stay in the shadows, following him, but keeping a little distance. There is a lot of light in this area. He has to take a right in a few blocks. The street he lives on isn't as well lit, and there are only a few houses that are all spread apart and his is at the end near the trailer park. This area of town is such a fucking dump. Who chooses to live in a tin can? There is no way I would live like a sardine. We get to the darkest part of his street, and I jump him from behind. He's on the ground before he even knows I'm there. He tries to wiggle and twist away from me, but I straddle him, keeping him in place while I punch him in the back several times. Idiot should know that I am way too strong for him to get away.

"Get off of me," he chokes out between blows. I let him turn himself over, and I see recognition in his eyes as I land a fist to his jaw. I punch him in the face a few more times before I get up.

"Stay the fuck away from my brother, cocksucker. He doesn't need you making him any more of loser," I yell, kicking him in the ribs for good measure. I leave Sam crying on the ground in the dark, and head toward the rocks. This is turning out to be a great night! I had the pleasure of bringing a beat down on the king of the losers, and now it's time to get laid.

Tension is still high at home, and my round of sex with Ashley on the beach did nothing to calm my anger. Things with Carey haven't gotten any better, and everyone is on edge. Sean has been giving me shit for the past couple of days. I don't know if it's just because of Carey or if Sam said something about me jumping him. It doesn't matter. Sean won't confront me.

Dad is home early for the first time in weeks and is expecting all of us to have a nice family dinner. He's been cooking for an hour and actually sounds happy as he whistles away in the kitchen. It's a little creepy if you ask me. Jason and I are watching a movie and Sean is playing *daddy's* helper in the kitchen. Carey has been gone most of the afternoon. My brothers and I have barely spoken in days.
Every conversation turns to anger so it's just not worth it.

"Jason, text Carey and tell him dinner will be ready it ten minutes," Dad calls from the kitchen

"Like that will do any good," Jason whispers where only I can hear him.

"Yes, Dad," Jason rolls his eyes as he responds, but as usual does what *daddy* says.

"Thanks. He knows I expect him home."

He's probably right about Carey. I can't remember the last time we all sat down to eat together. It might sound strange coming from me, but I like having dinner with my family.

When things are good, we have a great time together, but things haven't been good in a long time. Jason's phone dings less than a minute after he sends the text. He stares at the response with his mouth hanging open.

"Everything okay?" I ask.

"Um...yeah...he's on his way," Jason sounds as confused as I feel. Carey always has an asshole response or doesn't bother answering at all.

"He's on his way, Dad," Jason calls.

"Good. You two come set the table. We'll eat as soon as Carey gets home."

We are setting out the last platter of food when Carey comes in the back door.

"Smells good, Dad. I'm starving," he says, taking his seat. I look at Jason and Sean to make sure they are as weirded out as I am by Carey's attitude. He's calm, and being nice. I think he's even sober. This is kind of freaking me out. My brothers stare at him in disbelief.

"Sit boys," Dad says, pulling the three of us out of our trance.

"Are you boys ready to go back to school?" Dad asks as we pile food on our plates.

"Hell no! I am ready for the season to start. I need to find a way to have football without school," I say.

"Good luck with that," Jason retorts.

"What do you know about school?" I goad him. He hates it when we bring up his failed attempt at college.

"Or a job," Sean piles on.

"Damn, little Seany with the insults," I laugh and high five him.

"Both of you shut up," Jason says, pointing his fork at us.

"*Have* you found another job?" Dad asks.

"Not yet, but I've been looking. I have some ideas. Maybe I can run them by you later?"

"Sure, Jase. I would love to hear them. If you aren't going to go to school, you need to work and take on some responsibility around the house."

"Oh, don't worry, he works," Carey jumps in. "Well, if you count chasing girls, he works more than the rest of us put together," Carey says nonchalantly. Jason elbows him in the side.

"Watch it, little brother," he tries to look serious, but I can hear the laughter in his voice.

"He has a point," I add.

"What's wrong? Can't handle the truth?" Carey continues, "You know you could make a lot of money if you just start charging the girls."

"Enough, Carey," Jason starts to get annoyed. He doesn't like it when his little brothers gang up on him.

"What? I'm just saying, you obviously have the skills to make a lot of money as a male prostitute. Is your job idea a male escort service? You and Brody could make millions. I'm just trying to help. It's no secret that you're a sure thing," Carey shrugs. "Oh, wait. Nevermind. You probably need to wait until that little problem clears up."

"Shut up, Carey," Jason says through gritted teeth as he hits his fist on the table.

"What are you talking about? What problem?" Dad asks.

"It's nothing," Jason tries to blow it off, but the angry glare he gives Carey says it's definitely something.

"Talk. Now," Dad says.

"How did you know?" Jason asks, ignoring Dad. Carey just shrugs. I don't know what's going on, but I have never seen Jason squirm like this.

"I'm serious! How the hell did you know? Have you been in my room?" Jason lunges toward Carey, but Carey is out of his chair and across the room. Jason catches him by the door and pulls him back to the table, forcing him to sit. "Answer me, you little shit!" Carey is laughing his ass off. Damn this is fun to watch!

"What? I saw the meds and did a little detective work," Carey says through his laugh. Jason looks like he going to rip Carey's head off.

"What were you doing in my room?"

"I...um...I...was just..." Carey stops laughing and stumbles over his words. Jason grabs a fist full of Carey's shirt and gets in his face.

"What. Were. You. Doing. In. My. Room!" Jason yells.

"Nothing," Carey mumbles.

"Pills or money?" Jason asks.

"I didn't take anything."

"You had no business snooping." Jason shoves Carey as he lets his shirt go and sits back down. "Stay out of my room."

"Jason is right, Carey. You shouldn't be in his room without his permission. We'll talk about privacy when I'm done with your brother. Don't think you're off the hook," Dad says. "Now, tell me about this little problem you have," Dad continues, turning his attention to Jason.

"It's nothing, Dad."

"I'm not dropping this, so you can tell me or I can have Carey tell me," Jason rolls his eyes at Dad's words.

"I may have a little infection. It's not a big deal. I'm taking care of it."

"Infection? You told me you had an STD," I whisper to Jason.

"An STD is an infection...wait, you have an STD?" Dad yells, but Jason just shrugs.

"Shit, Jason. What the hell is wrong with you? Please tell me you are not having unprotected sex."

"Well, *obviously*, I did," Jason starts to get angry, then takes a deep breath and continues more calmly. "Most of the time I *am* careful, but there have been a few times when I haven't used a condom. I know it was stupid. Now, I'm paying the price."

"How bad is it?" Dad asks.

"It's just a little bit of gonorrhea. That's the only thing that showed on the test, but the doctor is treating me for chlamydia, too. You know, just to be on the safe side. I have to get rechecked next month. Really, Dad, it's nothing to freak out about," Jason explains.

"Don't act like this isn't serious, son. Please tell me you haven't had sex for the past few weeks," Dad pleads. Carey and I snort. Jason's look shuts us both up.

"Dammit, Jason. How stupid are you?" Dad yells.

"I'm not going to infect anyone else." Jason whines. "I've been using condoms since I found out," Jason tells Dad. Then, he turns to our brother. "Thanks, Carey. I really needed this today," He says angrily.

"Don't be mad at me. I'm not the one screwing everything that moves."

"No, you're just the one screwing up his life"

"Jason," Dad warns.

"You just can't stand it that the three of us actually do something with our time. I mean other than get high. You had to open your big mouth. Thanks a lot for once again turning everything to shit. I hope you're happy," Jason yells at Carey.

"Fuck off," Carey says, getting up.

"You're not walking away from this. You caused the problem. You're going to deal with it." Jason blocks Carey's path.

"Get out of my way," Carey says, shoving Jason. Jason pushes back and Carey stumbles. As soon as he recovers, he takes two steps toward Jason and then takes a swing at him. Jason sees it coming, ducks, and tackles Carey. Jason has Carey on the ground in seconds. Carey is yelling, cursing, and fighting against Jason. Someone should probably step in, but we just let them handle it. Surely, Dad will stop them before someone actually gets hurt. Jason finally pins Carey down and holds him there for a solid minute before Carey tires out and quits fighting. I know because I timed it. When Jason lets go, Carey gets up and immediately storms out, slamming the back door behind him. I knew family time wouldn't last long.

Jason

I left the house not long after Carey and ended up at Brody's. I am so pissed at him for calling me out in front of my family. It's not a big deal. I took all of the antibiotics the doctor prescribed. I should be clear by now. If I'm being honest, I'm angry at myself. I shouldn't have said that stuff to Carey about being a screw up.

"Want to talk about it?" Brody asks, handing me another beer.

"No," I tell him for the hundredth time. Why won't he back off?

"Sorry. It's just that I've never seen you care about anything other than yourself and your car. Your *baby* is in the driveway, so I know she's fine. The only thing you love more than that car is your dick, so unless it fell off, I can't understand what has you so upset."

"I'm not upset! I just don't want to talk about it," I yell at him and then down the beer. I open another one immediately. All I want to do is get wasted and lose myself in a nice piece of ass. "Get some girls here, now," I tell Brody.

"Is that going to help?" he asks.

"Now!" I yell, glaring at him. He must know I'm about to beat the shit out of him because I have never seen him move that fast.

It doesn't take long for the girls to show up. It never does. If Brody or I call, the girls come running. They can't get enough of us. Tammy walks in like she owns the place with Mia and some girl I don't know following her.

"Hi, hot stuff," Mia says, straddling me. "This is my friend from college, Debbie," she says this even though she knows I don't care. Mia starts kissing me with that magic tongue and the world is suddenly a better place. We kiss for a few minutes before she starts removing clothes; hers and mine. I look over at Brody, and he already has Tammy on her knees sucking his dick. He smiles at me, and I turn my attention back to Mia. When I do, I realize that her and Debbie are both naked and on their knees in front of me. They both start licking up and down my cock. Damn, it feels good. Debbie's tongue works just as well as Mia's. They take turns sucking my length into their throats. If they keep this up, I am going to come too soon.

"Kiss," I tell them, pushing their faces toward each other. It gives me a chance to calm down, plus it's hot to watch girls make out. They don't even hesitate before their tongues are in each others mouths. Soon, Mia breaks the kiss and takes one of Debbie's nipples into her mouth. Debbie moans in pleasure, and it's obvious this isn't the first time these two have fooled around. As Mia makes her way down, kissing Debbie's stomach and thighs, I stroke myself and watch.

Brody is watching Mia and Debbie while Tammy continues to suck him. Debbie moves to the couch and spreads her legs for Mia. Mia immediately starts licking Debbie's slit, and I almost blow my load at the sound of her pleasure.

"Come here," Debbie smiles and motions me over. I oblige, standing on the couch and pushing my aching length into her mouth. The vibration every time she moans is about to send me over the edge. I'm glad these two found each other. I will definitely call on them again. After a few minutes, Brody motions for me to join him and Tammy. I am more than happy to join them since the other two seem fine without me. Debbie pulls Mia onto the couch and kisses her way down to Mia's breasts. She spends time sucking one nipple and then the other into her mouth. Mia moans as she guides Debbie's head down lower. I know the instant Debbie licks Mia's folds. The sounds of her pleasure fill the room. Tammy's mouth feels great, but watching those girls get each other off is the hottest thing I've ever witnessed. I'm mesmerized by the action on the other side of the room while I fuck Tammy's mouth. Brody is banging her from behind. A thought occurs to me.

"Hey, Brody, this takes me from 199 to 202. Where you at?"

"Fuck you, you bastard. You can't count this as three. You're only jizzin' in one."

"Bullshit! They all sucked my dick."

"Rule number 1 states you have to finish even if she doesn't. We set these rules so your lying ass couldn't cheat."

"Clearly, you've never been blown by Mia *and* Debbie. But whatever, I'll claim 200. You're just pissed off because you're losing. What's your number again?"

"195," Brody mumbles.

All Tammy can do is take the assault as we pound her harder and harder. She loves it. This isn't the first time we've shared her. We're both close, and it isn't long before we are filling her from both ends.

"Swallow it all," I command as I explode into her mouth. Tammy always does as she is told.

If the screams of pleasure are any indication, it sounds like Mia and Debbie have reached their peak as well. Brody and I hand the girls their clothes as quickly as possible.

"Thanks girls," Brody says as he pulls on his shorts. He opens the front door, motioning for them to leave.

"Any time, boys," Mia says, making her way out with her friends in tow.

"Damn, that was awesome. Thanks," I tell my friend as he closes the door.

"Feel better?" he asks.

"Yep." I open another beer and soon I am well on my way to reaching my goal of forgetting about tonight.

Carey

Since all hell broke loose a couple of weeks ago, my dad and brothers have been on my case constantly, causing the last two weeks of summer to *suck*. After the night Jason tackled me, I stayed away for two days. During the day, I found some secluded shade on the north end of the island, and at night I slept on the soft couch on the porch at the bookstore. Mrs. Watson must have known because both mornings I found bottled water and a small bag of snacks waiting for me.

I didn't even bother calling or texting. My dad probably used that stupid app he has to keep track of my location. No one came for me, so I stayed out until I needed a shower and some real food.

The last thing I wanted to do was face Jason. He had no right to treat me that way. I know I'm a screw up. I don't need him rubbing it in my face. My dad grounded me for a week when I finally returned; like that matters. He isn't home enough to know what I do or where I go.

As much as I hate the thought of going back to school, it has to be better than being in that house all day. School starts back tomorrow, and I'll need more than a few pills to face it. It's gonna be impossible to avoid Seth. The entire island only has a population of about 5,000, so the high school isn't that big. I know we'll have some classes together. He's a year ahead of me in school, but we always choose the same electives.

It should be some comfort to have Sean and Nick there, but we still aren't getting along. They're still being jerks to me. I've spent the past few weeks avoiding them as much as possible. I've been civil, but tried not to spend much time at home. Okay, that's a lie. I've tried to be civil, but my family makes that too damn hard. Especially since the night Jason tackled me. That was totally unnecessary and just proves to me once again that my family doesn't care about me. All they want to do is attack me and tell me all the shit I do wrong, but they never care when I do something right. Hell, no one even notices when I do something right.

I've spent most of my time at the Watson's. I've written a few more songs and worked on my novel. Last night, I researched how to sell a song even though I know I'll never follow through. I have all the information I need to send my novel to be rejected by publishers, but I know I'll chicken out and never do anything about it. I want it to be good enough to fulfill my dream, but I have too many doubts.

I spent the last few days of my freedom getting high, and now it's the night before school starts. My brothers keep trying to pick fights with me, and it's putting me on edge. I decide to head up to my room early since they won't leave me alone. It makes me want to punch someone in the throat. A couple of pills should calm my nerves.

As I make my way through the halls on the first day of my sophomore year, I'm glad to have Sean and Nick at school despite the way I've been treating them. As much as I hate admitting it, I love my brothers and know they will always be there for me, even when I just can't stop being a jackass. I hate the way I've been treating them, but I can't get my life together. I am miserable because of the choices I've made over the past few years, and the secret I keep is weighing heavily on me. My brothers would probably help me if I asked, but I won't drag them into my messed up world. Instead, I push them away more each day. Maybe if I push them hard enough, it will hurt less when they cut me out of their lives.

I'm in my own head, navigating the halls and trying to get to homeroom. As I round the corner at the end of the hall, Seth is only a few steps away. Damn my luck. He's talking to our friend Travis. They must be standing outside of their homeroom. This hallway has all of the sophomore and junior homerooms and Seth and Travis are always in the same one. For the first time, I'm glad that Seth is older. Not sure I could stomach beginning every day this year with him. Seth freezes when he sees me. He looks as nervous as I feel. I pause when we make eye contact, but quickly try to pull myself together and act nonchalant. Before I can get past them, Travis calls out to me.

"Hey, Carey. What's up?" he calls. I would be a total ass if I ignore him. The thought of being near Seth makes my skin crawl and pisses me off all over again.

"'Sup, Travis?" I nod quickly in his direction, wishing I didn't have to talk to him.

"What happened to your hand?" he asks, looking at the splint. The cast was removed a few days ago, but Riley said I should wear the splint for another week.

"Oh...I...um," He caught me off guard, and I am stuttering like an idiot. Seth's presence is making me nervous because I have no idea if he's already told Travis anything. I finally go with the story I gave my family, "I broke it a few weeks ago playing basketball."

I shrug as if it's no big deal, daring a look in Seth's direction. He winces a little but looks relieved at the same time. Probably thankful that I didn't say more. He must be keeping secrets now, too.

"I see your face healed." My words are dripping in sarcasm. It pisses me off that his face shows no sign of his broken nose, and I am still stuck in this stupid splint. I turn to walk towards my classroom without another word.

I have no doubt Travis is wondering what is going on with us, but thankfully the bell rings before Travis stops me.

This day could not have passed any slower. I have two classes with Seth and for the first time in my life I made sure to sit as far away from him as possible. We always sit next to each other, unless a teacher separates us for cutting up. I've never been as relieved as I am when the final bell rings. I make a beeline for my locker and then quickly head to the parking lot. Nick's football practice doesn't start for forty-five minutes, so he'll drive Sean and me home, then come back. As I near the parking lot, I notice a group of guys hanging out near Travis' silver Jeep.

"Shit," I mumble as I get closer and see that it's Seth, Travis, my brothers, and a few other guys we hang around. I'm not in the mood for this so I keep walking toward Nick's car and act like I don't see any of them.

"Carey," Sean calls as I pass them, but I don't acknowledge him. I hate treating my other friends this way, but that's the price they pay for being around Seth.

"Hey, Carey. Wait up," Seth calls, catching up to me, but I keep walking. "Stop," he grabs my arm, forcing me to stop. My rage is ready to explode. I jerk my arm free.

"Can we talk, man?" he asks. Crossing my arms, I just glare at him.

"Look, I get it, Carey. I screwed up, but it's not what you think," I snort my disgust and turn my back on him. Seth steps around me. "You need to let me explain."

"Dead friendships can't give an explanation."

Seth doesn't move so I leave him standing there, dumbfounded.

"Carey," Nick calls, catching up as I reach his car. God, why won't people just leave me alone? "What's your problem? This shit with Seth has been going on for weeks."

"Can we just go home?" I reply as a non-answer. I light a cigarette mostly because I know Nick hates it. I take a few drags, waiting for Sean to make his way to the car.

"That was awkward," Sean says as he reaches us.

"Drop it," I say angrily.

"What's your problem?" Sean asks defensively. I blow smoke in his face instead of answering.

"Asshole!" he says, hitting my shoulder with his as he passes. Anger erupts within me. I drop my bookbag and cigarette, grab the front of his shirt, and slam his back against the car as hard as I can.

"Ow," he groans.

"Don't ever push me, you son of a bitch!" I yell in his face still holding onto his shirt. Without thinking, I let go with one hand and pull back to punch him when someone grabs my arm.

"Let. Him. Go," Seth speaks firmly and deliberately, stepping between Sean and me and putting his hands on my chest. I do as I'm told, noticing it's my injured hand I'm threatening to hit Sean with. All I need is to break it again.

Rage floods by body when I realize Seth is touching me.

"Get your disgusting hands off of me!" I growl, shoving Seth back. He stumbles, but quickly gains control, taking a step toward me. I hold my ground, ready for a fight.

"Get in the car, Sean," Nick calls over his shoulder, stepping between Seth and me. I have never seen Sean move that fast.

"This isn't going to solve anything." He tells me. "I don't know what's going on with you, but don't take it out on Sean," I drop my shoulders and study the ground as Nick lectures.

"If you ever lay another hand on Sean, I'll beat the shit out of you. Get. In. The. Car." Seth orders. I don't say a word as I pick up my bag and get in. Who the fuck does Nick think he is getting between my fist and Seth's face? I could have taken him. And when did it become Seth's job to protect Sean. This is all bullshit!

Nick says something to Seth, and Seth nods then heads toward his jeep. Nick gets in the car without a word. The air in the car is thick with tension as we silently head out of the parking lot.

After a few minutes, I calm down enough to realize that Nick might be right, and I feel bad for what I

94

did to Sean. I hate seeing the fear on Sean's face. Fear I put there. I didn't mean to scare him. I just reacted without thinking again. I do that a lot and people always get hurt.

Nick

Things are getting worse with Carey. I've never seen him treat Sean that way, no matter how angry he gets. I've seen him treat others like shit, start fights, and lay into Jason and me, but never Sean. Some bad stuff must be going on for him to threaten our baby brother. The car ride is silent and uncomfortable, but I can't let this go. I have to confront him.

"What the hell was that, Carey?" I ask.

"Nothing," Carey retorts.

"Nothing, my ass. You almost hit Sean."

"I'm fine," Sean pipes up from the back.

"Shut up, Sean," I tell him, "This doesn't concern you."

"Actually, it does concern me. I'm the one who almost got clocked."

"Why are you pissed at Sean?" I ask Carey.

"I'm not mad at Sean."

"Then why did you attack him?"

"I didn't attack him! God, Nick!" Carey yells with exasperation.

"Yes, you did. Whether you want to admit it or not you're turning into a real bastard. You kind of remind me of Riley."

"I am nothing like that fucking asshole," he yells, coming out of his seat and taking a swing at me.

I duck, and he misses, but I swerve into oncoming traffic while avoiding his fist. I recover before I cause an accident. My heart is racing as the car I almost hit passes us, and the guy driving lays on his horn.

"Son of bitch, Carey. You could have gotten us killed."

"So, no one cares if I die," he mumbles, returning to his seat.

"Whoa, what's that supposed to mean? We would all care if something happened to y…"

"Stop shoveling the shit, Nick. You know everyone would be better off if I wasn't around."

"That's not true," Sean whispers from the backseat, clearly hurt.

"Don't *ever* compare me to Riley," Carey say, ignoring Sean.

I know it was low because he hates our uncle, but it's true. He is starting to remind me of him. Riley is a pompous ass who thinks he's better than all of us because he's a doctor. He treats all of us like crap, always trying to get the upper hand. Ryan and Reid take it in stride, but they grew up with him. Sometimes Dad will step in if Riley gets too out of line, but usually he just let's it go. I don't know what it is, but they're like oil and water. It's gotten worse over the past few years. Every time Riley is around, they end up in an argument. More than once, we have expected it to come to blows. Carey and Riley are both like bombs just waiting to explode.

Carey

Sean immediately goes to the back porch and parks himself in a lounge chair overlooking the beach; his safe place. It's the place he always re-treats to when he needs to pull himself together. I shouldn't have snapped at Sean. It isn't fair that I'm taking my anger out on him. I should follow him and make amends, but I've been sober for too many hours. It's just too hard to deal with reality when I'm not high.

I'm glad Nick has to return to school. He's getting on my nerves. I can't believe he said I remind him of Riley. That was the worst insult he could have used. I hate Riley, and I will never be anything like that shithead.

Grabbing a six pack from the fridge, I head up to my room. What I said in the car is true. I've thought about it several times recently. My family would be better off without me. Nick wouldn't admit it, but he knows I'm right. I close the bedroom door and take out my pain pills so I can get lost for the night. The first day of school was worse than I expected. I can't do this all year. There has to be a way to avoid Seth, keep my brothers off my case, and have friends. Actually, maybe I don't need friends. I could just ig-nore everyone. I have my writing, music, and drugs. Who needs friends?

I pop a few pills into my mouth and wash them down with a beer. It doesn't take long before I start to feel the effects. I know I shouldn't mix the pain meds with alcohol, but I take a few more pills with the second beer. Fog clouds my head, and I can barely stand up by the time I open the third beer. Finally, I'm on my way to where I want to be.

Sean

The back door slams behind me, and I drop into a chair overlooking the beach; my go to place when I need to be alone. It isn't very private, but no one will bother me today since Nick will go to practice and Carey is upstairs, angry. He's barely spoken to me in two weeks. Why would this afternoon be any different?

I'm still reeling from the events of the past few minutes. I can't believe Carey almost hit me! He would have if Seth hadn't stopped him. We've argued and wrestled over the years, but he has never tried to punch me in the face. I hate the person Carey has become; angry, sullen, mean, and now he's escalated to violent. I hate sharing a room with him because I'm afraid of what he will do. I'm not sure if I'm more afraid of him hurting me or himself. I wipe the tears with the back of my hand. More than anything, I just want to be able to save my brother. I am tired, so very tired. The constant worrying is wearing me out. I need to find a way to get through to him, but I just don't know how.

"Hey, little brother, you okay?" Jason asks, startling me. I must have zoned out. The sun is lower, and I didn't even hear the door open.

"Yeah, I'm fine," I wave him off.

"Was the first day of high school that bad?" he asks.

"No, the day was fine."

"Then, what's up?" he asks, taking the seat next to me, "You don't look so hot."

"What do you think is wrong, Jase?"

"Carey," he says knowingly.

"He was an ass to Nick. He almost punched me, but Nick stopped him. Then he tried to hit Nick *while* he was driving. Nick almost lost control of the car. It scared the shit out of me." The pitch of my voice rises with each statement as I get more upset.

"Damn. That's bad even for Carey."

"He's becoming violent, Jason. It's starting to worry me. I think I need to tell Dad what happened in the car."

"Are you sure you want to deal with that fall out?" he asks.

"I don't know," I shrug, "I guess not." Jason is right. Carey will make life even more miserable if I tell Dad. "I'm just getting sick of him."

"We're all sick of Carey." We sit in comfortable silence for a long while; both lost in our own thoughts. Finally, I speak my worst fears.
"What if we can't save him, Jason? What happens then? I can't stand the thought of him ending up like Mom."

"He has already turned into Mom," Jason says sadly.

"I meant dead," I whisper.

"We won't let that happen, Sean," Jason says, as if he actually believes the lie he's spinning.

"How are we gonna stop it from happening?"

"I don't know, but we'll figure out something, Seany. I promise." We sit quietly for a few minutes. I watch the waves while warring with myself, trying to think of a way to save my brother. Is it even worth trying? Maybe I should start sleeping on the couch. I don't know how many more nights I can spend in the same room as Carey.

"Are you going to be okay if I leave? I can cancel my plans if..."

"Just go, Jase. It's fine." I forgot he was sitting next to me.

"Are you sure?" he asks reluctantly.

"I'm sure," I insist.

"Call me if you need me," he says, heading down the back steps. I don't really want to be alone with Carey, but I'm not going to ask Jason to cancel his plans.

There's no telling when Dad will get home. He's a detective for the county. Even though our beach town has a low crime rate, there's a larger city about twenty minutes inland in the same county. Their crime rate is much higher.
He's been investigating three big cases over the past month, and working late most nights.

I head inside to cook something shortly after

Jason leaves. Jason and Nick will be starving when they get home later tonight. I chop up veggies for homemade spaghetti sauce. I enjoy cooking, so when Dad isn't here, I take care of it. It takes about an hour to make the sauce, but I don't mind. Cooking relaxes me and gives me time to think. This is a recipe I found online. I've tweaked it a little and added some things I like.

Once the noodles are ready, I head upstairs to get Carey. I hope I can convince him to eat something, but I'm not sure how he will react to me. He might still be angry. If he tries to hurt me, no one's home to stop him. I shake those thoughts away. I shouldn't be afraid of my brother. I take a deep breath to calm my nerves. I shouldn't feel the need to knock on my own door, but Carey is already irritated. I have no desire to add fuel to his fire. He doesn't respond, so I knock again, but there is only silence.

"Real mature. Just ignore me," I mumble, rolling my eyes. I probably should leave him alone for the night. He'll come out when he gets hungry. I start to walk away. But, you know what? Screw that! It's my room, too. I have every right to go in, and I know he needs to eat something. I barge in before I lose my nerve.

"Carey, I cooked dinner," I say, opening the door. That's weird, I don't see him.

"Carey?" I call again, entering the room.

As I walk around my bed, my whole world implodes. Carey is lying face down between our beds.

"Shit! Carey!" I yell, turning him over.

I'm freaking out, screaming his name, and crying. He isn't moving, and he is pale. I mean *really* pale. I can't tell if he's breathing, and I don't know how to check for a pulse. Even if I did, I'm probably shaking too much to feel it. I pull my brother's head and shoulders into my lap and cradle him in one arm while I dial 911.

"Please don't be dead. Please don't be dead," I keep saying over and over as I wait for someone to answer.

I give the dispatcher all the information she needs and hang up. She tries to keep me on the line, but I have to call my family.

Jason

I probably should have stayed and comforted Sean, but I had this smoking hot girl waiting on me. We met this morning at the beach, and now we're at the condo she's renting for the week. Her friends had big plans to go to dinner and then to some club in town tonight so we have the condo to ourselves for the next several hours. She cooked me dinner, and we shared a bottle of wine.

I'm thrilled to find out that this chick's a true redhead. In my experience, redheads are usually wild and a little crazy. I am balls deep in her when my phone rings on the bed next to me. I ignore it and keep pounding this girl. It rings again, but I continue to ignore it. When it starts ringing for a third time in less than a minute, I reach for it, not stopping what I'm doing. If this is Brody fucking with me, I'm going to kill him. It wouldn't be the first time he interrupted me just because he can. I pick it up, and I'm about to turn it off when I see Sean's number. He never calls me, and he was upset when I left.

I slow my thrusting while I debate whether or not I should answer it. The ringing stops, so I figure the decision is made for me. As soon as I pick up the pace, the phone rings. I'm staring at Sean's number again. This can't be good.

"Sean...I'm a ....litt...," I say between thrusts. I just need to get him off the phone so I can finish.

"Jason. Help me!" he cuts me off.

"Sean, what's wrong?" I ask. Everything stops when I hear the panic in Sean's voice.

"It's Carey. I think he's dead," he cries into the phone. Please tell me I misheard him. Please tell me he did not just say those words.

"What happened, Sean?" I ask, fearing the answer.

"I don't know. I found him unconscious in our room."

"Is he breathing?" I ask, jumping off the bed.

"I don't fucking know, Jason. Somebody needs to help me. Please, Jase. He can't die in my arms." Sean is losing his mind on the other end of the phone, and I am completely helpless. I *knew* I should have stayed at home.

"Did you call an ambulance?" I manage to get my clothes on as I question him.

"Yes, I can hear them coming."

"Stay on the phone, Seany, but go let them in."

"I can't leave Carey."

"It's okay to leave him for a minute," I try to stay calm for Sean, but I am freaking out as I grab my keys.

"Where are you going? We aren't done," the girl whines behind me. I turn and just glare at her. "What? I didn't come," she says, like that matters when my brother could be dead.

"Find someone else, whore," I tell her, slamming the door behind me. I hear Sean talking to the paramedics, and then he's back on the phone with me.

"Jason, the police want to talk to me. Am I in trouble? Did I do something wrong?" His words are full of terror and confusion.

"Sean, they just want to know what happened. Tell them everything you know. You didn't do anything wrong, okay," I try to calm him.

"I think he took too many pills, Jase. Why would he take too many pills?"

"Sean!" I yell, gaining his attention. Then I speak calmer. "Hand the phone to the officer." I talk to the officer as I speed home. All I can think about is that I have to get to Sean.

Carey

My eyes are heavy, and I find it hard to open them. There is a haze in my brain as I try to wake myself up. I feel like I've been asleep for years. I slowly begin to hear a strange beeping and every so often the swish of forced air. The sounds are far away at first, but soon it's all I hear. I try to concentrate, but my head's killing me. Something squeezes my left arm. What the hell? I look that way, but can't focus. I blink a few times hoping to wash away the haze, but it doesn't do any good. I try to move my arms, and find they are strapped down. What the fuck? I'm in a bed in a room that I don't recognize, tied down with machines hooked to me. When realization hits, I immediately freak out. Holy shit! What's going on? Where am I? I try to scream, but there is no sound. I can't move or talk. What the fuck is happening? I close my eyes hoping this is just a bad dream. My mind races with fear and confusion. When I open them again nothing has changed. I start to thrash and pull at the straps. I have to get out of here.

"Hey, Kid, calm down," I hear a voice I recognize to my right.

My uncle, Ryan, is the only one who calls me Kid. He's my father's much younger brother. I mean younger by sixteen years. He lived with us for a year when he was a teenager. I was only five, but we had an instant bond that has only grown stronger over the years. He's more like another brother than an uncle. When Ryan comes into view, he smiles, and I relax a little.

"Finally awake," he seems relieved. "You scared the crap out of us, Kid," he continues. "Don't try to talk or move. You have a tube down your throat helping you breath, and they have your arms strapped to the bed so you don't hurt yourself again."

Hurt myself *again*? What is he talking about? I didn't hurt myself. I look at him hoping he can see the question in my eyes.

"Don't worry. You're safe now." He rubs a comforting hand through my hair and smiles again. It's a nice gesture, but doesn't really help. I need to know what happened. I need to be able to talk. I need to be able to move my arms. I pull on the arm straps again and try to sit up. Of course that's pointless, since I'm tied to this damn bed!

"Kid, you need to calm down. You don't want your blood pressure to go up. They just got it stabilized."

IIe really isn't helping me be less confused or scared. The only reason I'm not in full panic mode is because Ryan is the one talking to me. His presence can calm me down instantly.

"Try to relax, Kid. The doctor should be back in a few minutes. As long as you're stable, he's going to take the tube out of your throat." At least I know I'm in a hospital. Hopefully, I can get some answers once I'm able to talk.

I close my eyes, but I can't relax. What happened that earned me a visit to the hospital and made my family think that I hurt myself? I remember being at school and everyone was on my case, even Sean. I went home and had a beer and a few pills to take the edge off. That's all; the last thing I remember is drinking a beer. Ryan is quiet. Maybe he thinks I'm asleep. I continue to rack my brain, but nothing else makes it through the fog.

The door creaks open, and I hear my dad ask if anything has changed, and Ryan explains that I woke up for a few minutes. I keep my eyes closed and just listen. I need information. Maybe if they think I am sleeping, they will continue to talk. But then it's quiet for so long, I begin to think the conversation is over before it really got started.

"The boys reluctantly went to school. I didn't think I'd ever get them out of the house this morning. I know they want to be here with Carey, but they've got to get back to normal. They have already missed two days, and it's only the first week of school," my dad starts.

Two days? Have I really been unconscious for two days?

"It's best that they stay on track. There's nothing they can do here," Ryan agrees.

"Reid, you don't really believe that Carey did this on purpose?" I can hear the concern in Ryan's voice.

"I don't know what to think. He was unconscious, and you saw the toxicology report. I can't imagine *this* was an accident. Not with that level of narcotics in his system and a blood alcohol level of .12." My dad sounds frustrated and defeated. He's not usually one to worry, but I can hear the fear in his voice. I put that there. Once again, I did something stupid and upset everyone. *Apparently*, this time it went too far. It sounds like they think I drank too much and took a lot of pills. I mean, I like to take pain pills to take the edge off, but I wouldn't over do it.

"Sounds like you are siding with the doctor," Ryan brings me out of my reverie.

"I didn't say that," Dad retorts.

"You didn't have to, Reid," Ryan snaps.

"So you think all of this is just an accident? He overdosed, Ryan. My son is strapped to a bed with a tube down his throat. He's been in a coma for two days. He almost died!" Dad yells. Then, calmer, "Hell, maybe he wants to die, and all of this is pointless. If that's what he wants, he'll find a way." There is a long pause, and I can hear someone pacing. My dad is convinced that I overdosed on purpose. I would never do that. I don't want to be dead. I don't think I want to be dead. I'm not sure what I want any more.

"I don't believe that Carey tried to kill himself," Ryan finally speaks.

"That makes one of us." My dad sighs heavily, like the weight of the world is on him. "Sometimes I wonder if we would all be better off if Carey would just go ahead and do it."

"Reid!" Ryan yells.

My heart sinks. Oh my God, my dad actually wishes I was dead. If that's what he wants, I can make it happen. It's not like I haven't thought the same thing countless times before.

"I didn't mean it that way. I do NOT want my son dead!" My dad exclaims and then continues to speak barely above a whisper, "but, I'd be lying if I said similar thoughts haven't crossed my mind. I am truly afraid Carey thinks overdosing is his only way out. I often wonder if he just wants to escape it all and won't stop until he succeeds. He's always so angry. He's been fighting depression for months, maybe longer, and I haven't done enough to help him. I thought it was a silly phase of puberty-induced rebellion. Now that my fears have become reality, I know how wrong I was. I would be devastated if I lost Carey, and his brothers would never recover."

"None of us would, Reid. I know these past months have been tough. I can't imagine what it feels like to watch your son fight his own demons."

"Helpless and hopeless, Ryan. I feel helpless and hopeless all of the time."

"Then step in and do something. He doesn't have to fight alone. You never gave up on me. You fought so hard to keep me from letting my own stupid choices ruin my life. You fought for me; you fought with me. You did everything to get me back on track and focused on the future even when the present seemed impossible for me to overcome. Why are you giving up on Carey?" I don't know what Ryan is talking about, but apparently he had some kind of trouble in his past.

"I'm not giving up on him."

"Yes, you are, Reid. Whether you want to admit it or not, it's true."

"You make it sound so simple," Dad bites out sarcastically.

"It can be simple. Take one thing at a time. Start with the depression. If you think he's depressed, take him to see someone."

"Like Carey would agree to go," Dad says, caustically.

"Quit making excuses and be the fucking parent, Reid! Make him go," Ryan snaps. I rarely hear my uncle curse. He must be really pissed at my dad.

"You're not a parent, Ryan. It's easy for you to tell me what to do. Tell me how easy it is when you have kids of your own."

"That sounds like a cop out."

"Think whatever you want. You seem to have it all figured out. Maybe you should raise him."

"Jesus, Reid. Listen to yourself. Can you honestly tell me that you want to give up? You want to just hand Carey over to me? Wash your hands of all of his problems?"

"No." He sounds more crushed than I have ever heard him, "I want to help him. More than anything, I want to keep him safe; protect him. I love him so much. But I feel like I'm failing him and

I don't know what to do." My dad's voice catches, and he has to clear his throat before continuing. "When I got that call from Jason, I thought for sure Carey was gone. I thought I had lost him, Ryan." My dad's breathing changes and he starts to whimper quietly. At first, I don't realize that he's crying, but suddenly he is sobbing uncontrollably. He tries to say more, but can't seem to get any words out. It's weirding me out to hear all of this from my dad.

"It isn't too late. He's still here with us. We can help him, Reid. I'll do anything I can. Whatever he needs, I'm here for him," Ryan promises my dad. The room is quiet except for the beep of the machines and my dad's crying as he slowly gets himself under control. I don't know what to think. He was all over the place in that conversation. Does he really love me and want to help, or would he just be better off if I was gone? I don't know what to believe.

"Did Nick or Sean tell you anything else about what happened on Monday?" my uncle asks.

"Not much. Either they really don't know or they are keeping quiet. You know they have this weird bond thing. They never rat each other out. God, I hope they are telling the truth. I hate to think that my boys would keep something this serious a secret. Nick did say that Carey wasn't acting like himself on Monday; he was angry and wouldn't even talk to his friends. That sounds suspicious to me," Dad says. "Sean hasn't said much of anything since he found Carey. You know he was the only one home, and he has just shut down. Jason agrees with me."

"Of course, he does."

"What's that supposed to mean?"

"It means that Jason always agrees with you. He never expresses his own opinion to you." Ryan is getting angry again. I'm glad someone is sticking up for me even if it isn't doing any good.

The door to the room opens, and my dad and uncle stop talking. Even in the silence, I can feel the tension between them.

"He's stable now. The most life-threatening of the detox symptoms are subsiding. There could be some additional side effects of the drug use, but for now, his blood pressure is back in normal range. We've weaned him off of oxygen, and he has been breathing room air on his own for a couple of hours. I think we can remove the endotracheal tube."

"Carey, can you hear me?" the doctor gently shakes my arm, "Can you open your eyes for me?" I do as I'm asked and have to blink a few times to adjust to the bright light. I try to act as if I'm just waking up. I don't want my dad to know I heard everything he said.

"You're in the Pediatric ICU, son," the doctor says as he comes into focus. "You have a tube in your throat because you were having some trouble breathing when they brought you in. I'm going to remove the tube. Your throat will be sore for a few days, but that's nothing to worry about," he continues.

The doctor speaks quietly and calmly; quickly putting my fears to rest. He tells me everything that he's doing, and how it will feel. I'm so glad to have that thing out of my throat. He's right, my throat is dry, and it feels like sandpaper when I swallow. I want to sit up, but I'm still strapped down. I have to try several times before any words actually come out.

"Water," I finally manage. Ryan pushes a button and sits my bed up a little so I can sip some water. My dad didn't even speak to me before he followed the doctor into the hallway to talk about me privately.

"Straps," I plead

"I can't...," he starts.

"Please. I didn't hurt myself." My voice is hoarse, and it hurts to talk, but I need to plead my case.

"Eavesdropping?" Ryan forces an uneasy laugh. I manage a guilty smile, knowing I'm caught. "I guess you weren't asleep after all," he says, shaking his head.

"At least, you believe me," I croak out.

"You heard everything, Kid?" he questions. I nod my head without looking at Ryan.

"He hates me."

"He loves you. Your dad is just scared. He..."

"He wishes I died," I cry, cutting Ryan off.

"Stop. That is NOT what he said. That is NOT what he wants," Ryan takes my hand. I want to pull it away, but I can't so I have to allow it. His voice is full of emotion when he continues, "Is this what you want, Kid? Is Reid right? Do you want to end it all?" Ryan blinks back tears as he struggles with the reality of what he's asking. I look away again.

"I don't know," I answer honestly. It's possible that on some level I did this on purpose. I didn't plan it, but I'm well aware of the dangers of taking pills and how much worse the effects can be when they're mixed with alcohol.

"Fair enough," he makes no effort to let go of my hand, "I won't ask anymore questions right now, Kid. The doctor said you need to rest your voice. I'll see what I can do about the straps. Maybe I can convince them to untie you if someone is in the room." That isn't what I want, but it's better that nothing. I nod to indicate my agreement. Ryan squeezes my hand and lets out a sigh.

"You scared us, Kid. Don't ever do that again. Sean thought you were dead when he found you. Hopefully, seeing you awake will help him. He's been a mess for days." I know my uncle isn't trying to make me feel bad, but knowing how much I hurt Sean guts me. It's hard to fight back the tears. First, I treated him like shit, then I almost punched him, and if that wasn't enough, he found me unconscious. Of course, he's a mess and it's all my fault. The one who's been sheltered and kept in the dark had his whole world turned upside down in a matter of hours. He must *hate* me.

Reid

When I get home, Nick and Jason are watching highlights from last week's scrimmage and last night's game and discussing what the team can do better. They won both, but neither was pretty. If they don't make some changes, they won't keep winning. There are some good teams in their division. If they want to come out on top this season, they need to step up their game. Nick loves playing defense, and he's very good. For the past year or so, he's gotten interested in the coaching side. He works with the defensive coach to call plays. His advice was pivotal in some big decisions made last year. They were risky, but helped lead the team to win the state championship.

"Boys, can I talk to you for a minute?" I ask.

"Sure, Dad," Nick says, pausing the game.

"Where's Sean?" I ask. I was hoping to talk to all three of them.

"He went somewhere with Sam," Nick states, rolling his eyes with disgust.

"Good for him. I'm glad he's making some friends," I say honestly. I don't know why Nick hates Sam so much.

"Okay then, it's just the three of us. I know Carey has been angry for awhile," I get straight to the point, "I knew he was going down hill, but I never stepped in and now he's in the hospital. I need you boys to be completely honest with me. Do not sugarcoat this at all." I take a few deep breaths as I pace in front of the windows. This is difficult for me to ask; especially from my children. "Am I different with Carey? Do I really treat him as differently as he says? I try to be fair to all of you. I just need to know where I went wrong."

"You haven't gone wrong, Dad," Jason tells me. "You never treat Carey differently. It's all in his head."

"You've always been hard on all of us. Strict, but fair," Nick adds.

"You ride me all the time about flunking out of college and not being able to keep a job. You pulled me aside and handed me my ass when you found out that I had gonorrhea."

"Yeah, and you are always on me about keeping my grades up so I can get a scholarship," Nick tells me.

"You ride Sean's ass for not being social and losing himself in video games and anime," Jason continues.

"Honestly, you're more lenient on Carey. You let him get away with stuff that you would have never let us get away with because it's easier than dealing with his shit. We all do it. I guess we do treat him differently, but not in a mean way," Nick says.

"Maybe that's the problem. Maybe he needed discipline, and I just ignored his choices so I didn't have to deal with it."

"Don't beat yourself up, Dad. Carey has made some crappy choices lately. It's not your fault," Jason tries to make me feel better. I appreciate his attempt, but it doesn't help.

"Thanks, Jase, but you're wrong. It is my fault. I should have known he was in trouble. I should have seen the signs and stopped him long before he OD'd. I have failed my son," I tell them. I've spent countless hours helping families in similar situations, but I don't know how to help my own son.

"We all failed him," Jason says. Nick rolls his eyes. Nick's phone buzzes, and he quickly reads the text.

"Got to go," Nick says, rushing out of the door before I have a chance to stop him.

"You might as well go, too," I say with a heavy sigh. Jason doesn't wait for me to change my mind.

I take a seat on the couch and stare aimlessly at the frozen image on the television. I hate seeing my boys having such a hard time dealing with everything that's happened over the past few weeks.

Nick is letting his anger fester and taking it out on everyone around him. His anger won't let him agree with Jason and me when it comes to Carey. He played dirty on the field last night and almost got ejected from the game. I've heard that he bullies some of the kids at school. Hopefully, they're just rumors, but I worry that there is some truth to them. I've seen how he treats Sean. If there is really a problem, the school will call. I'll step in then.

Sean has closed himself off more that he normally does, which really scares me. He's only going to be able to hold onto his anger and resentment for so long before he blows. I'm afraid of what will happen when he finally breaks. I just hope it isn't too late to save him. Sean has always been a little socially awkward. He was a late bloomer compared to his brothers. Truth be told, he's still behind most kids his age. Smart as hell, but small and immature. Sam has been good for him. He needs someone with similar interests so he doesn't feel alone. His brothers don't realize how inept they make Sean feel. In their eyes, they are protecting him, but the reality is they make him feel like he isn't good enough. Like he is something less than them. I hate that he feels this way. Of course, Sean would never tell me these things.

Jason covers his emotions by acting like he doesn't care. Girls, cars, and parties are his drugs. When Jason isn't under the hood of his car, he's chasing down another party looking for his next girl. He uses all of these as an escape. Technically, he is an adult so there's not much I can do. If I'm being honest with myself, I'm losing all of my boys in different ways. They all need me for different reasons, but I can't seem to find a way to heal my family.

Carey

I'm moved to a regular room the day after they remove the ventilator. I spend the next few days in the hospital being evaluated by doctor after doctor. It's getting old. At least I finally convinced the shrink that I didn't try to off myself. I'm no longer strapped to the bed, but he wants me in counseling since, *apparently*, I have a drug problem. Now I have to meet with him and get drug tested once a week. Hopefully, that won't last long. I just need a little something to take the edge off, but if I test positive for any drug, my dad threatened to send me to rehab. Who knows if he will actually follow through on that threat? That's all I need right now.

My family has finally stopped hovering. Dad and Ryan are back at work, and my brothers are in school. It's nice not to have a constant babysitter. It's time to get Sean alone and start patching things up with him.

R u in class

It doesn't take long for him to respond to my text, and I'm relieved. He isn't my biggest fan right now, and I was afraid he would ignore me.

On my way to English

Skip

Why?

Come see me

Dad will kill me

He's at work. Don't tell him.

No response comes. I watch the clock while I wait. Two minutes pass. Why did he just end the conversation? Come on, Seany, answer me. Four minutes. Class will start soon, and then he'll never get away. Seven minutes. I'm about to give up when the phone rings, and Sean's number appears.

"Hey. What took so long?" I ask.

"I ran into Nick and some of his asshole friends."

"Did you skip?"

"Yeah, I had to get rid of them, and then sneak out. Do you think I can be back by three?"

"Sure, why?"

"No reason." I can hear the smile in his voice. "Hold on," he says, and I hear a door close.

"Okay, I'll be there in five minutes." Five minutes? It will take at least fifteen to twenty to walk here. What is he doi...

"Did I just hear a car crank?" I ask, catching up.

"See you soon."

"Wait. Bring me some food. I'm starving."

"Okay, bye."

"Wait, whose car did you take?" he laughs at my question.

"What makes you think I took a car?" he questions innocently.

"I heard the door close and the car crank." There is a pause, and I start think he isn't going to answer me.

"Nick's." he finally says reluctantly.

"How do you know how to hotwire a car?"

"I don't. I may or may not have my own set of keys. You know, just in case."

"You what?" I yell.

"Calm down. It's no big deal." Sean blows me off.

"Sounds like this isn't the first time you have 'needed' those keys."

"Probably not," he says with pride, "Nick deserves it. I am so sick of the way him and his football douche-bags treat me and my friends."

"Just get here safely," I say, shaking my head. Sean is definitely my brother. I may be rubbing off on him and not in a good way. Stealing a car at fourteen sounds like me, not Sean. Who am I kidding? I've been "borrowing" cars since I was twelve. How come I never thought to get my own set of keys? I think I just might like this new Sean. I also think I'm going to have a little talk with him for being a hyp-ocrite. He let me have it a few weeks ago when I drove myself to the hospital, and that little shit has his own set of keys.

I need to remember to talk to him later about that last comment. I know Nick and his friends are ass-holes to a lot of the kids at school. They think they run this town, but I had no idea Sean was involved. It sounds like they're pushing him around, and that's low even for Nick.

About fifteen minutes later, Sean walks in. "Here you go," he says, tossing the fast food bag to me.

"Thanks," I open it and take out a burger, "I can't wait for something worth eating. I am so sick of hos-pital food."

"Yeah, well don't tell anyone I brought it to you. You're not supposed to be eating it."

"I'm not eating that crap anymore," I point to the tray of unidentifiable lunch. "I'm going to starve if I stay here much longer." I finish off the large order of fries and two burgers in a matter of minutes. I don't stop to talk until the bag is empty. Then, I wipe my mouth with the sheet. I haven't been this hungry in a long time. I guess being strung out all the time makes you lose your appetite because now that I've been sober for a few days, I'm constantly hungry. To be honest, the hospital food isn't that bad. I was just craving a big, greasy burger.

"That was amazing," I say with a moan.

"A little hungry?" Sean laughs.

I nod in response to his question.

"So are you pissed at me like everyone else?" I ask, getting to the point. I know he needs to get back to school soon.

"I'm not mad, Carey."

"Well, you're the only one."

"I think you're an idiot, but I'm not mad."

"Ryan seems to be the only one not ready to disown me," I say sadly. I hate what I've done to my family. It's going to get worse. I have too many secrets for this to end well.

"I'm not going to disown you, but I can't speak for the rest of the family. Dad is flipping out and of course Jason is such a kiss ass that he always takes Dad's side. Riley is adding fuel to Dad's fire as usual."

"He hates me." I can feel the anger start to bubble up.

"Riley's a jerk. He doesn't like anyone. Don't let him get to you."

"Those reactions don't surprise me. It's Nick who has me confused." We've always gotten along. Now he can barely look at me. It's driving me crazy to feel the anger and disappointment from him.

"He's madder than anyone. He was yelling the other night about how stupid you are and how could you do this to us. I think it was more fear than anger, but he isn't handling this well and we're all suffering."

"What do you mean? You're all suffering."

"It's nothing. He's just angry. He'll get over it when all of this passes," Sean dodges the question. That is so like Sean to hide his feelings. I won't push him now because we have other things to deal with, but if I find out that Nick is taking this out on Sean, I will kick his ass.

"Thanks for not laying into me, Sean."

"This doesn't mean I agree with the drug use. I think it's bullshit, and you need to stop. I just don't see the point of yelling at you. You're not alone with this. I want to help you, but you have to tell me what's going on with you. You just keep everybody out, and it's not healthy."

"Sean, can we not do this now?"

"That's what I mean. You never want to do this."

"Sorry, I just don't see the point in complaining about the crappy hand we've been dealt."

"We haven't been dealt a crappy hand. I know there was a lot of stuff with Mom, but we've had a good childhood. Dad's a good man, and he loves us. The four of us were close growing up and got along for the most part. There's more to whatever you're dealing with, and you're using our childhood as an excuse to dodge the truth." I don't know what to say to that. He's right, and I should have remembered that he's so intuitive. When I keep quiet he continues.

"You're just like Mom," he mumbles under his breath.

"What did you say?" That was a low blow, and he knows it.

"You heard me. You're turning into Mom," he shrugs, "Sorry if the truth hurts."

"I'm nothing like our mother. She was a junkie who had an affair and walked out on us." I'm not thinking clearly about what I'm saying to Sean, and the words pour out of my mouth before I can stop them. "She didn't deserve us, and now we are left to pick up the pieces of the lives she screwed up. It sucks knowing that your mother was a junkie and a whore." He jerks back as if I've slapped him.

"What are you talking about? Mom didn't have an affair."

"Yes she did," I whisper. He's visibly upset. I've kept it to myself for years, and it's screwed me up. Now I'm dropping it on Sean just to get back at him for saying I'm like our mother. He has every right to say that. She died from a drug overdose, and here I am lying in a hospital bed because I took too many pills.

"When?" he asks.

I sigh before continuing, "It was a long time ago. It started before we were born, and it continued on and off for years."

"How do you know?"

"I just know, Sean," I snap.

"How?" He persists.

"I found some papers a few years back."

"You've known for years?" His words are both angry and accusatory. "How many?"

"Just over three," I respond quietly. There is a long pause as Sean processes what I've just said. I know I should try to change the subject, but there is no way he's going to let that happen.

"That was before Mom died." He takes a deep breath and exhales slowly. "Did she know you knew?"

"I confronted her a few months before she died..."

"You talked to Mom?" He cuts me off.

"Yeah, she lived in those run down apartments near the schools. For a couple of years before she died, I would sneak over there during or after school and visit her. I just wanted to get to know her, Sean."

"So did I, but I never got the chance." Sean's words cut like a knife. I've wished for three years that I could go back and change what happened.

"I'm sorry, Sean. I thought there was time for you to get to know her. We talked about it. She wanted to meet you again." I give Sean a minute before I continue. "I wanted to tell everyone I was getting to know her and she was clean, but she said we had to keep quiet." I'm about to cry, and that is the last thing I want to do, so I shrug as if it isn't a big deal.

"Did she kill herself?" he asks in a whisper.

Her death had been ruled an accidental overdose.

There was always speculation, especially from Jason and Nick, that she knew what she was doing.

"No." It isn't a lie. I'm not ready to tell him the truth, but it looks like there isn't going to be another choice.

"Who knows about the affair?"

"Dad and..."

"Dad knew?" he yells, cutting me off. "Who else?"

"Sean, you don't want to know," I shake my head.

"Tell me," he says. I shake my head again. "Tell me!" he yells, "What does it matter now? It can't get much worse." He has no idea how much worse it is going to get.

"Riley knows."

"And Ryan?" he questions.

"I don't think so."

"How do you know Dad and Riley know all of this?" I don't answer at first. This is going to kill Sean.

"I found some paternity papers in Dad's desk. He had us all tested when you were one." He runs a hand through his hair as he paces the room a few times.

"That was right after Mom left the first time," he speaks to himself so I stay quiet. He needs time to work through this. "Riley did the test. That's how he knows."

"No. Well, maybe. I don't know who did the test."

"Then, how do you know that Riley knows?" I can't answer.

All I want is for Sean to drop this. I wish I could take back everything I have told him, but I have to get this off my chest and Sean is the only one I trust.

"Carey, answer me!"

"He...Riley..." How can I break this to him?

"What?" he stops and stares, trying to piece this together, "Wait...are you trying to tell me that Riley had an affair with Mom?" I'm relieved that I don't have to say the words. I nod, unable to confirm the truth out loud.

"Oh, shit! He got Mom pregnant, didn't he?" I nod as he comes to the correct conclusions.

"Who?" he whispers in contrast. "Who?" he asks louder when I don't respond. I can hear the fear in his voice. "Is it me?" he whispers again as the magnitude of this is setting in. He won't even look at me right now.

"No!" I say emphatically. I am not ready to do this, but I can't let him believe it is him. I blink back the tears that threaten to overflow. Sean slowly looks at me, and I can see it in his face the moment he sees the truth in my eyes.

"You," he manages as his tears start to silently fall. Sean looks more crestfallen than I have ever seen him. My silence is all of the confirmation he needs. The paternity test confirmed that I am not Reid's son, and Reid has kept this from me for my whole life.

"I wish it was me," he whispers, shaking his head.

"Wait," he speaks louder, grabbing my attention. "Are you sure Riley saw the test results?"

"I don't know if he saw the results, but I know that he knows."

"How can you be sure?"

"A few weeks after I confronted Mom, I went back to see her. I wanted to talk to her some more because I'd been trying to convince her to tell everyone the truth about me. I wanted Dad to know that I knew about the affair and the paternity test. I was just a kid, I was confused, and I wanted someone else to know. When I got there, Riley's car was parked in front of her apartment. I snuck up to the front window and could hear them arguing. Mom was starting to agree with me. She was trying to convince Riley to come clean. He still didn't know that I knew the whole story. He told her to keep her mouth shut about everything. I left before Riley came out, and only saw her alive one other time because she was dead a few days later."

"I know she was a junkie, but it's still hard to believe that she overdosed. We should have been more important than drugs. Part of me hates her for what she did," Sean tells me his true feelings. He rarely mentions our mother. He was just a baby when she left. I'm not even sure he remembers what she looked like.

"She was clean, Sean. She had been clean for about two years. She was trying to get herself together so Dad would let her be a part of our lives."

"Sure she was, Carey."

"I know it's hard for you to believe, Sean, but it's true. She loved us and wanted to be part of our lives." His eyes soften at my words. I think I see a little hope there, like he wants to believe my words are true.

"Does Dad know you know about the paternity test?" Sean moves the conversation along.

"No, just you...and Mom."

There's a long pause as he stares past me toward the window, and we both try to process this conversation. I think Sean is in shock, he looks a little out of it. I never meant to put all of this on his shoulders. I asked him to come see me so I could convince him that I didn't overdose on purpose. Telling him all of this was never part of my plan. I know I can trust Sean, but I should have waited until things with me were a little more stable. At the same time, part of me is glad to share this with someone else. I've been keeping this secret for over three years. It's been too much for me to handle on my own. I hate Riley, but acting like nothing's wrong every time he's around is killing me. The longer I keep quiet, the more I hate him and the harder it gets to keep my emotions in check.

"Are you going to tell Dad you know?" Sean finally asks.

"Eventually, I think I will."

"I don't know what to say."

"I'm sorry. I didn't plan to..."

"Stop, Carey. I'm glad you told me. You shouldn't have to carry this burden alone." He looks at the clock and sighs.

"I don't want to leave you, but I have to go or I'm not going to make it back before three. I'll be back later. I'm here for you, Care." he promises.

He leans down and hugs me. A real hug, not one of those quick bro hugs. I need it more than I want to admit. I can't remember the last time someone hugged me.

I hate that he has to leave after I just dropped this bomb, but he needs to have Nick's car back in the lot before the last bell. Sean leaves without another word. It's after two thirty, but he has time to make it back. It feels really good to share my secret with Sean. I relax and turn on the TV. Settling back against the semi-hard pillow, my eyelids get heavy almost immediately. I try to fight it, but soon I start to doze off.

Sean

I'm in a daze walking back to the car. If everything
Carey just told me is true, it's no wonder that he's
in this downward spiral. I can't believe our mom
had an affair with our uncle. Is Riley really Carey's
father? This is all so screwed up. I'm beginning to
understand why Carey is so angry all of the time.
I'm pissed, and I'm not even the one most affected
by this news.

My mind is a mess as I drive back to school. I have
plenty of time, but I gun it as soon as I turn onto
Green Street. This road is full of curves, and I know
I'm taking them much faster than I should, but the
speed helps calm some of my anger. As soon as I hit
the sharpest curve, I know I've made a huge mistake. Shit! I'm going too fast. The car starts to slide,
but I overcompensate and lose control. Panic sets in
as the car careens off the road, and suddenly there's
a huge tree right in front of me. There's nothing I
can do. I don't even have time to brace myself before
the violence of the impact throws me forward, and
my head is smashed against the steering wheel with
entirely too much force.

Everything is foggy. My head is killing me, and
there is blood running down my face. I'm scared to
move because my whole body hurts. I try to reach
for my phone in the cupholder. How in the hell did
my phone managed to stay in place? The simple

movement causes excruciating pain to shoot through my side.

Fuck! I need help. It's getting hard to breath. My chest feels like it's closing in on me. I am so scared! This is bad, really bad! The front of the car is wrapped around a tree and smoking. The steering wheel is pushing into my abdomen, and I can barely move. I try opening the door, but it won't budge. Oh, shit! I'm trapped. I try the door again and again. I'm trapped in a smoking car. I have to get out or I am going to die!

"Calm down, Sean," I say out loud, trying to get myself under control. It doesn't do much good. I try to reach my phone again. It takes longer than it should because I can't use my right hand. The pain is unbearable, and it is hanging at an odd angle. My heart is racing and my whole body is shaking. I hit the button for the last number I called, hoping I can stay awake long enough to talk to Carey.

Carey

My phone startles me out of a nap. I look at the screen and see Sean's number. It's already ten after three.

"Did you get caught?" I laugh as I greet him.

"I'm..in...trouble," he sounds out of breath. I will laugh my ass off if Nick caught him sneaking back to school. Only Sean would sneak *into* school. Nick is probably ready to pound him. He's probably out of breath from running from our brother.

"What? Was Nick waiting for you?" I begin to smile thinking about Nick chasing Sean around the parking lot.

"Wrecked...car." My blood runs cold as soon as those words leave his mouth.

"What?" I sit up too quickly and get light-headed. Holding onto the bed, I try to focus on Sean, "Are you okay?"

"Not sure." His breathing sounds laboured. "Green...stree..." I can barely make out what he is saying.

"Sean, did you call the police? Are there other cars involved?" Sean doesn't answer. "Sean. SEANY!" I panic when he doesn't answer.

I have to calm down and quit yelling or the nurses will be in here. I keep trying to get Sean to respond while pacing next to my bed, and frantically looking around for the answer as to what to do.

Sean needs help, but I'm not about to end the call. My eyes land on the hospital room phone sitting on the table next to the bed, and I can't get to it fast enough. I dial Ryan's number and will him to pick up even before it starts ringing.

"Officer Oliver," he answers on the second ring, but it isn't fast enough.

"Sean's in trouble. He needs help. There was an accident," the words rush out even though I can't get my brain to focus.

"Carey, slow down. What are you talking about?"

"Sean wrecked Nick's car. I think he's somewhere on Green Street. I was asking him questions, but he sounded like he was having trouble breathing, and then he quit answering me." I tell Ryan everything I know.

"I'm already on my way. Do you still have him on the line?"

"I think so," I answer.

"Keep trying to get him to respond. I'll call an ambulance."

"Hurry, Ryan. You have to help him!"

"I will help him, Carey, just keep talking to him." With that Ryan hangs up. The silence is deafening. I continue to talk to Sean, but there is nothing from his end until I hear the sirens approaching. Good. He isn't alone anymore, but I still can't relax. My hands are shaking, and I have to sit down. I can hear voices in the background, and then Ryan is finally on the line with me.

"Kid, you still there?" he asks.

"Is he okay? Please tell me he's okay, Ryan."

"The paramedics are with him. I don't know any-thing other than he's breathing, but unconscious." I breathe a small sigh of relief.

"Try to relax a little," Ryan continues "Your dad is on his way to get Nick, and they're going to meet the paramedics at the hospital."

"Okay." I drop the phone and sit back on the bed. I rub my hands over my face trying to clear my mind. What have I done? Sean's hurt, and it's all my fault. He was upset when he left, and was probably driv-ing too fast or not paying attention. He had plenty of time to get back to school. There was no need to rush. Why did I tell him all of that stuff? I knew he would have to drive back to school. I'm so furious with myself. I'm ruining everything. If Sean is seri-ously injured, I will never be able to forgive myself. I turn on the television, but end up staring blankly at the screen. I pick up my book, but throw it across the room after I read the same sentence for the fifth time. The wait is endless, and I have nothing here I can take to calm my nerves. Every nurse I ask refus-es to give me anything, even though my headache won't go away. I just need something to help me escape until I know Sean is okay. If I could just get my hands on a couple of pills...

After almost an hour, there's a knock, and I look up expectantly. It's just the nurse coming to take my vitals. At least, it's Claire. I like her, and I'm pretty sure Ryan does, too. She's funny, and can always get me to relax. Claire was off yesterday and the nurse on the day shift was a complete bitch.

"Hey, Carey." She says brightly. "How are you feeling today?"

"Hi, Claire, I'm okay." I respond absently, watching the clock as the seconds crawl by and thinking about Sean.

"Are you sure you're okay?"

"Yeah, I'm fine."

"I just need to take your vitals and get some blood." She always tells me what she's doing. Claire begins taking my temperature, pulse, and blood pressure. She takes my blood pressure more than once. I can't see the monitor, but why would she check it three times? Could it be off because I'm upset? Probably, but I don't want to tell her about Sean. She's obviously worried even though she tries to act like everything is fine. I just keep quiet while she goes about her business, drawing a vial of blood. She doesn't stab with the needle like that one yesterday, but I still have to look away. I hate needles, and have passed out after getting my blood drawn. She's just leaving when the door opens and my brothers appear.

"How's Sean?" I ask, not giving them a chance to speak first.

"He'll be okay." Jason answers. "He has a bad

break in his wrist, a deep gash on his forehead, a concussion, and a few cracked ribs. There's some bruising on his abdomen where the steering wheel pinned him in the seat, but there doesn't appear to be any internal bleeding. He's going to need surgery on his wrist, but the doctors are going to watch him for the next twenty-four to forty-eight hours then reevaluate. They want to make sure the concussion isn't too bad before they put him under. He should go home a couple of days after the surgery. He's still in the ER. Dad's going to stay with him until they get him in a room."

"It could have been much worse. Ryan showed us pictures," Nick trails off, shaking his head.

"I guess the car didn't fair as well."

"It's totaled. They had to cut the door off, and the steering wheel out to get to him," he says sadly. He doesn't love his car like Jason does, but he's still bummed to be without it. I'm not sure how we'll get back and forth to school now.

"After seeing the car, it's hard to believe Sean wasn't more seriously injured. He's lucky to be alive," Jason continues for Nick. I'm so relieved to hear that Sean will be fine. He scared the crap out of me.

"I'm going to kick his ass the first chance I get. What the hell was he doing driving my car?" Nick's mood switches to anger now that he knows Sean is going to be fine.

"He didn't tell you where he was going?" I ask, hoping Sean kept quiet about being up here.

"Nope, but I'll get it out of him."

"Give him a break," I sigh.

"Shocker, you're on his side; the druggie and the thief."

"Sean isn't a thief!" I yell defensively, "He just borrowed the car without asking, and I'm not some damn druggie. I might take a few pills when things get bad. Sometimes, people need something to help them get through a rough patch." When I say it out loud, it does sound bad. "It isn't like I can't stop whenever I want," I add quickly. Although, waiting to hear news about Sean almost sent me over the edge, and I was desperately hoping for something to calm me down. God, maybe I do need help.

Reid

When I arrive at Mel's, my brothers are already in our usual corner booth. I mostly enjoy our weekly lunch, but I'm dreading it today. Hell, I dread everything these days. Life with Carey has become a nightmare. Frankly, I'm terrified for him. Sometimes, I'm even afraid of him. I don't think he'll hurt any of us on purpose, but he gets so angry at times that I'm afraid one day he'll do something stupid.

"Hey, guys," I greet Riley and Ryan as I collapse into my seat, sighing heavily and studying the table.

"You okay?" Ryan asks.

"Yeah," I wave him off and pick up a menu.

"The boys are fine, Reid. You can stop worrying," Riley rolls his eyes and groans. He has never wanted children so I guess it's hard for him to understand.

"I know Sean is fine, but I'm not so sure about Carey," I tell them honestly.

"Carey is medically fine, but let's be honest, he's a worthless, little prick," Riley says nonchalantly.

"Watch it, Riley! That's my son you're insulting," I reply angrily.

"Carey will never amount to anything. He should have taken another handful of pills last week."

"Riley!" Ryan yells. I'm too shocked to say anything.

"Come on, Reid. Can you honestly tell me that you disagree?" Riley asks.

"Yes, I disagree!" I fist my hands in my lap and take a few calming breaths, trying not to punch my brother. I know Riley and Carey don't get along, but I keep hoping one day they will start. If I'm being honest with myself, part of Riley's observation is correct.

"My son is *not* worthless." I bite out. "I just wish he could see his worth. Then, maybe, we wouldn't be in our current situation. I do agree that he can be difficult sometimes. We all can," I say, looking Riley directly in the eyes.

"Sometimes?" Riley retorts, ignoring my comment and gaze. "That stupid shi..."

"Enough, Riley," Ryan says through gritted teeth, "Carey's a good kid. He has a ton of potential. He's just lost his way right now. Kids make mistakes. Sometimes they fall, and that's when they need their family to be there to pick them up. The last thing Carey needs right now is for us to fight about him. He needs to know we're all on his side."

"I'm not on his side. I don't give a fuck," Riley says curtly.

"Not about anyone but yourself," I agree. Riley is so self-righteous. I love my brother, but sometimes I want to punch him in the mouth.

"Can we just have a meal without the arguing and

name calling? Can we at least pretend to be adults?" Ryan asks, sadness thick in his voice.

"Sure Ryan, you're right. We're all adults. What do I know about raising kids anyway?" Riley laughs at his own joke. "Let's order some lunch."

Ryan looks from Riley to me and back. He's worried about Carey, too. We had several conversations while he was in the hospital. Maybe Ryan can help him if I can't. After all, Ryan and Carey have always been close. Man, I hope Carey won't shut him out.

We order and eat in uncomfortable silence. This sucks. My family is being torn apart. I see it my line of work all the time. Drugs ruin lives and not just the user's life.

"I've got to get back to the station," Ryan says when he finishes his sandwich. "Are we still on for tomorrow?" he asks as he stands to leave.

"Yeah, five o'clock," I confirm.

"You gonna be there, Riley?" Ryan asks.

"I'll be there," Riley nods.

"See ya, brother," he pats me on the back and leaves.

"Can you try to be nice to Carey tomorrow?" I beg.

"We'll see," Riley shrugs. "If that little bastard starts something, I'm not holding back," he tells me rising from his seat.

"I'm serious, Riley.

"So am I," he snaps, walking away before I can respond.

I sit in my car for a few minutes before heading back to work. I was hoping to get some advice from my brothers, but lunch didn't exactly go as I planned. There is someone else I've considered talking to, but I don't know if it's a good idea. Officer Cooper has two boys in their late twenties, and they turned out to be good men. Maybe she can offer some advice on raising teenage boys. But then I hit the steering wheel in frustration. I can't tell another officer about Carey's drug problems. That will just put her in a compromising position. It's bad enough that Ryan and I know. What am I going to do?

Out of habit, I patrol my neighborhood on the way back to the station. When I get to the four way stop at the corner, I see Melody Kelley in the distance, working in her flower beds. Melody and Emmett have been wonderful friends to me for years. The four of us enjoyed some great times together before we had children. My friendship with the Kelley's grew stronger after Sarah left. I don't know what I would have done without their help with my boys. Melody loves them as much as I do. As I pass her house, I suddenly know who to talk to about Carey. Melody will listen and advise me without judgment. I make a quick u-turn and pull into the Kelley's driveway.

"Melody," I call as I get out of my car.

"Hey there. Overlook my appearance, I have been working all morning battling these weeds. I just don't have the same green thumb as my mother.

I think weeds are actually scared to grow in her beds."

"She's always had a way with flowers." We both laugh, but mine is forced.

"If I may be so bold, Reid, you look rough. Are you feeling okay? Are the boys all okay?" Melody is instantly in mother mode, worrying over everyone. That's just her sweet disposition.

"Well, actually, no. Everything is going to hell, and I don't know how to stop it."

"Is it Carey? Is it Sean?"

"It's a lot of things Mel, but mostly Carey." I hang my head. I feel so helpless.

"I am going to get us a glass of iced tea, and we can sit in the shade." When Melody returns, we both take a chair on the porch.

"What's going on?" she asks.

"I don't even know where to start." I reply, shaking my head.

"Let's start easy. How is Jason?"

"Same, too many girls and not enough jobs," I say with exasperation.

"He's still finding his way, but he'll settle down one day with a good job and a nice girl. How's Nick?"

"He can't see anything but football and himself," I say, shaking my head.

"Football is going to pay his way through college, and he's going to make a difference one day. How is my sweet little Sean?"

"Sore, but he will make a full recovery. The first week of school was rocky. He's made a few friends, but he still struggles socially."

"He has a protective heart of gold," Melody has an amazing way of always seeing the diamonds under the rough exterior of my boys.

"Now let's talk about you and Carey."

"I don't know what to do, Mel. Everyday, he slips farther and farther away. He's pulling away from everyone; friends and family. No matter how hard I try to reach him, he's always running away; literally and emotionally."

"Well, he's always been a runner. Every time the going gets tough, Carey runs and hides," she says smiling, "Even if it's just three houses down, but I haven't seen him in weeks."

"It's so much worse now. I mean he's always been a difficult child but...," I shake my head and drop my eyes. Admitting all this out loud is hard. "He is using drugs. That's why he was in the hospital. He over-dosed, Mel. I thought for sure I had lost him. Now I live in constant fear that I will wake up one morning and find him dead."

Melody gasps at my words. "Oh, Reid. I am so sorry. Seth didn't tell me." She drops here shoulders, and I can see the concern in her eyes. I know this news is hard for her to hear.

"I'm not sure Seth knows. He hasn't been around much lately. I don't know what happened between those two, but they haven't spent much time together in the past several weeks."

"Seth has been going through a hard time. I haven't seen Carey in weeks, and Seth doesn't want to discuss him."

"Carey is using, Sean is an introvert to a fault, Jason is an extrovert to a fault, and Nick is so full of Nick that he can't see anyone else. Sometimes, I'm afraid I won't see any of them make it to adulthood! Raising them without their mother has been hard, but I wouldn't trade those rotten ass boys for all the money in the world. I'm a good cop, but I might be a complete failure as a father," I confess my fear to her.

"You stop right there, Mr. Oliver!" Melody scolds me, sounding just like her mother. In a gentler voice, she continues, "You are not a failure. We all make mistakes no matter how much we love our children." She reaches out and takes my hand, waiting until I look up into her eyes. "Reid, everyone knows you love those boys. They are your life. I'm a firm believer that as parents, we do the best we know how to do at the time. Is every choice we make correct? Probably not, but we make every single one the best we know how to keep them safe and loved. The Good Book says raise them up in the right ways and when they are grown they will not depart from it. Our job is raising them up right. Their job is not departing."

"I think mine have already departed," I laugh at my attempt at a joke, even though it isn't funny. Melody smiles at me, "Deep down, they are all good boys, Reid. They just have to find that part of their heart and nurture it. They'll get there eventually. I have faith in them and you should, too." She is always able to see the positives.

"Thanks, Melody. I don't know what I would have done without your help over the years. You're a great friend, and I'm truly thankful."

"No thanks necessary. That's what friends are for. Plus, I love those boys. Is there anything else I can do?"

"Listening was what I needed right now. If I think of anything else, I know where to find you. I better get back to work. Thanks for listening."

"Anytime, Reid." We walk down the steps of the porch and into the yard.

"Thanks again." I say, hugging Melody before she heads back to her flowers, and I walk to my car. I still don't know how I'm going to reach Carey, but with Melody's positive words to fuel me, I'm more hopeful than I've been in a long time.

Carey

Sean and I have been home for almost a week. We were released from the hospital on the same day, and are planning to return to school on Monday. It's just my opinion, but I'm not sure Sean needs to spend a whole day at school yet because he's still getting headaches.

My uncles are coming for dinner. We grill out most Saturdays and often Ryan, Riley, or both join us. We all need some normal. I've been stewing over the paternity test even more now that Sean knows. Everyone is expecting a calm evening, but I'm considering screwing that up for all of us. I've been staring at this paper on and off for an hour. The more I look at the test results, the angrier I get. The last thing I want to do this afternoon is face Riley. I *hate* that man.

My dad and brothers have been downstairs cleaning and prepping food for tonight; something we usually do together on Saturdays. My dad expected me to help, but I refused to come out of my room.

I just keep second guessing myself. I'm not sure that I really want to bring this up today, but every time I unfold the paper, I get angry all over again. It's almost five and Riley and Ryan will be here soon. Ryan is bringing Claire, the nurse who took care of me in the hospital. No, that's not weird at all.

I love hanging out with some hot, older chick who has seen me naked and totally strung out lying in my own piss and vomit. Riley is coming alone as usual. He doesn't do commitment, and he never brings his whore of the week around.

I know I'll have to join them when the others arrive, but I'm putting that off as long as I can. I pull on my ripped jeans, mainly because my dad despises them, and head for the bathroom. After I splash some water on my face and brush my teeth, I run my fingers through my hair a few times trying to work out some of the knots. My hair has gotten a little longer than I usually keep it so I pull it into a man bun, but it looks completely stupid so I take it down. I go back into the bedroom and find my *Assault Lab* t-shirt and pull it on. Dad hates this shirt more than any other because he thinks it condones violence. He gives me crap all the time about my taste in music.

I pick up the paper one more time and turn to put it in my desk. As I'm unlocking the drawer, I hear a car door close. When I look out the window, Riley is walking up to the house. Another wave of rage hits me. I shove the paper in my back pocket and grab a pack of smokes. I head for the stairs hoping I can sneak out for a quick one before joining the others. Standing at the top of the stairs, just out of sight, I listen and try to place everyone. My dad asks

Jason to open the back door for him, and then Riley offers to grab the other tray. That only leaves Nick and Sean since Ryan hasn't arrived. I walk down the stairs hoping Nick won't stop me. Thankfully, he's watching TV and has his back to me. Sean is sitting at the table drinking a soda and reading that manga crap he likes. He looks up as I reach the bottom of the stairs, and I put my finger over my lips telling him that he should keep quiet. I nod my head towards the door, indicating that I want him to join me. He follows and silently closes the door behind us. We walk to the side of the house out of sight and wait for the others to go back inside.

About five minutes later, we are crossing the last dune and walking onto the beach. We walk for a few minutes in silence before I take out two cigarettes and hand one to Sean. I light mine then hand him the lighter.

"Need a break before things even get started?" Sean questions.

"I hate him so much, Seany. Just being in the same house with him makes my skin crawl."

"Dad or Riley?"

"Yes," I answer and Sean shakes his head.

"I get why you are so pissed off at Riley, but why Dad? He's been a great father to you."

"Yeah, right," I bite out sarcastically. "He's always treated me like I'm stupid and worthless. He's on my ass all the time. He smacks me, and he lied to me about all of this shit with Riley."

155

"He didn't lie. He just never said anything."

"Omitting is lying." He can't possibly understand how I feel about the situation, and I can't expect him to feel the same hurt and resentment that I feel.

"You know all of that's in your head. I don't mean the issues with Riley, but the stuff about Dad treating you differently. He's always been good to you. You make it sound like he was abusive. He disciplined us all when we got out of line, but it wasn't like it ever hurt us or left a mark. He's on all of us about something, Carey. He just wants us to grow up to be good men. It can't be easy to raise four boys alone." Somewhere deep inside I know Sean is right, but I can't bring myself to agree with him so I keep quiet. We continue down the beach in silence, smoking our cigarettes.

"You know you shouldn't smoke," Sean deadpans. I raise an eyebrow at him.

"Really?" I say, motioning to his cigarette. "Hypocrite."

"It's just that I can quit anytime. I mean, I only smoke when I'm with you. You, on the other hand, have an addictive personality. It will just be harder for you to quit." Is he seriously going there tonight? I take a deep breath and try not to lose my temper. Then, he starts laughing. Not just a little laugh, but a full on, doubled over, stomach-grabbing laugh.

"Oh...man...," he continues, laughing. "You should...see...your face," he starts to get himself together. "I'm just kidding, Carey. Wow, you were

156

mad. I thought you were going to take a swing at me." I laugh, but then punch him in the arm for good measure.

"Ow," He says, rubbing his arm, but still laughing.

"Speaking of you being a hypocrite, want to explain why you had keys to Nick's car? You gave me so much grief about taking Jason's car, and then I find out this shit."

"Are you jealous that you didn't think of it yourself?" he asks with pride.

"Yes, but that's not the point."

"What is your point, Carey?"

"I don't know," I sigh. "Do you have keys to the other cars?" I ask. He smirks yet won't meet my eyes. Damn, he's full of surprises. His silence speaks volumes of truth.

"Sometimes, I need to get away," he shrugs.

"What are you saying, Sean?" I put my hand on his shoulder. Now, I'm really concerned. What the hell is he thinking? He stops and looks at me, but quickly focuses on the sand at his feet.

"I have keys to all the cars. Sometimes, when things get bad between us, I can't sleep.
I like to go for a drive to clear my head," he admits in a whisper.

"I thought you went to the back porch for that."

"Yeah, when people are around, and I can't hop in a car, but not in the middle of the night," he confides, still not meeting my eyes.

"Running off without telling anyone where you're going is really dangerous, Seany. What if something happens, and no one knows where you went?"

"That's the pot calling the kettle black," he retorts.

"I'm just worried about you," I confide.

"Quit playing big brother." Sean looks me in the eye. "I can take care of myself," he says with finality, and I know he isn't going to continue this conversation. I let it go for now because it's worth it just to have finally had a real conversation. I don't want to screw this up.

We walk the rest of the way to the pier in silence. I sit down on a bench near the end of the pier and Sean joins me. We watch the waves for a few minutes. I always enjoy hanging out on the beach with Sean. He knows silence is sometimes the best medicine.

Sean

"Do you think they've noticed we're gone?" I ask.

"Maybe," Carey shrugs, studying his shoes. He looks so lost. I want to hug him, but I know he'll just get angry and push me away.

"You can talk to me, Carey," I say, hoping he'll tell me what's on his mind.

"Just thinking about all the shit in our lives. Telling you all that stuff about me almost got you killed. I don't want to break my family apart. I just need some answers. I can't understand why Reid and Riley kept this from me," Carey spills. It's such a relief he's finally talking.

"I've been really worried about you. I hate seeing you like this, Carey. I'm scared something bad is going to happen. Like, you're going to take things too far again and next time it'll be too late to save you," I tell him my fears. I hate seeing any of my brothers hurt or in trouble.

"Nothing's going to happen to me," he says quietly, but he doesn't sound like he believes his own words.

"You've been hiding in our room all day."

"You worry too much. How are your wrist and ribs? Still getting headaches?" he asks, trying to change the subject, but it isn't going to work.

"I'm fine," I sigh. "Sick of the cast. Ribs hurt more than my head, but I'm still getting some headaches. Nothing you don't already know, and nothing I haven't dealt with before. Quit trying to change the subject." We sit in silence for a few minutes before I get up the nerve to say what's been on my mind for weeks; okay, months.

"Carey, I'm being serious about how worried I am for you. Whether you want to see it or not, you're in a downward spiral. You have been for months. Maybe years, and I just didn't want to see it."

"What the hell are you talking about, Sean?" he asks angrily.

"The drugs, Carey. You overdosed! You're an addict!" I yell.

"I am not an addict! I get high once in awhile. It's no big deal."

"No big deal! Let's start with the pot you left in Nick's car last year that almost got him kicked out of school and arrested. Do you have any clue what would have happened to him if I hadn't taken the blame?"

"No one asked you to take the fall."

"Well, you sure as shit weren't going to help him. As soon as your strung out ass stumbled through the front door and saw the cops, you high tailed it out of there."

"What was I supposed to do, Sean? I was high and had drugs on me. I would have gone to jail."

"Are you even listening to yourself? You don't care that I got in trouble or that Nick could have gone to jail. All you care about is yourself. No, I don't think you even care about yourself. The only thing you care about is your next high. Have you even looked at yourself lately? You look awful. You're losing weight, your clothes don't fit, your hair is greasy and getting stringy. You have huge circles under your eyes. I watch you, Carey. You rarely eat, and you either spend more time sleeping than is normal or more time awake than is normal."

"You're wrong, Sean. Now, you're just making stuff up!" he yells.

"You are slowly killing yourself," I whisper as I wipe my tears. "You almost died in my arms. What if I hadn't come upstairs that night? Do you realize that I walked away from the door several times before I got up the nerve to come inside?"

"I don't want to do this right now," Carey turns away from me.

"You never want to do this! That's the problem. You never listen to anyone. Last year, for a whole month, Dad made me go to work with him." He knows this story, but I didn't tell him everything last year, and now he needs to hear it. "Some scared straight shit he was trying to pull on me. Except, I wasn't the one who fucking needed to see it. Carey, it was bad. I saw some stuff that really scared me

161

There were kids our age who were drug addicts, dealers, rapists, and murderers. I don't want you to turn into one of those guys. More than anything else, I just want my brother back," I say, getting up and walking toward the house.

"Seany! Sean, wait!" Carey calls behind me.

"We should head back," I say over my shoulder, not slowing down.

Carey and I have been spending more time together over the past week. I was basically on bed rest and couldn't do much due to my injuries, and he might as well have been on house arrest. Dad barely lets Carey out of his sight. He won't let Carey be home alone, and he's pretty much grounded until the apocalypse. Since more often than not we've been the only two home in the past week, Carey and I had a choice to talk or ignore each other. I'm glad we decided to talk. I'm the only one who knows the secret he's been keeping.

Even though we share a room, we'd barely spoken in the weeks before he overdosed. I was so over his drama, and he was too angry to talk to me anymore. I finally told him all the stuff I have been keeping inside so I thought things were better between us. I guess I made a mistake. He runs to catch up, and we walk back in silence.

When we reach the dunes behind the house, we see Nick, Jason, and Ryan on the porch. It won't be as easy to sneak back into the house.

"Can you at least pretend not to hate me when we get home?" Carey asks as we make our way over the dunes. His words stop me in my tracks.

"I don't hate you," I bite. "I love you, dammit. That's why I'm so worried. I'm losing you, and it is breaking me." Carey flinches at my words like I slapped him in the face.

Carey

"Where have you two been?" Jason calls as we clear the last dune.

"We just went for a walk," I say with a little more attitude than necessary.

"Sean needs to rest and you aren't allowed out of the house," he continues.

"Give it a rest, Jase," I say, knocking his shoulder as I pass. He turns to grab me, but Nick stops him.

"They're fine, and they're home. Let it go," Nick says pointedly, not breaking eye contact with Jason. I can't believe that Nick is sticking up for me.

"Whatever," Jason shakes his head and goes inside. He's probably going to tattle to his daddy.

"Thanks," I mumble to Nick.

"I didn't do it for you. I did it for Seany." Wow, he should have just let Jason hit me. It would have stung less.

"Are you okay?" Nick asks Sean.

"We're *both* fine," Sean says, emphatically. "I just wanted to get some fresh air, so I asked Carey to go for a walk with me," Sean lies.

"Right," Nick says, clearly not buying Sean's story. He goes inside without another word. I am so sick of their high and mighty bullshit. Ever since they found out about the drugs, things have been different between us. I'm suddenly the black sheep. Who am I kidding? I've always been the black sheep, but the drugs took it to a new level. Ryan is still standing there looking at Sean and me like he has something to say. Apparently, he changes his mind because he turns toward the door. Nope, this isn't awkward at all. He's about to open the door when he turns back to me.

"They're just worried about you, Kid," he says.

"Sure they are," I say, rolling my eyes.

"Your brothers love you," he tries again.

"I can tell," I say sarcastically. Ryan runs his hand through his hair and sighs deeply. He walks inside knowing he isn't getting anywhere with me. I'm not buying that "love and worried" crap. Nick and Jason are jerks and should mind their own business along with everyone else in this family.

"He's not wrong, Care," Sean says almost inaudibly. I don't know how to respond. I guess somewhere inside I know that my brothers worry about me and love me. It's just so much easier to be angry. Why is anger always easier? I may never understand. Sean looks lost standing there willing me to respond. He just wants to fix his family, but he can't. I'm already too broken.

"Let's go watch the game and forget about the last few minutes." Sean suggests, patting me on the shoulder.

"You go."

"You can't avoid Dad and Riley forever."

"I know." He's right. I'll have to face everyone eventually.

"Go," I nod toward the door. "I'll be in soon." Sean heads in the house. I take a few deep breaths to try to calm myself. The folded paper in my pocket feels like a hot iron, branding me as an outcast. I want to run back to the beach and forget about everything in my life. I turn back toward the water and watch the waves for a little longer. I wish I had something with me to take the edge off.

Finally, I decide if I don't head in someone is going to come get me. As I enter the house, I see my brothers sitting on the couch watching a game. I don't even know who's playing. My dad and Ryan are at the kitchen counter slicing tomatoes and onions for the burgers. Claire and Riley are sitting at the table. Claire is talking and has everyone's attention.

Seeing Riley makes the rage inside of me rise toward the surface. I *try* to force it down, but he makes eye contact, and mimics smoking a joint. As if that isn't enough, he mouths the word "druggie." That does it. I explode! I rush across the room, grab him by the shirt, and start punching him in the face.

"You son of a bitch!" I get a couple of good hits in before anyone has a chance to stop me. "Get the hell out of my house!" I shout as I go for another hit.

Riley reacts, grabbing me by throat, and slamming me down on the kitchen table. When my back hits the table, it knocks the breath out of me. I see the horrific rage in his eyes, and I'm certain he's

166

going to kill me right then and there in front of my entire family. He squeezes my throat harder when I try to push him away. I try to get some air to my lungs, but he's too strong.

"What the hell is your problem, you little prick?" he yells. I can't breathe. The room is darkening and all I can see is stars. The more I try to take air in, the harder he squeezes.

"Riley, let go of my son!" I hear my dad scream. He and Ryan are trying to pull Riley off of me. When my eyes dart toward the knife still in my dad's hand, Riley notices immediately. He manages to keep me pinned as he grabs the knife from Dad and replaces his hand with the blade.

"Back the fuck off!" Riley yells at my dad and Ryan. They both let go of him and take a step back, probably hoping to keep him from slitting my throat.

"Control your fucking son before I kill him!" Everyone freezes. I try to keep the tears from coming, but I can't. I am terrified. Riley leans down into my face.

"You better be scared, you worthless, piece of shit. Don't ever put your hands on me again or I will cut your fucking throat." He puts some more pressure on the knife. Enough to draw blood, but not enough to do any real damage. I'm still trying to catch my breath, my throat hurts, and it's getting difficult to stay focused. My back is hurting from being slammed onto the table, and the cut on my neck is starting to sting. I'm scared to move much less try to get away. Riley still has the knife to my throat and isn't showing any sign of letting me up. Everyone remains frozen in place. Time stands still. Ryan finally speaks.

"Give me the knife, Riley," he says calmly. Riley looks at him like he doesn't understand what Ryan is saying. After a few endless moments, he leans closer until his nose touches mine.

"This isn't over," he growls where only I can hear him.

He drops the knife on the floor and shoves me hard, causing me to hit my head against the table. Then, he casually sits back in his chair and wipes blood from his lip before picking up his beer and sucking it down as if nothing has happened. Sean and Ryan help me stand up. I rub my throat and blood coats my fingers. Seeing the blood makes me feel a little faint so I lean against the table and try to get my breathing to return to normal. Sean puts an arm around my shoulder.

"What the hell was that about?" my dad shouts at both of us. I cross my arms over my chest and stare at him. There is only one way to handle this now.

"Tell them, asshole," I say to Riley as I shrug Sean's arm off to throw the paper from my back pocket onto the table.

I use my shirt to wipe the blood from my neck, but

the cut keeps bleeding. Sean puts his arm back around me, and nods his support. Nick and Jason stand on the other side of the table in shock and confusion. Claire is slightly behind them. They must have stood in front of her to protect her during the fight.

"What is this?" Riley snaps.

"Read it. It won't be news to you." He opens the paper and reads it in silence. I watch his face go from smug to rage.

"Where did you get this?" Riley roars, standing as if he's going to come at me again. Everyone except Claire and I take a step toward him, and he stalls.

"Don't worry about where I got it," I bark, gaining a little confidence. "Do you hate me so much that you can't stand for it to be true?" I continue through tears that I can't stop, even though I don't want to show weakness. I'm angry, but I also feel hurt; un-loved, unwanted. The same way I have felt for the past three years.

Riley runs his fingers through his hair and lets out an angry laugh. "I didn't want this," he shakes the paper in my face. I flinch at his words, knowing he means that he didn't want me. "Kids were not in my plan and telling you or anyone would have caused a lot of problems, especially for me."

"What is that?" Reid interrupts Riley, reaching for the paper. Riley pulls it out of his reach.

"Like you don't already know!" I yell at him now. "You had the tests done."

"Carey, I don't know what's going on," he pleads.

"How long have you known?" Riley asks quietly.

"I found the paper about two months before Mom died."

Riley stands and begins pacing in front of the windows in silence, his hands clenching. No one speaks or moves.

"You should have told him," Riley finally says, locking eyes with Reid, and pushing the paper toward him. As he reads the paper, Reid stumbles back into a chair.

"Oh, God," he says. "Carey...," he blinks back tears as he reaches for me. I take a step back. "I didn't know..."

"I can't believe you're still lying about this," I cut him off.

"Son...," he's as pale as a ghost.

"Don't call me that," I snap.

"I never opened the envelope. I was angry when I found out about the affair. I had the tests done, but by the time the results came in, I didn't want to know. It didn't matter what was in the envelope. All of you boys were mine. I swear I never opened it," he explains. It's true that the envelope was still sealed when I found it.

"How did you know?" Reid asks Riley, his tone changing to anger.

"Sarah and I did the math. It wasn't that hard to figure out. We knew there was a good chance," He smirks and shrugs as if this situation means nothing. Then, he looks me in the eye and says, "I told her to take care of that problem."

I *can't believe* he just said that. He's wanted me dead since I was conceived.

"Will someone fill us in? What affair? What is on that paper?" Nick asks. He and Jason are thoroughly confused. Sean stands unmoving next to me. I didn't realize how much I needed his strength and support.

"You need to leave," Reid growls at Riley, ignoring Nick's questions. Riley doesn't argue, but takes his time sauntering away. He acts like all of this is no big deal, like he didn't just attack me with a knife. Claire whispers something to Ryan and he hands her his keys. She kisses him on the cheek and leaves.

"Sit down, boys," Reid says. No one argues. "When you boys were bab…"

"I'll tell them," I interrupt.

"Carey?" He questions.

"I said that I will tell them," I say louder. He nods his approval, and I start the story. I tell them about the affair and how I found the papers. I tell them about confronting Mom and trying to convince her to tell everyone. As I finish the story, I can see that Nick, Jason, and Ryan are all in shock. No one knows what to say. Sean breaks the silence by telling them about finding out in the hospital before wrecking Nick's car.

"So that's why you've been such a pain in the ass," Jason laughs, trying to break the tension.

I shrug. I confess to them that I've been having nightmares for years and how I found that the pills helped. I don't tell them that I could have saved her, but I didn't have the balls to do anything. I don't tell them that I believe my mom's death is my fault.

"You know this doesn't change anything," Jason says.

"It changes everything," I retort.

"We're still brothers," Nick counters.

"Sort of," I put my hands in my pocket and study the floor.

"You're still my son," Reid says adamantly.

"No, I'm not," I reply angrily. "I think part of you has always known the truth. We've never gotten along. You even said I act just like Riley."

"You're my son, and I love you. That piece of paper doesn't change one damn thing for me," he says, leaning over and touching my arm. I pull away.

"Don't," I say with tears in my eyes. I push off the table and head for the stairs.

"Where are you going?" Reid asks.

"I need some time." I rush up the stairs to my room, take out a duffle bag, and throw in some clothes. I don't know where I'm going, but I'm not staying here. I grab a few books I want to read, my tablet, and phone. As I'm shoving those things into my backpack, there's a knock at the door. Ryan enters the room without waiting for a response.

"What are you doing?" he asks, closing the door behind him.

172

"What does it look like I'm doing?" I respond bitterly.

"We're still your family. You can't run away from this."

I fall onto the bed as tears stream down my face. I don't even bother trying to wipe them away.

"I don't know who I am, Ryan. I don't belong here. I never have." I put my head in my hands and cry harder. My body shakes, and Ryan pulls me into his arms. It's one of the few times I allow anyone to get this close. I stay like that until I can't cry anymore. My eyes hurt, and I have a headache. It's the first time I've let myself cry about this. I'm scared and alone; like an outsider in my own family. I wipe my eyes on my shirt and walk over to my desk. I take two packs of cigarettes, put them in my backpack and zip it up. I put the backpack over my shoulder and reach for the duffle bag.

"I'll carry it. I texted Claire, and she's coming to get us. You'll stay with me while we sort this out," he walks out of the room without even giving me a chance to argue. I'm thankful for the offer because I don't have anywhere else to go. He also knows I would have *never* asked. I follow Ryan downstairs. When I reach the bottom step, my brothers and Reid are still at the kitchen table. Sean walks over, hugs me, and whispers 'I love you' before he runs up stairs. His voice cracks when he speaks. I know

173

he doesn't want me to go, but I also know he understands that I need to get out of here. He's scared and hurt, too. Jason walks toward me as Nick and Reid stand.

"Don't bother," is all I say before I walk out of the door. The last thing I need is more fake sympathy from Nick and Jason. They didn't even try to help with the drugs. They never asked why; just assumed I was nothing more than a loser junkie. Ryan says something too low for me to hear when they try to follow. I'm relieved to see that Claire is waiting in the driveway.

We drive in silence the few miles to Ryan's house. When we arrive, Claire kisses him and gets in her car and leaves. I like her more than I did before. I appreciate that she's staying out of our family drama and giving Ryan and me some space. Ryan unlocks the door and leads the way into his house.

"Leave the bags here for now. We can put them in the guest room later," Ryan tells me. I sit on the couch, lean back into the cushions, and close my eyes. I'm exhausted, the cut on my neck is throbbing, and I still have a headache.

"Here," Ryan says. I open my eyes and sit up. "Take these," he hands me a glass of water and some ibuprofen. "Did the cut stop bleeding?"

"Yeah, I think so," I swallow the pills and hand the empty glass to him. "Thanks."

"Are you hungry?" He asks, walking into the kitchen.

His house is small, but I guess it's perfect for one. There is a bar separating the living room and the kitchen. The living area and dining room are opened to one another. There's a door across from the kitchen that leads into a small hallway with a bedroom at either end. There's only one bathroom between the two bedrooms.

"I can order a pizza," he states. Suddenly, I realize we never ate. I can only assume the burgers burned on the grill during the drama.

"Sure, pizza sounds good."

I hear Ryan in the kitchen ordering our food while I sit staring out the window. My mind is racing. I can't wrap my head around the past few hours.

"Take off that bloody shirt and let me clean the cut, Carey." Ryan returns with some cotton balls and hydrogen peroxide. I lie back on the pillows and close my eyes while he works. I try not to wince, but dang it burns.

"That should do it," he says, handing me a clean shirt.

"Thanks, Ryan. For everything," I say, blinking back more tears. Why can't I pull myself together? He nods slightly and retreats to the kitchen. I throw an arm over my eyes to block out the light that's making my headache worse. I just can't seem to keep them open no matter how hard I try.

I must have fallen asleep because the doorbell startles me. I sit up a little too fast and get dizzy.

I'm disoriented and can't figure out where I am at first.

"Pizza's here," Ryan calls as he closes the door. "You okay, Kid?" he asks, approaching the couch.

"Yeah." I hope I sound more convincing than I feel. I'm still a little out of it.

How can I face my brothers now? I sit at the table and try to think of something to say as we eat the pizza. Considering the silence, Ryan must not know what to say either. Somehow, we manage an uncomfortable evening of avoiding all issues with a little television and even less small talk.

Reid

I'm still at the table where I was sitting when Ryan and Carey left. I have no idea how long it's been. Nick and Jason haven't said anything, and I have no idea what to say to them.

Now I'm more worried than ever about Carey. No wonder he's been a mess for years. I probably should have figured it out sooner. Carey is more like Riley than I care to admit. They're both time bombs just waiting to explode. I guess Carey is a lot like his mom, too. He clearly has a drug addiction, even though he refuses to acknowledge it.

If I'm being honest, I've been turning a blind eye to his problems for far too long. He's unhappy and depressed. He keeps himself locked away from everyone who cares about him. He's cut his friends and brothers out of his life. It's been weeks since I've seen Seth, and those two have been inseparable their whole lives. I'm afraid he's going to kill himself, whether by accident or on purpose.

Riley, on the other hand, has always been an asshole. After the incident with Carey, I'm beginning to realize these might be sociopathic behaviors, but I would never have thought he was capable of murder. Now I'm not so sure. I'm still reeling from seeing my brother pull a knife on my son.

I wasn't lying to Carey when I told him that I didn't know the paternity results. I never opened that envelope because I didn't want to know. He doesn't believe me and now may never trust me again. Those four boys are my sons, and I knew if I ever learned a different truth, it would change all of our lives. Still, I'm not shocked to find out that one of my sons belongs to my brother. I knew about the affair. It went on for years. I think they were still sleeping together after our divorce. Maybe even until Sarah died. I quit keeping tabs on her after a while.

"Dad?" Nick sounds so young and unsure when he speaks. His confidence is frayed.

"Yeah, son?"

"I...is...I don't know," he shakes his head and fights back tears as he struggles to work through what just happened. Jason doesn't look much better, and Sean hasn't returned from his room where he retreated when Carey left with Ryan.

"Is Riley really Carey's father?" Nick finally asks.

"Yes."

"Did you know?"

"No. I suspected it was possible when I found out your mom was having an affair with Riley, but honestly, I thought it was Sean. I thought the affair started early in her pregnancy with Carey," I tell them the truth. I'm done keeping things from my children. They have all grown up so fast in the past few months. It's time to treat them like the men they are becoming. I was fooling myself to think the affair had only lasted a short time.

I didn't want it to be Sean, but he would have been able to handle it better than Carey. Carey has always had a volatile personality. He never handled change well or liked surprises; still doesn't. I don't know how to help Carey heal from this. He thinks I hate him because he isn't biologically mine, but he doesn't understand how wrong he is to feel that way. He. Is. *MY*. Son. I raised him. I love him. I will never look at him as anything other than my son. His own father hates him, and just threatened to kill him. I can't imagine the doubt and resentment he must feel.

"You could have told me." I didn't hear Sean come back downstairs.

"You were just a baby when I had the tests done. I haven't thought about it in a long time, Sean."

"I'm not a baby anymore, and I'm tired of everyone treating me that way. You shouldn't have kept this from us."

"Are you being serious? I kept it from everyone, even myself. But you're absolutely right, Sean. I shouldn't have kept the tests a secret. I thought I was doing the right thing. Even though the results never mattered to me, it was wrong to keep them hidden. Boys, I swear I never opened them. I have four sons who are my entire world. I don't give a shit what those papers say."

"What happens now?" Jason pipes up. Jason always tries to make light of stressful situations because he can't handle the pressure of silence. He isn't making jokes today.

"We start by giving Carey some time and space. He needs to know we love him, but he doesn't need us to pressure him to talk to us or come home. He's safe with Ryan. Text, call, talk to him at school, but if he isn't responsive, back off and try again another day. Don't get angry with him."

"We were complete asses to him and treated him like shit. How can he ever forgive us?" Jason questions.

"He will. Give it time boys. We aren't going to heal overnight." I have no idea how to handle this. All of my sons are hurting, and I'm still trying to process this new reality. I don't even know if I'm giving them the best advice.

"He won't forgive you; us." Sean tells us. "Not anytime soon. None of us wanted to see that he had a real problem. We just wanted to ignore it in the hopes that it would go away. I wasn't any better. I knew there was a problem. I confronted him, but I was never man enough to tell anyone else. I found drugs in our room over a year ago. Long before the cops found them in Nick's car."

"Why the hell didn't you say something?" My voice is full of anger, not that it will help the situation now.

"I didn't want to deal with the fallout. I thought I could help him on my own." I've never heard Sean sound more shattered than he does right now. His words are wracked with sadness and guilt.

"Sean, you cannot take the blame for any of this. None of this is your fault."

"Bullshit!" he yells, gaining the attention of his brothers. Sean doesn't usually yell and cuss.

"How can you be so passive about this?" Sean continues to yell, taking a step toward me. I back up a little, finding my back against the door. Sean gets closer to me with each line he speaks.

"You act like this isn't a big deal. Like we aren't all to blame. We *should* feel guilty. All of us, especially you," he pokes his finger into my chest. My jaw drops. I have never seen Sean get physical with anyone.

"We all ignored Carey's issues. All. Of. Us." Sean hits the back of the front door in emphasis. I flinch at his unexpected outburst.

Sean takes a ragged, deep breath and continues in a fragile voice. "He could have died in my arms when he OD'd. He could have died so many other times when he was strung out or drunk, but we kept ignoring it. You turned a blind eye because it was too hard to deal with him," Sean's anger builds again. "I call bullshit on you and all of your shit. By failing Carey, you failed us all!"

"You need to calm down and watch how you talk to me. I know you're angry and scared right now, but that does not give you the right to speak to me that way." I have to stay calm. I know Sean is hurting, but I can't allow him to behave this way.

182

"Yeah, and I'm not taking the blame for this. It's all on Carey," Nick adds.

"Shut up, Nick," Sean tells him.

"Watch it, baby brother," Jason says, taking a step toward Sean.

"Dammit! I'm so sick of everybody's shit. You want to fight me. Fine! Come at me! Both of you! I dare you!" I have never seen Sean act this way.

"Enough, boys!" I move in between them to diffuse the situation. "Nothing good will come from us being at each other's throats. We can't blame ourselves for the choices Carey made, but yes, Sean, you are right. I should have stepped in sooner. I'm the parent, not you three."

"Damn right. You need to deal with your son. I'm done with this shit," Nick yells, throwing his hands up, and heading for the door. Nick always deals in anger when he doesn't know how to handle a situation. I don't try to stop him. I just let him go. A few minutes later, Truck pulls up in front the house, and Nick leaves with him. Knowing those two, they'll spend the rest of the night getting drunk.

Jason leaves not long after Nick. Probably to get laid. Will he ever learn that sex does not solve your problems?

Sean returned to his room after his outburst. I know I should check on him, but what would I say? I can't change what's happened. He blames himself for Carey's problems, but none of this is his fault.

I'm the one to blame. How many times have I ignored Carey's shit because that was easier than dealing with the consequences? Avoidance just seemed like the better option. I see now that was a selfish choice and look where it got us.

It took hours for me to move from my seat at the kitchen table. None of us ever ate. The burgers were burned to a crisp when I finally found the energy to go clean the grill. Have I driven all of my children away? We were once happy and whole. I remember how close the boys were when they were younger. They always got along so well. Even with their differences, they were inseparable. I never thought that bond could be broken.

It's after midnight as I lie in bed, staring at the ceiling worrying about my boys and what will happen next for all of us. I'm so completely exhausted, but I can't find sleep. At some point during the night, I hear the front door. I can't be sure if Sean left or one of the other boys returned. All I can hope is they'll all be home safely by morning.

Carey

The next morning things aren't any less awkward, but thankfully Ryan has to go to work. I have some time alone to sort through everything. It doesn't take long for me to realize that time alone is not what I need. There is school work to do because I've fallen behind. Missing the first few weeks wasn't good. I have too much to makeup, but screw that. Why should I bother doing any of it? My grades were crap last year. I barely passed, and I don't really care to make this year any different. It isn't as if making good grades will make things better for me. It's not like I'll ever graduate. I'm thinking about just dropping out. Life sucks too much for anything to matter. It all seems pointless right now. I wish there was a way out.

I spend hours on Ryan's front porch reading, writing, and working my way through a pack of cigarettes. Since no one knows about my writing, I have to find time to work when they aren't around. The peaceful, solitude of a quiet outdoor spot always helps me concentrate. I hate being cooped up inside.

When I start to get writer's block, I get frustrated because then my mind wanders to my family. Ryan's acoustic guitar was in the guest room where I slept last night. I grabbed it this morning before heading to the porch. Playing the guitar helps, so I spend some time picking at the strings. Music has always centered me. Whether I'm playing or listening to it, music keeps me out of my own head.

I've smoked most of the pack, but the cigarettes aren't doing shit for me. I don't even really like to smoke. I prefer something that can make me forget. I need something stronger, but I have my first meeting with the psychiatrist tomorrow, and it includes a drug test. I can't fail my first drug test after being released from the hospital because I still can't figure out if Reid was serious with his rehab threat.

My body is stiff with pain when I stand up to stretch. Looking around at the mess I've made of the porch, I make quick work of cleaning up all of the papers and shoving them back into the backpack where I keep them. Then, I get rid of all the cigarette butts. When I go into the bedroom to return the guitar, I notice that it's already after five. Wow, I've spent the whole day writing and never even stopped to eat. Ryan should be home soon, so I go to the kitchen to find a snack while I wait. I sit on the couch with a soda, a bag of chips, and the remote, but there's nothing worth watching. How can someone have access to over 200 channels and there still not be anything to watch? I really hate television. It's never interested me. My phone dings alerting me to a text, so I grab it off the table.

Caught at work. I'll be late.
There's leftover pizza if you get hungry.

Guess I'm on my own. Might as well eat something more than chips. I'm not a big fan of leftover pizza so I rummage through the kitchen to see what I can find. There isn't much in the way of food in the house. Does Ryan ever go to the grocery store? I find a jar of peanut butter and a loaf of bread. I consider making a sandwich, but I'm just not that hungry. I decide to have a couple of beers and eat later. Surely, Ryan won't miss one or two. It's not like Reid has ever had a problem with us drinking.

As I down the first two beers, I began to think about my brothers and what I've done to them. It's been twenty-four hours since I screwed everything up for us. As proof of the havoc I caused, no one has tried to contact me. Not Reid. Not Nick. Not Jason (which I expected). But, Sean hasn't called or texted either. I thought he would at least care enough to try.

I spend more time than I realize wallowing in my own misery. When I see headlights shine through the front window, I almost crap my pants. It's after nine, and there are easily ten empty beer bottles on the table. I stand up thinking that I can clean up the mess and get to my room. No such luck. I'm completely wasted and can barely walk. I manage to pick up a few bottles and stagger to the kitchen. By the time I reach the trash can, the door jamb, table, and a chair have jumped into my path. I'm going to be bruised as hell tomorrow. The door opens as I'm heading back to the living room for more bottles.

I stand there wide eyed, staring at Ryan. His eyes widen when they land on the empty bottles, not to mention the fact that it's taking everything in me to keep from falling over. I don't even try to speak. I mean, what can I really say? The situation is obvious. I brace myself for a lecture, but Ryan just sighs and shakes his head.

"Let's get you to bed."

"I'm not tired," I slur as he takes my arm.

"Would you rather sit and talk about what the hell this is?" He asks, gesturing to the bottles.

"No," I sulk. He tries to help me again, but I pull away. "I can do it myself." After two steps, I trip over the air and start to fall, but the end table stops me.

"Shit!" I cry out. I stumble a few more steps, but Ryan catches me before I completely lose my balance. He helps me to the bed and as soon as my head hits the pillow, the room starts spinning. I moan as Ryan starts to take off my shoes.

"I'm gonna...," I can't finish my sentence before I hurl all over the bed and floor. Ryan gets me to the bathroom and leaves me there to finish. I puke a few more times and I think some of it even makes it in the toilet. When I finish, I lie down on the cool tiles hoping for some relief.

When I wake up, I have an excruciating headache. The room is still spinning, and my stomach is in knots. Slowly, the previous night starts to come back to me. Great, now I'll have to face Ryan. He's going to be pissed and may even make me leave. I open my eyes and roll over to check the time. It's after ten, and I'm thankful that Ryan didn't wake me for school. Somehow, I have to get myself together before my appointment with the psychiatrist.

Ryan must have cleaned up because the last thing I remember is lying on the bathroom floor after coating everything in vomit, but I woke up in a clean bed. When I enter the bathroom, I am thankful to find that it's been cleaned, too. I use the bathroom and then splash some water on my face. I hardly recognize the guy in the mirror. Man, I look like hell. My eyes are bloodshot, my hair is sticking up in weird directions, stiff from vomit, and I stink like some disgusting combination of stale beer, puke, and body odor. Gross, I think wrinkling up my nose.

As I wash in the hottest shower I can stand, I find several bruises from all the furniture I tried to take out. I'm sore, but I feel a little more human now that I'm clean. After I dress, I head for the living room. I might as well face Ryan and get this over. He's at the kitchen table going over what looks like bills.

"You look like hell," I say, wondering if he got any sleep last night.

"Right back at you," he deadpans. "You hungry?"

"No! God, please don't ever mention food again," I say, holding back the dry heaves.

"You need to eat. It will help," he laughs, getting up from the table.

"I'm so glad you find this amusing."

"Drink this, and I'll fix you some food," he says, handing me a cup of coffee.

"No, thanks," I push the cup away.

"Yesterday, you tried things your way, and it didn't work out too well. Today, we try it my way. Drink!" he states, pointing to the coffee. His tone doesn't really leave any room to argue, so I drink the coffee. It's bitter and disgusting, but I force it down. I prefer a little coffee with my cream and sugar, not this black tar. By the time I finish, there's a plate of dry toast, eggs, and grits in front of me.

"Thanks," I mumble as I slowly start to force the food down. Except for the few chips I had yesterday, I haven't eaten since the pizza on Saturday night. I do feel a little better once I get some food on my stomach. I leave my dishes in the sink and head for the couch. All I want to do is take a nap.

As I walk across the room, Ryan asks, "What happened last night?" Damn, I was hoping to avoid this conversation. I sigh heavily.

"I had a couple of beers. I'll pay you for them." I say, taking a seat on the couch.

"You had more than a couple. You were plastered, Carey," he states. "You're fifteen years old. What the hell were you thinking?" Ryan asks, standing over me with his arms crossed.

"I was thinking that my life's falling apart!" I yell. "I'm not in the mood for this, Ryan."

"We're talking about this, Kid."

"What do you want from me? I screwed up. Again. It's what I do, Ryan. I screw everything up for everyone who has ever mattered to me."

"Your dad and brothers are worried about you. Frankly, so am I."

"Did you tell them about last night?"

"No. I told Reid that you didn't feel well this morning, and I thought another day home would do you some good. He wasn't happy, but I didn't give him a choice. Right now you are in my care, not his."

"Have you actually talked to my brothers? I doubt they even care how I'm doing."

"Check your phone. There have been texts coming in all morning. I didn't look at them, but if I had to guess, I would say they're from your family."

I grab my phone from the table next to the couch to find that Ryan is right. There are text messages from Reid, all of my brothers, and a few friends. Some of the messages came in last night, but I was too wrapped up in myself to pay attention to my phone. I read through some of the messages and don't realize that I'm crying until Ryan hands me a tissue. I put my phone down to wipe my face.

"As I've said before, your family cares about you. They need time to work through this, too. This news changed them. Nick and Jason feel terrible for the way they treated you."

"Yeah, right," I laugh sarcastically, although the texts do confirm what Ryan is saying. I can't bear to read anymore of the texts so I pick up a book and start to read, hoping this conversation is over.

"Put the book down," Ryan tells me, but I ignore him and keep reading.

"Put the book down, now," he says a little firmer, but I keep reading. Exasperated, Ryan leans over, takes the book, and tosses it onto the chair across the room.

"I was reading that," I say, standing up to retrieve it.

"Sit. Back. Down." he says, stepping in front of me. I listen because I have never seen Ryan in parent mode. It's kind of scary. He pulls the coffee table closer to the couch and sits on the edge facing me. He leans toward me and puts his hands on my knees. I look away. I'm really uncomfortable, and he knows it. It's no secret that I hate people in my space like this.

"You can't drink in my house," he starts. "I'm not going to lecture you, and it's not my job to punish you. I'm not your parent."

"Who is?" I mumble. He ignores the comment and continues.

"You will not drink alcohol in my house, period. End of discussion."

"How about on the porch?" I ask. He gives me a dirty look and I retreat. "Fine," I start to stand, but he stops me.

"We're not done."

"You said 'end of discussion,'" I remind him.

"We're not done. Sit!" He points to the couch. I sigh and roll my eyes, sinking back to the couch. He starts to speak, but then stops. This happens several times, and I'm getting a little annoyed. I wish he would just spit it out.

"What?" I ask heatedly.

"I don't know where to start. I have so many questions, and so much that I want to say."

"Let me help. I am a worthless piece of shit. The family screw up. Don't worry, I'll be on my way soon, and none of you will have to put up with me anymore."

"That's not how any of us feel. I don't want you to leave. I told Reid when I talked to him earlier that you're staying here indefinitely. He has no say in this decision," he pauses, and I just stare at him. I can't believe he said that to my dad, no my uncle. Whoever he is to me now.

"Thanks," I manage. I can feel the tears burning my eyes, and I fear I'm going to break down again. I have to hold it together so I swallow a few times, trying to control myself.

"Why did you wait so long to say something about this?" he asks.

"I don't know," I shrug. "I thought Reid and Riley both knew. At first, I wanted to say something. Mom and I talked about it, but she didn't think it was a good idea. It took time, but I finally convinced her to tell the truth. She confronted Riley and told him that she wanted me to know the truth. He didn't agree and kept telling her to keep quiet. That's all she told me."

"Your dad and I talked last night. We both think you and your brothers should give a statement to the police. We aren't pressing charges right now, but it's best that there's an official police report after Saturday's events."

"What? Why?" I'm not sure how I feel about talking to the police. Riley scares the shit out of me.

"We all saw Riley pull a knife on you and threaten to kill you. I hope this is a precaution we'll never need, but after seeing the rage in Riley, I don't know what he's capable of doing," he pauses and takes a deep breath. This has to be so hard for him.

"You understand that they aren't going to allow Reid or me take your statement. You have to be honest and tell whoever interviews you everything that happened that night."

"Everything? Ryan, I attacked him. Am I going to be in trouble?"

"Tell them everything. Even what you did. I seriously doubt Riley will try to press charges."

"I will," I promise, even though I'm not sure I really want to admit my part in the fight.

"I spoke to my partner this morning, and he's working on a restraining order. Reid and I don't want Riley near you or your brothers. You, Sean, and Nick can't go anywhere alone. We prefer, for the time being, the three of you go to school and home. That's it. Jason, Reid, or I need to be with you if you go anywhere other than school. Starting tomorrow, Nick can come pick you up and take you to and from school."

"I'm not riding with him," I say a little louder than intended. "I can walk. It's only three miles," I add a little calmer.

"Then I'll drive you. It isn't safe for you to walk. We don't know if Riley will try anything else. Keeping you and your brothers safe is our top priority right now," I want to argue, but I understand they're just trying to keep us safe.

"I'm sorry I brought this on our family."

"Stop. This is not your doing. Sarah and Riley did this. You will not take the blame for choices that were made before you were even conceived," I nod my head in agreement even though I still disagree.

"I'll go take care of those dishes. You should rest before your appointment this afternoon."

Sean

It's been just over two weeks since I wrecked
Nick's car. I'm still grounded, and after everything
went down with Carey and Riley none of us are allowed to go anywhere alone. Dad and Ryan are both
working late on cases, and Jason has been tasked
with keeping tabs on me. Of course, he's off with
Brody and some girls, so I snuck over to see Carey.
He wasn't happy about me sneaking around alone,
but I needed to get out. When I'm not at school, I'm
either stuck in the house alone or, worse, with Nick.
He's becoming more and more of an ass every day.

The visit with Carey was good. It's the first time
we've spent time alone since he moved out. He was
sober and sounded happy. Well, maybe not happy,
but he wasn't angry. We spent a few hours playing
video games so we didn't have to talk about anything serious. Carey insisted that I leave when it
started getting dark. I didn't want to, but he's right,
I need to be home before Dad. Carey offered to walk
with me, but it's probably safer for me to be out
alone than him. I refused his offer and promised to
text when I made it home.

As I head around the bend where Shore Drive and
Ocean Boulevard meet, I see Nick's friend Truck
heading my way. I would recognize his obnoxious,

tricked out, lowrider anywhere. He slows down and glares at me as he passes, and my heart begins to race. Suddenly, I realize this was a mistake. I shouldn't be alone. I risk a glance behind me and see he has turned the corner heading into his neighborhood. I take a few deep breaths trying to stop shaking. That was close.

I'm about a mile from my house when I stop in my tracks. Truck is leaning against the giant oak tree that is famous for being the oldest in the state. He must have cut through the park. I can keep walking toward my house directly in front of him or turn around and run like a coward. Either way won't end well for me. Truck has cornered me before when Nick wasn't around. He even had the nerve to shove me into the wall one night when he was at our house. I almost lost my balance and fell down the stairs. Truck scares the shit out me. I put on a brave face and continue walking toward my house. Maybe I can outrun him if he tries anything. Yeah, because I have so much stamina, especially since my ribs and wrist are still healing, and I have a concussion from the wreck. Not that it would matter. I would be no match for Truck in my best physical health on his worst day. I don't make eye contact as I pass him. I'm a few feet past the tree, when he acknowledges me.

"Hey, Oliver," he calls from behind. I keep walking, praying that he will leave me alone.

"I'm talking to you, boy," he calls louder. I don't stop and try my best to seem casual. Truck is like a rabid animal. I think he can smell my fear.

"Dammit, you little fuck, answer me when I speak." He grabs my arm and turns me toward him. When he squeezes my arm in his vice like hand, I whimper involuntarily. Truck laughs as he slams my back against the nearest tree.

"Ow," I moan as I blink back the tears.

"Damn, Nick's right. You really are a fucking pussy." His breath smells like a mix of alcohol and weed, a combination I smell on Carey often when he stumbles into our bedroom in the middle of the night. I'm not prepared for the fist to my stomach and almost hurl. Before I can recover, I'm blindsided with a right hook to my jaw. That's going to leave a mark. I would be on the ground if Truck didn't still have a strong grip on my left arm. I take another hit to the stomach and two to my already injured ribs. When Truck finally lets go, I fall to the ground, landing painfully hard on my knees. I don't have the energy to keep myself up, so I fall onto my side and put my arms up in defense, but it doesn't do any good. He hits and kicks me several more times and I'm afraid I might pass out from the pain. I just stay on the ground trying to cover my face, taking the assault while he laughs with delight. His laughter borders on hysteria as he pummels me. Eventually, he tires out or gets bored and just walks away.

There are no other words, just the beating and then silence.

As the crying subsides, I begin to feel the pain of what Truck did to me. I risk a look to see if he is still there. As I focus on his retreating figure, I see his drunk ass run face first into a street sign. He stumbles backwards, regains his footing, and staggers around the corner. I wince when a laugh escapes.

When Truck is out of sight, I carefully push myself up and sit against the nearest tree for support. I gingerly touch my side, and I'm certain that he damaged my healing ribs. He only hit me in the face once, so the concussion probably isn't any worse. My chest, ribs, and abdomen are throbbing, and I know there will be plenty of bruises forming. Hopefully, I can keep them all covered. The last thing I want to do is explain this to anyone. I hate Truck for making me feel like such a wuss. I hate myself for being such a wuss. Most of all, I feel betrayed by Nick for allowing his friends to treat me this way. This isn't the first time, and I bet it won't be the last. I slowly push myself to my feet and begin to walk the last painful mile to my house. As I reach the end of our street, I see headlights approaching and quickly step into the shadows afraid that it's Truck. Whoever it is must have seen me because the car slows as it nears. My heart feels like it's going to beat out of my aching chest. I'm frozen with fear when the car stops. It doesn't belong to Truck, but that doesn't calm my nerves.

What if it's another one of Nick's friends? I can't take another beating. I step behind a palm tree hoping for safety.

"Sean? Is that you?" Seth's familiar voice asks.

"Yeah," I choke out before stepping back into the light cast by the nearest street lamp. My ribs are killing me, and it hurts to breathe.

"Shit. Are you alright?"

"Yeah," I lie.

"Get in the jeep, Sean. I'll drive you home."

"It's only a few houses away, I can walk." I take a few steps, but I have no idea how much farther I can make it on my own. I try to cover a wince because I don't want Seth to tell my dad how bad I look.

"Get in. It isn't a request," Seth is out of the jeep and by my side. His tone is gentle but full of authority.

"If you insist," I use sarcasm to hide how grateful I am for the ride. I let out a moan as I take my seat.

"What happened to you?" Seth asks, looking me over.

"Nothing," I mumble.

"Okay, then. Who happened to you?" he tries again, more firm this time. "You can tell me, Sean. I can help you, " he adds more gently.

"You can't help me," I snap. "Please, just drop it," I can tell he wants answers, and I know this conversation is not over with him. He drops it for now and circles the jeep to the driver's side. Thankfully, we make it to the front of my house without any more inquiries.

"Thanks for the ride." I get out as quickly as my injuries will allow.

"You know where to find me if you need anything," I nod and start to close the door. "Anything, Sean. I mean it," Seth finishes not breaking eye contact.

"I know. Thanks." I turn and walk away before I lose it. Seth waits until I am inside before driving away. I make my way upstairs, collapse onto my bed, and fall into pain-filled dreams.

Reid

Things feel like they will never get better. Even though I know it's for the best right now, I hate that Carey is living with Ryan. I just want my son home. I want my family together. We haven't spoken since he moved out. I've reached out several times, in several ways, but he hasn't responded. Sean convinced him to come over today and help work on the car I bought Nick. It needs engine and body work. Carey is a genius when it comes to cars. If he can stay focused, chances are good he'll have the engine running by the end of the day. By focused, I mean sober. I have so much hope for this day. I hope he doesn't have any drugs on him. I hope today helps us begin the healing process. I hope today will help the boys begin to rebuild the bond they had when they were younger.

"Hey, Dad," Sean says as I walk into the kitchen from the storage building.

"Good morning, Sean," I respond, handing him a bag of tools. "Take this out to Carey." I follow him out into the garage carrying a set of ramps.

"Look at this piece of shit. Couldn't Dad find something worth a crap," I hear Nick tell Jason as I walk up behind them.

"You're lucky to have a car at all." He jumps at my words, but quickly recovers.

"I'm not the one who wrecked the car so I shouldn't be the one suffering," he bites out, staring at Sean as he speaks.

"Suffering?" I question. "Do you know how many hoops I had to jump through with the insurance company to get a penny? They don't exactly line up at the door to hand out checks when a fourteen year old wrecks a car. Not to mention the red tape I had to wade through to keep your brother from getting arrested."

"I don't care about hoops or red tape. Maybe Sean should have been arrested. You know, teach him a lesson," Nick continues. "I shouldn't have to settle for something that looks like a rust farm and practically needs a new engine because that little thief stole my car and wrapped it around a tree."

"NICK!" Jason yells. "Enough! You know it was an accident. It's not like you haven't taken a pre-license drive. Just be thankful Sean wasn't seriously injured or killed."

"Jason's right. You need to calm down and watch how you talk about your brother. At least Carey can do the work. I was barely able to pull together enough money to buy the car. I got lucky that I found a seller who wanted to dump it as fast as possible and was willing to take less than the asking price. Otherwise, you'd be walking everywhere. I am not made of money, Nick!" Nick needs to understand that he can't just have everything handed to him in life.

"It doesn't feel like luck. It feels like a sick joke! I'm getting a drink," he pouts and heads to the cooler of water I brought out this morning.

"Ignore him, Dad. He's just pissed off that he got knocked on his ass in the game last night by a guy smaller than him," Jason tells me when Nick walks away.

"I'm glad you're here," Sean whispers to Carey setting the tools down beside him. Carey gives a slight smile and nod. Then, he turns back to the car. He hasn't said much since he arrived a few minutes ago, but at least he's here.

"What? No beer?" Nick complains to the opened cooler.

"No!" I yell back. He must accept my simple response because he grabs a water and heads back to the car. First of all, it's nine in the morning and second of all, the last thing I need is a cooler full of beer with Carey here. Carey spends the next thirty minutes with his head buried in the engine, occasionally asking for this tool and that tool.

"Can you two push the car up onto the ramps? I need to get under it," Carey asks Nick and Jason before turning to Sean.

"What happened?" he asks, pointing to the bruise on Sean's jaw. I'm glad Carey asked. I've been trying to get Sean to tell me for the past two days. Maybe Carey can get it out of him.

"Nothing," he shrugs it off.

"Get in a fight with your girlfriend?" Nick questions with a laugh.

"Shut up, Nick," Sean glares at his brother.

"Come on, Seany. You can tell us," Nick says in the most condescending voice I have ever heard.

"I said it's nothing," Sean snaps.

"Sean?" Carey asks, his attention now fully on Sean.

"Ever been blindsided by a football player?" Sean asks.

"OH! MY! God! Widdle Seany can't even pway fag football in P.E. wiffout getting a widdle bwuise." Nicks starts laughing, and Sean looks completely beaten.

"That's enough, Nick. Don't be an ass." Nick can be so rude. I turn my attention to Sean. "You aren't even supposed to be participating in P.E. yet. You haven't been released from the orthopedist. First thing Monday morning, I'll call the school and take care of this. Don't you worry, Sean." I turn to head into the house to make a note in my phone.

"That's not necessary, Dad. We had a sub, and she didn't know. It won't happen again."

"How are you really feeling, Sean?" Carey asks.

Sean gives a sarcastic laugh, "Like I was hit by a truck."

The tone of his voice has me turning around, but he already has his back to us and is heading out through the open garage door.

"I've got to meet Sam to work on a project," he says without turning around.

"What is up with Sean?" Carey asks in a very defensive voice.

"He's a wimp who can't take a hit," Nick laughs.

"I don't know what your problem is, but I will not put up with you bullying your brother!" I tell Nick through gritted teeth.

"Bullying Sean? I have never laid a hand on him," his words sound like the truth, but I can tell there is more he isn't saying.

"I agree with Dad. You can't be bullying our brother," Jason pipes in.

"Kiss my ass, Jason! Oh wait, you can't because you're too busy kissing Dad's! I've had enough of this shit! I'm outta here. Truck and I have things to do anyway." Nick storms out.

"Nick! Get back here. We are not done!" I yell to Nick.

"Well, I'm done!" he yells back.

"We aren't going to fix your car without you," I yell to his retreating form. He just keeps walking in the direction of Truck's house.

"Don't listen to him, Dad. He's just mad because we're right." Jason tells me when Nick is out of earshot.

"Is it okay if I keep working on the car?" Carey asks, disappointment evident in his voice.

I did this for us to bond with him and now the day is ruined. The last thing I should do is finish Nick's car. He doesn't deserve it. On the other hand, I would love to spend some more time with Carey.

"Come on, Dad," Jason interjects. "The three of us can probably get the engine running. I'm just going to run go take a leak. Then, we can get started."

I pat Carey on the back. "Of course you can keep working, son. Jason and I will help," I agree. Carey smiles at my words. Probably, the first real smile I've seen on him in months.

"What's going on around here?" Carey asks as soon as Jason closes the door behind him.

"What do you mean?" I ask.

"You can't be serious."

"So, it isn't just my imagination. Sean was acting weird today," I confirm. He seemed off, but I thought it was just me.

"Sean has been acting weird for weeks. He's made a couple of comments to me, implying that shit's going on with Nick and his friends, but he will never come right out and tell me." Carey sounds worried.

"I know, son. I'm going to talk to Sean and get to the bottom of it. Don't worry. I'm sorry today didn't go as planned. I was hoping the five of us could spend the day together."

"I could have told you that wouldn't work. Nick's an asshole. Him and his football entourage make life hell for a lot of kids at school, not just Sean. Sean will never say anything even when point blank asked about it. Jason kisses your behind all the time which makes Nick angrier. None of us get along anymore. A car isn't going fix us," Carey calls all of his brothers out as if he's innocent in all of this. Today, yes, but he's had his share of ruining days.

"None of us are perfect, but we can find our way back to what we once had, Carey."

"Do you really believe that? Look at all of the damage. Can anything be salvaged from this wreckage?" Carey looks like he's completely destroyed. He was so hopeful when he arrived this morning.

"I hope so, son."

"Me, too. I miss my brothers," Carey and I both turn at Jason's words. Neither of us heard him come back.

"How long have you been there?" I ask.

"Long enough to know I like to kiss ass," he deadpans "You aren't wrong. I do like to kiss ass, just not Dad's," he winks playfully at Carey instead of taking offense to the conversation he overheard. Carey laughs uncomfortably.

"Can we just work on the car?" Carey asks hesitantly.

"Sure," Jason and I say together.

Nick

Skin wanted a rematch, so here we are getting ready to race again. I don't know when he'll learn that he can't beat me. After Sean wrecked my last car, Dad bought me this one. I loved my Fastback, but this '70 Corvette Stingray is the bomb. Well, it will be when Carey finishes working on it. After I left last weekend, Carey got it running. Even after all that crap Dad said about not working on my car without me, they still spent hours on it. I knew I had nothing to worry about. During the week, Jason and Brody helped me make some modifications that could have left my old car in its dust. All it needs now is a little body work and a coat of paint.

Tonight there's money involved. Most of the time it's just for fun and bragging rights, but a few times a year, people place bets on the racers. When I win tonight, I'm looking at at least two grand. I've already beaten my first two opponents and it's down to Skin and me. I knew long before we showed up that Skin and I would end up in the final race tonight. There aren't any regulars who can beat us.

"You ready?" Jason asks, sounding more concerned than anything.

"Yeah. No way that prick's gonna take me," I answer with confidence, eyeing Skin.

"Just be careful. I need you in one piece more than you need to win."

"Not true. I have to win. I need more than just bragging rights. Winning tonight proves that I'm the best and the cash ain't a bad bonus."

"Promise me you won't be stupid, Nicky," Jason puts a hand on my shoulder and looks me in the eye.

"I'll be fine," I shrug out of his grip and head toward my car.

"Not good enough."

"It's going to have to be good enough, Jase," I tell him, climbing into the driver's seat. I know Jason is worried, but I can handle Skin. He's mostly talk. I pull up to the starting line and rev my engine for show. I hear noise from the crowd because most of them are on my side. It's such a rush when people cheer my name.

The same girl who's out here for every race raises her red scarf. She's always here to start the races, but I don't know her name. I call her Curves because she has a body like a hourglass. She's hot enough, but a little old for me. Not that I would say no if she offered, but she's got to be at least thirty.

She drops her arms. Skin and I take off. I start off strong, leading by several car lengths going into the first turn. Skin falls a little further behind by the time we come out of the second turn. I have this race in the bag, I can already feel the money in my pocket.

As I approach the third turn, disaster strikes. There's a loud noise and suddenly black smoke is pouring out of the hood. Shit! I lose control, trying to see through the smoke and start to spin out. When I finally come to a stop, I am only inches from the pond. My heart is pounding against my chest and I'm shaking uncontrollably. That was close.

"Fuck!" I yell, punching the steering wheel.

Skin crosses the finish line with my bragging rights and my money. There is nothing I can do. The car is too hot to handle right now. I pop the hood to let out some of the smoke.

"Are you okay? What happened?" Jason asks, reaching me in record time.

"I don't know what happened, but the car is toast," I curse, kicking the tire. Brody, Tim, and Truck join us.

"Damn, boy. That sucks," Brody says, shaking his head. I just glare at him.

"I'll call Carey and see if he can come look at it," Jason says.

"Why, he's probably too busy getting high," Tim laughs.

"Watch it, Tim," I warn. It pisses me off for people to talk about one of my brothers, even if it is truth.

"What? It's true, and you know it," he continues. I start toward him, but Jason steps in my path.

"He said he'll be here in ten minutes," Jason says as he ends the call. I want to say "told you so" to Tim, but what good will it do. I try to look at the engine, but it's still smoking a little. I hope Carey can fix it. If I have to call a tow truck, I'll have to tell my dad what happened. I will be grounded for eternity if he finds out about the racing.

Ten minutes came and went, then twenty, then thirty.

"Where's Carey?" Tim asks a little too eagerly.

"He'll be here," I say.

"Come on, Nick, you know he's not coming," Truck adds.

"I'm telling you, he's getting baked. He probably doesn't even remember that Jason called," Tim continues to goad me. He knows it's pissing me off.

"Seriously, when was the last time he was sober?" Truck asks.

"Enough!" I yell, shoving Truck against the car.

"Calm your panties. You know you're only pissed because we're right!." Tim yells back. I raise my fist to punch him, but Jason stops me again.

"That's not going to help," he says.

"You two lay off," Jason tells my friends.

"Carey will be here, and he'll be sober," I tell them pointedly.

The wait is endless, and the longer I pace, the angrier I get. It's going on an hour since Jason made the call. Skin has long since collected his money, gloated, and left. The crowd has dispersed, leaving the five of us waiting. Finally, headlights approach. I see red when Carey stumbles out of a car I don't recognize. I can tell from here that he is half in the bag.

"What the fuck?" I yell, walking up to him.

"What?" he asks innocently, as if he doesn't know what he's done. "We've been waiting an hour, and you're wasted."

"I had to bum a ride." He pushes past me and staggers to my car. "What happened?"

"We don't know. That's why I called you," Jason says with exasperation.

"Well, I can't fix this shit tonight," he laughs.

"Told you he'd be high," Tim says, knocking my shoulder as he walks past me. I grab his arm ready to punch him when I notice the guy who drove Carey. He stumbles and has to lean on his car to stay upright.

"Go home, Tim, and take Truck with you," I growl, shoving him toward his car.

"Who the fuck is that?" I ask Carey.

"A friend," he shrugs.

"He's worse off than you," Jason says.

"What the hell were you thinking getting in a car with that guy? You could have been killed," Right now I am angrier than I have ever been.

"Back off, Nick. I'm fine. He's not even high."

"He can hardly stand up!" I yell. Carey and I are inches apart, and you can practically see the tension in the air.

"Look, this isn't getting fixed tonight," Jason steps between us. "You take my car and get Carey back to Ryan's. Brody and I will get this one home safely," he points to the other guy.

213

"Do you know him?" I ask in a whisper, not wanting Carey to hear.

"He does some dealing. Carey shouldn't be hanging out with him.He isn't a good guy, and he's several years older than me. I'm pretty sure he graduated a year or two before Ryan. Just get C home safely. We'll deal with the car tomorrow," Jason tells me.

"Fine," I say reluctantly. I don't want to leave my car. Damn, I hate when Jason's right.

Jason

Dad and I are the only two home today. He has a rare day off in the middle of the week, and my brothers are all at school. I haven't found a job since that gift shop gave me a permanent vacation. Most days, I at least pretend to look for a job, even if I just stare at a blank computer screen. I figure this is as good a day as any to talk to Dad about my plans for my future. Hopefully, he'll listen with an open mind.

He's sitting at the table with his cup of coffee, reading the paper. I watch him for a few seconds from the bottom step. My father is strong, loyal, and dedicated. He is the only completely unselfish person I know, having spent his entire adult life taking care of his family and community. He has never put himself first. I've always admired that about my father. I wish I was more like him. I wordlessly walk to the kitchen and pour myself a cup.

"You got a second, Dad?" I ask before I lose my nerve.

"Sure," he says as I walk to the table and take my seat.

"I thought we could talk about my future. I mentioned not long ago that I had some ideas." I know I sound unsure, but I'm really nervous. What if he doesn't take me seriously?

"I remember. Tell me about it. I'm all ears."

215

"Um...well...I...I want to open a strip club. I've been doing some research. I know I can't open it until I turn twenty-one, but I can start getting everything ready now. You know, find a place to rent, get loan papers filled out, apply for my business license..."

"A strip club?" he cuts me off. "Look, Jason. I'm glad you are thinking about the future. You definitely need to find something long term, but do you really think a strip club is a good idea? You've never held down a job for more than a couple of months. You don't know anything about running a business."

"I know enough, Dad. I took two business classes when I was in college."

"Did you pass them?"

"No," I sulk.

"No because you were too busy chasing girls and partying, which is likely what you'll do at the strip club."

"I'm serious about this, Dad. I kept those business books, and I've been reading them over the past several weeks."

"Well, I'm glad to hear that you're putting forth some effort. I think you should also consider taking some business classes online."

"I don't know. College didn't work out so well the first time."

"I'm not saying you have to get a degree, but a few classes will help. Just think about it."

"I'll think about it," I promise.

"You also have to be able to respect your employees and take care of them. You can't screw them every chance you get.
Business is business and pleasure is pleasure. Separate, always."

"DAD! I would never do that."

"Well, your track record says otherwise. For years all you've cared about is your next lay." He sits back, crosses his arms, and looks me dead in the eyes.

"I've heard the rumors, son. I always hoped they were just that, especially the ones about middle school. After the STD incident, I'm starting to believe all of the man-whore stories."

"Look, I know you don't trust me when it comes to work, or responsibility. I haven't exactly made the best choices since high school, but I am serious about this. I can make it work. I will be nothing but respectful to my employees. I've already thought this through, and I know I can't mix business with pleasure. I know I can't screw my employees. I can run this business, Dad. I know I can." We sit in silence while Dad mulls this over. It feels like an eternity before he speaks again.

"I know you can, son," he finally states. I let out a breath I didn't realize I was holding. "I've never heard you sound so passionate and excited about anything. If anyone can make this venture a success, Jason, it's you. I actually think it might be a good idea, as long as you keep your dick in your pants."

"You do?" I'm skeptical. Maybe he's just screwing with me.

"Yes son, I do. I think the best course of action for you at this point is working for yourself. Girls are the one thing that seem to keep your attention. If you can keep business separate from pleasure, I think you can be successful. If you can't, then you will fail and fail fast."

"I won't fail. I will make you proud, Dad. I promise."

"I know you will, Jason. If there's anything I can do to help, let me know. I'm here to support you."

"Um...wow....thanks, Dad." What just happened? Did Dad just give me his blessing to open a strip club? I never dreamed he would support this decision, but it feels damn good to have him on my side.

Sean

Since Carey moved out, I've been in the car alone with Nick every day. Nick's been more of an ass than usual, and I am sick of riding with him. Today, I decided to walk home with Sam. When Dad finds out, he's going to rip me a new one, but I'm done with Nick. He's still angry that I totalled his car, even though he knows now that I had just found out about Carey and Riley. Dad bought him another car the following week, so I don't understand why he can't let it go. He's still sneaking out and racing on the weekends. It's not like his life changed that much, just his ride.

Sam and I are almost to his house when a car pulls in front of us, blocking our path. Some guys in football jerseys file out. I drop my head in embarrassment when I realize Nick is with them. He hangs back while the other two approach us.

"Hey, losers," Tim says.

"Leave us alone," I say, starting past him. He grabs my arm and shoves me into Sam. We almost lose our balance, but somehow manage to stay on our feet.

"Did I tell you that you could go anywhere?" Tim yells in my face, but I don't respond.

"Answer me, freak!" he smacks me hard on the side of the head.

I look up at Nick for help, but he's laughing his ass off. When he sees me looking, he shakes his head slightly. I don't know if he is telling me to not answer or if he's ashamed I'm his brother.

"Speak, you little fuck!" Spit flies from Tim's mouth, hitting me in the face, as he continues his tirade.

"Are you disrespecting us?" Truck speaks up while getting in my face. This guy terrifies me even more after the beating he gave me a couple of weeks ago. He's the biggest high schooler I've ever seen. I cower at his words, which makes them laugh more. Why doesn't Nick stop them? How can he stand by and let his friends treat me like I'm nothing? I guess I am nothing to him now. I'm nothing to my whole family. I'm pretty sure that Sam is the only one in the world who cares about me.

"So, Nick, what's with the green hair on your brother?" Truck asks, yanking my hair and causing me to fall to my knees. Pain shoots through both knees as they make contact with the sidewalk. "Looks like a unicorn puked on him." I *hate* Truck.

"I don't know what's wrong with him," Nick says as he looks away from me.

"Sam sure seems to like it," Truck says, implying something is going on between Sam and me. This isn't the first time they have said stuff like this.

"You like your girlfriend's hair, little Sammy?" Tim asks.

"He's not my girlfriend. We're not gay. Just leave us alone," Sam says in defense, as if his words will matter to them.

"Are you talking back to me, boy?" Tim asks Sam.

"Come on, Sean," Sam ignores them and pulls me to my feet.

"No. You go. Sean is coming with us," Nick tells Sam finally stepping toward us.

"I am not going anywhere with you," I snap at Nick. He grabs the front of my shirt, and his face is inches from mine. From the corner of my eye, I see Sam flinch and back away.

"Get in the fucking car!" Nick says through gritted teeth. Then, he shoves me toward Tim's car. I push back, trying to get to Sam. It's no use. Nick is bigger and stronger than me. He easily forces me into the car. Out of the window, I see Tim and Truck on either side of Sam. They are saying something I can't hear and laughing at him. Tim knocks Sam's books out of his hand as Truck shoves him. Sam hits the ground hard.

"Let me out," I yell, trying to push past Nick. He holds me in place. I struggle against him, but it does no good. As Tim and Truck head back to the car, Tim kicks Sam's books and sends his papers scattering. They get in the front, and Tim drives away leaving Sam alone on the ground.

"Stay away from Sam. You need to find better friends, Sean. Sam is a loser, and he's dragging you down. You need to start hanging with us so we can make you cool." I see Truck give Nick a nasty look in the rearview mirror. It's clear that hanging with them is an idea only Nick wants.

"If being an asshole is cool, then, no thanks. I'll stick with Sam," I tell him. By the look of anger in his eyes, he wants to punch me. No matter how angry Nick gets, he has never hit me. As kids, we wrestled and smacked each other sometimes, but he's never purposely, physically harmed me. His words are a different story. I think I would rather be punched than belittled by Nick.

"You gonna let your brother speak to you that way?" Tim questions from the front.

"I'll take care of my family business in private. You just drive," Nick tells him. He wants his friends to think he is going to do something to me later, but I know he won't. He doesn't treat me this way at home. He'll probably even make up some story about what he did to handle me, but I don't care what he says to them. I can't wait for Nick to go to college, so I don't have to put up with him anymore.

Reid

"Hey, little brother," I greet Ryan, joining him in our favorite corner booth at Mel's.

"What's up, Reid?" he responds. I sit across from him and read over the menu that I long ago memorized. The waitress takes our order, but I continue to stare at the menu.

"You look like shit," Ryan finally says.

"How is he, Ryan?" I ask, ignoring his comment.

"He's okay."

"Don't lie to me." I look up, searching his eyes for the truth.

"I'm not lying. Carey has had some good days. He's been going to the psychiatrist. As far as I know, he hasn't used since he moved in with me."

"Are you sure? I just don't trust him, Ryan."

"He's tested clean for the past two weeks. He's been to school every day. I checked his grades this morning. Mostly C's and D's, but he isn't failing anything right now. I think you need to look at the positives. It's going to take time for him to heal, Reid."

"I worry about him constantly. Do you really think he'll ever heal?"

"Absolutely, Reid. Carey's a fighter. He'll get through this."

"No, Carey's a runner. He has *never* fought for anything, especially himself. He always runs when things get tough. You're wrong, Ryan."

"He sure as hell won't get better with that attitude. He needs your support, Reid. You sound like you've already given up on him. It doesn't sound like you even want to help him," Ryan says angrily.

"I do want to help him!" I yell a little louder than I mean and a few heads turn our way. "I do want to help him," I whisper, feeling completely beaten. "I just don't know how. I feel like I've let him down."

"Have you tried talking to him?"

"Why? He won't listen."

"He talks to me. Maybe he needs you to listen for a change. In the months before he overdosed, you spent a lot time on his case. Did you ever really stop to listen to what he had to say?" Ryan loves Carey so much. They've always had a special relationship, but he hasn't been there for everything that Carey has put us through.

"It wouldn't have made a difference, Ryan. You didn't live in that house. It was hell on all of us. Carey made everyone miserable, and frankly we all avoided him as much as possible."

"How did that work out?" Ryan snaps. He's pissing me off. I know he's right, but I don't want to hear it from my little brother. I'm tired of failing as a parent, and I don't need to hear it said out loud.

"It didn't," I admit. "The last thing I wanted was for him to move in with you, but I think it's been for the best. We all needed a break. If anyone can save him, it's you."

"Don't beat yourself up, Reid. You're a great father and those boys are lucky to have you. I know it wasn't easy on you being a single parent."

"Just because it was difficult, doesn't make it okay that I screwed up Carey's life."

"Stop, Reid. You know those words aren't true. The truth is Carey made his own shitty choices. That's on him. Now, he needs us to support him and guide him down the right path."

"Maybe." I sigh. "No, you're right. I want to help him find that path. Ryan, those boys were hard to raise and royal pains in my ass on a daily basis but dammit, I love them ALL with every ounce of my soul. They are my life. I don't care one iota that Carey's DNA is a little different. HE IS MY SON!" Even more heads turn this time when I yell.

"Anyone need a tea refill? I have a fresh gallon." From behind the counter, Brenda's sweet voice takes the focus off of us. She is a doll!

"I know, brother. In time, he'll see it, too. Just have some patience. Right now, Carey is lost and confused, but one day with our support, he will become a good man," Ryan is a wise man to only be in his twenties.

"I hope so."

"Have faith, my brother. In all things have faith! Don't make me quote Mom's scripture to you! You know I will!" Ryan promises.

225

"No, please, no!" We both have a laugh. "Pie?" Ryan asks.

"Always! What's the point of eating at Mel's?"

"Pie!" we say together.

Carey

I've been staying at my uncle's for a few weeks now. Nothing in my life is getting better. School is the same; avoiding Seth, being an ass to the teachers, and struggling in most of my classes. So really nothing has changed. Except, I have to do it sober.

I hate seeing the psychiatrist. It's two hours a week of him asking questions and me giving vague non-answers. I refuse to talk to that quack about my life. He sits behind his desk in a coat and tie acting all high and mighty, as if he has ever seen a day of trouble in his life. I am sure he was raised in a perfect, little, suburban family with 2.5 kids, a white picket fence, and a private school education. There is nothing he can say or do to help me with the problems I have in my life.

The only time I've spoken to Reid since I left his house was when we worked on Nick's car. He leaves messages daily, but I haven't responded to any of them. I haven't spent much time with my brothers outside of school. Things are strained between us. Nick and Jason have reached out and tried to mend our relationships, but I'm just not ready. That probably makes me an asshole, but what else is new. Sean has come over to Ryan's a few times. We played video games and watched movies to avoid conversation. I can tell he's worried about me, but if we actually talk, he'll know how messed up I am over all of this.

Things aren't much better with Ryan, but at least I don't want to beat the shit out of someone when he's around. Although, today, I may have put a wedge between Ryan and me because he got called to the school to come pick me up. I got into it with a girl in one of my classes who pissed me off. Nothing too bad; I would never lay a hand on a girl. She was being a bitch, and I told her as much. When the teacher stepped in, I simply told him to go fuck himself. Needless to say, that earned me a free trip to the principal's office where I was given a three day vacation. Ryan brought me back to his house, and I was hoping that he would drop me off and go back to work. Instead, he follows me into the house. I make a beeline for my bedroom.

"Carey, wait." I sigh with the frustration of not being able to get away from him fast enough.

"What?" I ask heatedly without turning around to look at him.

"Sit down, Kid. We need to talk."

"I don't need a lecture, Ryan. I already know I'm a complete loser," I continue towards my room.

"This isn't about you. It's about me." His words stop me in my tracks. Now, my interest is really piqued. I slowly make my way to the couch acting exasperated while hoping he doesn't realize that I'm actually interested in what he has to say. There's a long silence as Ryan paces in front of the couch. I can't imagine what could have him so nervous.

"Look, I need to tell you something that I've kept from almost everyone for ten years. Only a few people know what I'm about to say. I've debated on whether or not to tell you for the past few weeks. My hope is that it will help you see that you aren't alone. My fear is that it will make you hate your family more."

"I don't hate my family," I comment, but even I don't believe me.

Ryan is silent for too long, and I begin to think that he has decided to keep his secret to himself. With what he already said, I'm not sure I really want to know. Part of me wants to hear it, but the other part just wants him to give up, and let me go to my room. He's sat down and stood back up several times, and now he's pacing again. This can't be good. I have never seen Ryan this nervous and unsure. He always has it together. I'm really beginning to second guess my decision to hear his secret.

Geez, this is taking too long. "Just spit it out already," I say a little louder than intended.

"This isn't easy, Carey. I need you to listen to everything I have to say. I need you to understand that this was difficult for me when I first found out. It took some time, but I have accepted it. I'm grateful for the childhood I had; two wonderful loving parents and two brothers who I care about, and I know they care about me," I roll my eyes because there is no way he believes the bullshit he's spitting out

229

about his brothers. Reid, sure, but not Riley. Ryan ignores the eye roll. This must be serious.

"Do you remember when I came to live with your family when I was a teenager?"

"Yeah."

"Do you know why I came to live with you?"

"Not really. Dad...um...," I correct myself. "Reid said it was because you wanted to spend more time with us. We were kids, Ryan. He didn't really give us much information. I do remember that you seemed sad, and spent a lot of time with me. I guess that's when we became close. Dad said that I made you happy. I thought you hung the moon. I was only five, and I couldn't believe that you actually wanted to be around me." Saying it out loud sounds kind of pathetic.

"Reid was right. I did want to spend time with you and your brothers, but there's a lot more to the story. I was angry at my parents and hated everyone. I got into a lot of fights during that time, and eventually got expelled from school. The only time I was happy was when I was with you. I didn't understand then, but I seemed to have a different bond with you than with your brothers."

"That sounds really creepy," I joke. Ryan laughs, but it sounds forced.

"Carey," he pauses and runs a hand through his hair.

"I'm not who you think I am. I'm not really your uncle. I was adopted when I was born."

I am stunned to say the least. I can't even respond to that. I stare at Ryan in disbelief, trying to find words to express what I'm thinking. This does explain the age gap between Ryan and his brothers, but it doesn't make sense because he looks like he is related to us.

"Adopted or not, you're still my uncle," I insist. Instantly, I realize the similarity in my words and Reid's. We sit, staring at each other for minutes that feel like hours.

Ryan finally breaks the silence, "My biological parents were young, really young. My father was fourteen and my mother was fifteen when I was born. By the time they were ready to admit that she was actually pregnant, it was too late. My mother wouldn't get an abortion. My father refused to acknowledge that I even existed. He doesn't know what happened to me. My identity has been kept from him all of these years. My mother wanted me to have a good life, but her parents refused to allow her to keep me. My adoptive parents, your grandparents, signed the adoption papers the day I was born." Ryan pauses and sighs which makes me think that he isn't finished. I'm trying to piece this together because something doesn't feel like it's adding up, but I'm too confused and shocked to figure it out.

"I found out that I was adopted when I was sixteen. I know who my father is, but he doesn't know who I am. My parents told me everything, and I didn't take it well. I ran away, and it took them two months to find me. Reid was the one who finally tracked me down, and the only reason I agreed to come back was if I could live with him. After a year of being nothing but a waste of space, Reid handed me my ass and told me to get over myself. We had a big fight, but in the end I finally realized that he was right. I went back home to my parents and went back to school. I graduated high school a year late since I had to repeat the eleventh grade." He takes a deep breath before continuing. "It was hard to understand. I wished they would have told me sooner, but they wanted to wait until I was old enough to fully understand. My parents let me decide if I wanted to meet my mother and if I wanted to tell my father my identity. It took me years to make a decision, but I finally decided to meet my mother when I was twenty. We keep in touch, but don't have a close relationship. I've never told my father who I am even though he is a big part of my life. Carey, I want, no, I need you to know who I am because everything that has happened with you completes this story. It completes me. However, I need you to keep this between us. At least for now. Can you do that?"

"How the hell can I agree to that when I don't know what you're going to say? How does this affect me? I don't understand, Ryan." I'm scared to hear what else he has to say. For some reason, I feel like this is going to turn my world upside down again. I don't know if I can take anymore.

"Just hear me out, Carey," I nod my agreement. "I would have told you the night you moved in, but I was still trying to wrap my head around the news you dropped on us. I was in shock, too."

"Shit, Ryan, just tell me."

"My parents are actually my biological grandparents. Riley is my father." What did he just say? I know I heard that wrong. My head starts to spin. I feel like the breath has been knocked out of me. I lean over and rest my head in my hands. I feel like I am going to puke.

"Carey?" Ryan ventures.

"You're my brother," I state quietly.

"I didn't know. I thought we were cousins. I know this is a lot to take in right now. It was hard for me when I first found out. I felt lost and confused. Even though my parents loved and cherished me, I felt unwanted and unloved in that moment. It took me a long time to get past those feelings," Ryan pauses and smiles when I look up. "Want to know something?" he asks.

I nod at him in response.

"The best part about all of it was finding out I had a biological brother. You made all the mixed emotions worth it," Ryan looks sincere.

"I guess this explains that creepy bonding thing," I joke, trying to lighten the mood. It's stupid, but I don't know what else to say. Anger is usually my go to reaction. Surprisingly, I'm not angry. Confused as hell, but not angry.

"Are you okay?"

"I guess," I say, shrugging my shoulders. "It's cool that you're my brother. So no one else knows?"

"Reid and Riley know I am adopted. They were teenagers and obviously Mom wasn't pregnant. Neither of them knows that Riley is my father."

"Are you going to tell him?"

"No." He is quick and angry with his response. "I've thought about it for years, Carey. Riley hated me before I was born and said some awful things about my mother and me. He never even told our parents that he got a girl pregnant. Jenny, my biological mom, told my parents everything when she offered for them to adopt me. They never hesitated, but they knew Riley would treat me differently if he knew the truth. I think we all made the right decision."

"No kidding! He doesn't really handle it well when he finds out he has a kid," I say sarcastically.

"I won't tell anyone, Ryan. You can trust me on this," I tell him honestly.

"Thank you," he says. He starts to say something else when his phone buzzes. "Shit," he shakes his head, reading the text. "I hate to leave you after dropping all of that on you. My plan was to

234

spend the rest of the day here with you, but I'm needed at the station. I might be late getting in tonight, but there are leftovers in the refrigerator when you get hungry. I'm sorry to rush off."

"It's okay," I tell him. I think I need time alone to process this news anyway.

I sit straight up in bed and my heart is racing. What is that blaring noise? I shake my head trying to figure out the source and soon realize that it's my alarm. Why in the hell is my alarm going off? I have a three day vacation from school and should be sleeping late. The clock reads 5:32. Who set the alarm for this early? I don't get up until almost seven on school days.

"Good, you're awake," Ryan says. He is totally relaxed and leaning against the door jamb with a steaming mug of coffee.

"What the hell?" I bark in response.

"I have to leave for work in less than an hour. Get up so we can discuss your chores for the day."

"Chores?" I question.

"You didn't think I was going to let you sit on your ass all day while I work, did you?" he asks.

"I'm not doing your housework. This is bullshit! I don't live here," I tell him.

"Technically, you do. This isn't up for discussion. I've told you before that your way isn't working.

As long as you are living here, you need to take on some of the responsibilities. Be in the kitchen in fifteen minutes," Ryan says, closing the door and leaving me dumbfounded. I can't believe he wants me to spend my day off working. I put on some clothes, brush my teeth, and head out to the kitchen.

"You know today is my day off," I greet him.

"Getting suspended is not a vacation," he tells me.

"I beg to differ," I mumble.

"I made a pot of coffee, you can make your own breakfast. Here's a list of what you need to do today," he says, handing me a laundry list of chores. This is ridiculous, I think, reading over the list.

"This will take all day to complete," I say, tossing the paper on the table.

"That's the point." He walks out of the room.

"Can we talk about this?" I call, following him.

"Nothing to discuss, Kid. That list will be completed by the time I get home." With that he leaves for the day.

He's crazy if he thinks I'm doing anything on that list. I plop myself on the couch and pick up the remote.

The next thing I know, I'm startled awake by the sound of the front door opening. Ryan is going to be pissed if I slept all day.

"Hey, Carey," Claire calls as she enters the house. I look at my phone and see that it's almost noon. Oops, I guess I did take a little nap.

"Um...hey," I say reluctantly not sure why she's here. Her and Ryan have only been dating for a few weeks. Isn't it a little fast for her to have a key?

"Did you eat?" she asks sweetly.

"What? Are you my mother now?" I ask angrily.

"I'm just asking," she says, putting her hands up in surrender.

"No, I haven't eaten," I say with attitude. "I fell asleep after Ryan left for work."

"Why don't I make you some lunch while you get started on the list?"

"I'm not doing shit on that list."

"That list isn't going to complete itself."

"Well neither am I," I reply firmly. She's kind of annoying.

"Ryan will be very unhappy if you sit around all day. There's a reason he gave you the list." Her words are gentle, but they piss me off anyway.

"Yeah, so he can shirk his responsibilities. I am not his servant!" I yell. "Why are you even here? You barely know my brother, and you sure as hell don't know me. None of this is any of your damn business. Why don't you just butt out?"

She steps back as if she's been slapped. "I'm just trying to help," she says quietly as she fights back tears.

"Well you're not helping so why don't you get the fuck out."

I see the first tear fall as Claire turns and heads for the front door. Ryan is going to kill me now that

I've made his girl cry. Why do I turn everything to shit? I don't try to stop Claire. What would I say to her? It isn't as if I'm capable of making this better. I've proven that more than once. I grab a bag of chips and the list from the kitchen. As I sit on the back porch, I look over the paper. Dishes, laundry, yard work, vacuuming, there is no way I am doing any of this.

"Shit!" I yell, looking up from the paper. It just hit me that when I was yelling at Claire, I called Ryan my brother. I promised him I would keep that between us. I couldn't even keep my mouth shut for twenty-four hours. Once again, proving what a colossal screw up I am. Ryan is going to be so angry at me.

Instead of worrying about everything I managed to ruin lately, I open my backpack and pull the inside seam apart. There's a hidden compartment that's difficult to see if you don't know to look for it. I take out a joint and light it. Then, I burn the list. I spend the afternoon getting high and ignoring the problems continuing to pile up.

"What is wrong with you?" I hear from inside the house before the back door swings open. I try to stay calm and look serious.

"Why the hell were you a dick to Claire? She came over here because I asked her to check on you. I just wanted to make sure you were okay and had some thing to eat. In the five minutes she was here, you managed to upset her to the point that she spent the afternoon in tears. She has no idea what she did wrong, and doesn't believe me when I tell her it isn't her fault. You have to fix this," Ryan says with more anger than I have ever seen from him. I start laughing. I am high as hell, and it makes Ryan's angry tirade hilarious.

"This isn't funny. You were a disrespectful asshole to my girlfriend. I will not put up with that. I'm serious, Carey." Ryan takes a deep breath, but it does nothing to calm his anger.

"Get. In. The. Car. You are going to apologize to my girl...RIGHT NOW!" I continue to laugh because I can practically see the steam coming out of Ryan's ears, like he is some sort of cartoon character.

"CAR! NOW!" he yells, heading for the gate. I don't move. Opening the gate, he turns around and notices that I'm still cracking up from my spot on the back porch.

"Are you wasted?" he asks.

"No," I laugh.

"Bullshit!" he says angrily. "I am not putting up with you treating people the way you treated Claire or getting high at my house." His voice is more concern now than anger.

"Fine, but I'm not putting up with you thinking that I am YOUR servant." My laughter quickly turns to anger.

"I don't think you're my servant," he says. "Can't you see, I gave you that list to teach you a lesson."

"And what lesson might that be?" I bite out.

"Shit, Carey. I'm just trying to help. You are better than this," he says, pointing to me. Even high, I know I've screwed up yet again.

"You don't have to get high and treat the people who care about you like they're worthless. Your brothers miss you. They want to be in this with you, not working against you." I have no idea how to respond. I'm not worth their time. Why does everyone keep trying to make me into someone I'm not?

"I'm never going to be the person you want me to be. You don't understand, Ryan. I am messed up. I'm not worth anyone's time and energy. You have no idea," I say, feeling like I am going to start crying. I hate myself and the person I've become, but I know that I will never change. I've accepted that I'm just like my mother. Maybe that's why I was so drawn to her. More than any of my brothers, I felt the need to get close to her and have a relationship. All that did was cause more problems. Sometimes, I wish I could just end it all.

"Carey, there is nothing wrong with you. You've been dealt a rough hand, and you've made some bad choices. This isn't something that has to ruin you, now or in the future."

I roll my eyes at his response. He's just trying to help, but there is nothing he can do to save me.

I know I'm hopeless. I block out the rest of his pep talk, nodding and throwing in a "yeah" every now and then for good measure. Finally, he lets me head to the bedroom for the night.

The next few days passed without incident. I ended up doing some of the chores on Ryan's list. Mostly, because I got bored sitting around the house for three days. Ryan took all of my drugs and cleaned out his medicine cabinets. I haven't had a chance to buy more, so I haven't been high in several days. Today, I've been back at school for a week. I'm between classes when I get a text from Ryan.

Got an unexpected lead in this case.
Gotta follow the trail while it's hot. Sorry, Kid,
but I'll be late again. Can you fend for yourself
on supper?

Sure. No prob

It seems like an eternity before the final bell rings. I rush back to Ryan's with my mind intent on one thing. I searched when I was suspended without success, and Ryan claims to have gotten rid of all of the alcohol and medication in the house, but surely he hid something for a rainy day. I search for close to an hour, but come up empty handed. Pissed off and angry at the situation, I park myself on the back porch and put in my earbuds. I'm lost in the music when movement to the right catches my eye.

As soon as I see Riley, I bolt for the door. I can't believe he's here. There's no one home if he attacks me again.

"Wait, Carey. I'm not going to hurt you. I'll stay down here, just listen for a minute."

I freeze with my hand on the door handle, ready to run if needed.

"What do you want?" I ask. My heart is about to beat out of my chest. I don't want to be this close to Riley.

"I thought you could use a friend," Riley says, holding out a cold beer to me.

"You have two minutes before I call Ryan." Opening the beer, I take a seat on a porch chair. Riley saunters up the steps and takes the seat beside me. He opens his own and sets the rest of the six pack between us. I down over half of the beer before I speak again.

"What are you really doing here, Riley?"

"I just came by to talk to my son."

"Don't call me that." It makes my skin crawl when he calls me son. "Just get to the point." I open a second beer.

"I want to say I'm sorry for my actions that night at Reid's. You caught me off guard. I had a rough morning in the ER. I lost a patient. My mind was frazzled." He defends his actions.

"I think you said enough when you put a knife to my throat."

"Like I said, rough morning."

"That's no excuse," I mumble, reaching for my third beer. I notice there are still two sitting between us. Good. I'm going to need them.

"You're right, but it never gets easy to lose a patient." Riley takes a sip of his beer then changes the subject. "Carey, I know I haven't been much of a father to you."

"You'll never be a father to me."

"Fair enough," he pauses. "How are things here? Are you doing okay?" It's freaking me out a little to hear Riley pretend to be concerned.

"Fine. Everything is just great," I bite out sarcastically.

"I'm sure all of this has been very difficult for you. I mean finding out Reid isn't who he said he was, your mom overdosing..."

"She didn't overdose," I cut him off. "Someone killed her."

"That's quite an accusation. Do you have any proof?"

"Yes. No. I don't know."

"Who do you think would do that to her?" He hands me another beer.

"I was there the night she died. I saw someone leaving her apartment. I couldn't see a face, but I saw the shirt. It had this weird design. Something nautical like the outline of a sailboat. What really

243

caught my attention was that it glowed in the dark. I'll never forget what I saw that night."

"Wow. That's quite a story. Maybe I was right."

"Right about what?"

"I thought you might need something a little stronger than beer," he says, holding up a quart size bag of what looks like cotton twigs. It takes me a few seconds to realize what he's offering.

"We had a terminal patient, cancer. I was able to "borrow" a bag before we sent him home. It's not like he's going to be around long enough to need it all."

"Um...thanks," I say with amazement. Damn. I've never seen that much weed in one place. I'm practically salivating at the sight.

"This stuff is a little more potent than what you're accustomed to, so be careful. I wouldn't want you to end up back in my care." I notice a slight note of sarcasm in the last statement, but never let him see me waiver as I take the bag from him.

"You need to leave. Ryan will be home soon."

"Of course," he says, standing. When he reaches the bottom step, he turns around. I already have a joint in my hand searching my pockets for a lighter.

"Here, let me," he takes a step toward me and lights the joint. I inhale deeply, and start to cough. It hits me quicker than any other time. Riley wasn't kidding when he said this stuff is potent. "Have you told anyone about what you *think* you saw at your mom's?"

"Not yet. I might tell Ryan. I'm not sure," I shrug.

"No offense, kiddo, but do you think that's wise? You don't know for sure what you saw. You can't lie to the police, and Ryan is a cop. Plus, do you think anyone is going to believe a junkie? I'm not saying you have a problem, but some people would." With that last statement, Riley turns to leaves. He's probably right. Who's going to believe a "worthless, junkie?" I take another drag. I doubt even Ryan will believe me if I tell him, and he has more faith in me than anyone.

"Hey, Carey." Riley turns back toward me when he reaches the edge of the yard. "Don't worry, son. It will all be over soon." His smile appears genuine as he turns and steps through the gate.

Nick

As I predicted, we won the homecoming game. We are the best team in the state. I can hardly wait to prove it again come December, just like we have for the past three years. Of course, my family was in the stands. My dad has never missed a game. He loves watching me play. Jason played when he went to Paradise Cove High School. Having him in the stands isn't the same as taking the field with him, but I'm glad he was there. He comes to all of my games, and we often watch the highlights and talk strategy on the weekends after each game. Even Carey came tonight. He misses more games than he attends, but I like it when he's there. Sean sat with the family instead of with his faggot friends, and I felt a slight pang of guilt for all the shit I've been giving him lately. I love Sean, but I feel like he is making a mistake hanging out with Sam. High school isn't the place to stand out. He needs to find some cooler friends or he is going to spend the next four years in hell.

As soon as Coach finished his congratulatory speech, I rushed home. I've showered and changed into my clothes for the dance, and I look damn good. Not that I have to try too hard to look good. The constant girl drool proves that on a daily basis.

I'm meeting Ashley at the dance, mainly because she's a sure thing. I make my way to school as quickly as possible.

I stop in my tracks when I see Ashley on the other side of the dance floor. This year our Homecoming dance is in the pecan grove in the center of the high school campus. I thought it was a stupid idea when I heard about it, but a group of dads built a dance floor and white lights hang from the surrounding trees. It actually looks cool. Ashley is stunning in her long black dress. It hugs all of her curves and leaves little to the imagination. I feel everyone's eyes follow us as we close the distance.

"You are smokin' hot, babe." I whisper in her ear as I circle my arms around her waist. "I can't wait to rip this off of you later."

"You're not looking too bad yourself," she says, taking a step back and raking her eyes over me.

"I love how your muscles fill out this shirt," she rubs her hands over my chest and then down my arms. I lean in and kiss her deeply, pushing my erection into her so she knows how much I like what I see.

"Break it apart you two. Save room for Jesus," Mr. Raynor says, pulling me back a little.

"Seriously, what's the problem?" I ask, even though I know the school policy on PDA.

"You know the problem, Mr. Oliver. Either separate or leave," he scolds.

247

"Yes, sir," I roll my eyes to his back and take Ashley's hand, pulling her onto the dance floor.

We spend the next several songs dancing and every so often I cop a quick feel. She loves every second of it. Soon, it's time to announce the king and queen. As usual, several of the most popular guys and girls were nominated to run for king and queen. No one is surprised when they announced Ashley as the Homecoming Queen and me as the Homecoming King. We take our spots center stage, accept our crowns, and dance for the crowd. This is what it's all about. Proof that I run this school. Proof that I will go out on top. Something none of my brothers can say. I will leave this school a legend. As I look around at the crowd, I notice that Sean is still hanging with his small group of losers in the corner. If I don't accomplish anything else this year, I need to find him some new friends, better friends. I stare in shock as I make eye contact with Carey. He gives me a slight smile and then looks back at some girl. I can't believe Carey is actually here and dancing. He looks clean, and I don't just mean sober. He looks like he showered and washed his hair. It all seems so normal. I knew Carey moving in with Ryan was the best decision.

Things were good once, but that seems so far in the past. I hope we can find our way back someday. Even though things have been rough lately, I never stopped loving Carey. I'm happy to see him here tonight. Maybe there is hope for us.

Sean

The door startles me, and I almost fall off the couch. I must have fallen asleep while watching the movie. In the weeks since Carey moved out, I haven't been sleeping much.

"Sean? Nick? Anyone home?" My dad calls from the kitchen.

"I'm the only one here," I respond, sitting up and turning off the television.

"Where is everyone?" Dad inquires.

"I don't know where Jason went. Nick's on the beach with Truck."

"Are you okay, Sean?" Dad asks, taking the seat next to me.

"Yeah. I was just resting a little. I'm tired from the dance." It isn't exactly a lie.

"Are you sure? I know the last months have been hard on you. I'm worried about you, Sean."

"I'm fine, Dad," I roll my eyes, but he doesn't notice. Well, at least he doesn't call me out on it. Rolling our eyes at him always gets us in trouble. He finds it "disrespectful."

"This isn't going to work today, son." He looks me straight in the eyes.

"What isn't going to work?" I look away, afraid he will see past the fake truth I keep written on my face.

"Shutting me out. Keeping your feelings inside. I know you haven't been sleeping much." Dad takes my hand as he speaks.

"Wh...what?" I stammer as the unexpected contact startles me.

"I see the circles under your eyes. Sometimes, I hear you up at night," he tells me with concern.

"Sorry if I bothered you," I snap, standing up.

"You never bother me. Sean, please talk to me. Tell me what's going on in your head."

"Really, Dad. What do you think is going on?" I bite out sarcastically.

"I know you are worried about Carey. I'm sure all of this has been very confusing for you. A lot has changed in your life over the past two months."

"I'm not a kid, Dad. I understand everything just fine!" I yell, pushing past him. He lets me get to the bottom step.

"I think there's stuff you're hiding," Dad whispers, but I hear him loud and clear.

"I have homework," I say with my back to him, starting up the steps.

"Is Nick hurting you?" I freeze at his words, only making it two steps up. How did he know to ask that question?

"No," I say unconvincingly, without turning around.

"You can tell me the truth, Sean," he says calmly. I can feel his presence behind me, and all I want to do is run up to my room and hide from this.

"I can and will deal with Nick, but I have to know what he's done."

"He's never physically harmed me, Dad." He's standing right behind me now. I don't turn to look at him because I'm afraid he will see that I am lying.

"That doesn't answer my question. Is he hurting you in other ways?"

"Daaaad," I groan.

"Tell me," his voice is louder, but I know it's concern not anger that I hear.

"Sometimes, he says mean things to me. Calls me names and stuff. It isn't a big deal. Please don't say anything to him. It'll just make him mad at me. Then, he'll tell his frie...," I cut off the last word. I was so intent on convincing him not to talk to Nick that I didn't think through what I was saying.

"What do you mean, he'll tell his friends?"

"Forget it, Dad. That's not what I meant," I try to blow it off.

"That's what you said." He turns me toward him and then continues. "Did one of Nick's friends do something to you?"

"Dad," I plead.

"The bruise on your jaw a couple of weeks ago. Was that really from P.E. or did one of Nick's friends hurt you?" he asks. The doorbell saves me. I have never been so relieved.

"It's Sam," I say, moving toward the door. Dad touches my arm and turns me back to him. He puts a hand on each shoulder and looks me in the eye.

251

"This isn't over, Sean. Go hang out with Sam. Be home in time for dinner. Carey and Ryan are coming at six. We *will* talk about this tomorrow."

"Sure, Dad," I say, shrugging out of his grip. I have no intention of *ever* talking about this again.

"I'm serious, Sean," he says to my back as I escape with Sam.

Nick

Truck and I have been tossing the football back and forth for an hour. It's too hot for October, but that doesn't stop us from spending the day on the beach. We'll end up in the water when the heat gets unbearable.

My mind isn't right today, and I've missed more than I've caught.

"You suck, man," Truck laughs when I fail to catch the ball again.

"Fuck off!" I yell, throwing the ball at his head.

He ducks out of the way just in time for the ball to miss him. "Jesus, Nick. What's your problem?"

"Nothing." I sit down and stare at the waves. Carey and Ryan are coming for dinner tonight, but my family drama is none of Truck's business. I've seen Carey at school, but we rarely speak. When we pass in the hallway, I pretend he isn't even my brother. Someone who doesn't know us, would never guess that Sean, Carey, and I are related. Sean and I have the same blue eyes as our father, but that's where the resemblance stops. Carey looks more like Riley and Ryan. At this point, I wish no one in this small town knew that we share the same DNA.

"You want to find some action?" Truck asks as a way to avoid conversation. He knows I won't talk. Plus, he doesn't really care enough to listen.

"What kind of action do you have in mind?" I smile. "Sam and Sean just headed toward the pier. We could blow off some steam, then go find Taylor and Ashley."

"That sounds good," I say, standing up and wiping the sand off my shorts.

"Where's Tim?" I ask as we head toward the pier.

"Um...he's...out," Truck replies nervously.

"Please tell me he is not still tapping that freshman."

"I think he likes her. He's been a one woman kind of guy for the past few months." I figured as much when I saw them at the dance last night.

"What is wrong with him?" I say with disgust. "Why would anyone want to be with the same girl day after day?"

"There's nothing wrong with having a girlfriend. Ashley is practically your girlfriend. Look at Taylor and me, we've been together for two years."

"That hasn't stopped you from banging other girls." He looks shocked at my words. They were only rumors, and I didn't know they were true until I saw the look on his face.

"That's none of your business. Keep your mouth shut about it," he warns.

"I don't give a shit what you do."

"But you care what Tim does?"

"*Taylor* is of age. Tim's girl is jail bait. I've tried to warn him, but he won't listen. He needs to keep from getting arrested until after we win state."

"It'll be fine, Nick." Truck waves me off. I drop it, but the whole situation has already fueled my anger.

We quickly catch up to Sam and Sean. After following them for a few minutes unnoticed, Truck grows restless. He's ready for some release and usually when he gets this way, someone gets hurt. Today, I feel the same way. I want to punch someone or something. Good thing Sam is here because I'm not going to hit Sean, even though the urge to clock him has become more noticeable lately. He's such a little wimp that he has become an embarrassment to me.

"Hey, boys," Truck says, stepping between them and putting an arm around each of their shoulders. Sean jumps then stiffens with fear, but Sam just shoves away from Truck's reach.

"What do you want?" Sam asks.

Truck and I face the younger boys. Sean looks like he's going to lose his lunch. He's ghost white.

"We just want to talk," Truck says casually.

"Okay, let's talk about what happened to your face," Sam stifles a laugh. He's getting entirely too much confidence. Time to take this douche down a notch.

"Look, you little shit. You obviously have no idea who you are talking to." I take a step toward him.

"I know exactly who I'm talking to. I assure you, HE isn't much." The cocky bastard doesn't even see the hit coming. My fist makes contact with his face, and he's on the ground immediately.

"What the hell, Nick?" Sean yells, stepping toward me. Truck blocks his path, and Sean recoils.

"Stay out of this, Sean, or you'll be next." I don't know why I said that. I won't hit him no matter how much I want to, and I won't allow Truck to do it for me. Sam scrambles to his feet and faces us again.

"Leave us alone!" he yells. This boy has a death wish. Truck turns his attention away from Sean. He's on the warpath now. He hates when Sam tries to stand up to us.

"You're dead!" Truck yells, rushing Sam and knocking Sean's shoulder in the process. Sean looks like he is about to come undone. What the fuck is wrong with him today? As much as I hate the person he's become, I'm still his brother. I'm not going to let my friends physically harm him. Truck shoves Sam backwards and kicks him three times as soon as he's on the ground.

"Come on, Truck. Let's get out of here before we gain unwanted attention." I need to get away from Sean. The fear on his face is screwing with my head. Why is he so scared?

"This isn't over!" Truck says through gritted teeth to Sam. "I mean it!"

"That goes for you, too!" he says, getting in Sean's face before continuing down the beach. Sean lets out a small whimper that he tries to cover. What a wuss. I shake my head with shame and disappointment when my brother makes eye contact. Sean tries to go to Sam, but I step in front of him and get in his face.

"Why are you acting like such a moron? No one is really going to hurt you!" I tell him in a voice low enough Sam can't hear.

"Yeah, right! And Sam is laying there sunbathing. You're the fucking moron!" Sean spits back at me in just as low of a tone and steps around me.

"Dumbass!" I yell at Sean's back. Then, I turn to follow Truck. Damn, my brother's a fucking pansy.

Sean

As soon as I'm past Nick, I run to Sam. He's trying to get up.

"I got you, Sam." I pull him to his feet and help him sit on the nearest bench. "Are you okay? Do you need an ambulance?"

"I'm fine, Sean. The last thing I need is an ambulance. We both know it won't end well if the police get involved. What we need is for your brother and his band of hellions to leave us alone."

"Nick isn't the ring leader. That is all Truck!" I try to defend Nick out of habit, but I worry Sam is right.

"Bullshit!" I flinch when he yells. I never hear Sam curse and rarely see him get angry. "Truck is horrible. I know he's the main muscle, but Nick gives most of the orders."

"What do you mean?" I ask Sam.

"Don't play dumb, Sean. I know he's your brother, but you can't be that blind. You've been there when those guys stop us. Nick hangs back when you're there, but you've watched him whisper to Tim and Truck right before they attack one of us. It doesn't matter if it's physical or verbal. Nick is calling the shots. It's worse when you aren't around," Sam's words confirm my fears. He's right, I didn't want to believe my brother was capable of those things.

258

"Has Nick ever hit you before today?" I ask, even though I'm scared I already know the answer. Sam shakes his head.

"Can we just go, Sean?" Sam winces in pain as he tries to stand. I know he's lying, so I try again.

"You can tell me the truth, Sam. I need to know if my brother hurt you."

"Yes," he whispers, hanging his head.

"A few weeks back when you came to school sore, and you had some bruises on your face. You said it was from playing football with your dad. I knew something didn't add up."

"Nick jumped me after dark a block from my house. Just Nick. No one was with him, and he threatened to make it worse if I told anyone."

"You could have told me, Sam. I wouldn't have said anything to him."

"I can't expect you to choose me over blood."

"Blood doesn't mean shit anymore!" I yell. "Nick hates me. I'm just as scared of him as I am of Truck."

"Sean, you kind of freaked out when all that went down with Nick and Truck. They've hit you, haven't they?

"No, Sam. Nick would never hurt me or let his friends hurt me," I bite out sarcastically.

"Who hit you?" he asks with concern. Sam tries to stick up for all of his friends, and he hates it when any of us get hurt.

"Truck jumped me one night when Nick wasn't around. I was walking home from visiting Carey.I wasn't even supposed to be out alone," I tell him.

"So, the bruise I saw wasn't really from P. E.?" I shake my head in answer to Sam's question.

"I guess it wasn't too difficult to figure out. Even my dad figured it out." I laugh at my lame attempt at a joke.

"I wish I'd been there. You know you could have called me. I would have walked with you."

"I know, but my family disaster isn't really something I want on display."

"Sean, you know I don't judge you for your brother's choices."

"I know." Sam knows about Carey moving out and the drugs, but there is a lot I haven't told him. I just don't want anyone to know how bad things really are right now. Sam and I have always avoided talking about our home lives. I don't want to admit how much of a shit storm mine is, so I don't push him to talk about his.

"Do you feel like walking now?" I ask him.

"Yeah. Let's get out of here."

"How about a bite at Mel's? She has pie!" I say, raising my eyebrows.

"What is it with you and your love affair with pie?" Sam teases me, breaking the tension.

"What can I say? I love her!" I yell, jumping to my

feet, raising both my hands, and spinning in a circle. I'm making a ridiculous scene, but it makes Sam laugh.

Carey

I have no idea why I'm awake so early on a Saturday, but here I am lying in bed, wide awake at seven o'clock. I can't get the conversation with Riley out of my head. It's been keeping me up at night. I've tried everything to get my mind off of it. I even went to the Homecoming dance. Ryan informed me when I got home last night that we are going to Reid's for dinner tonight. We haven't had one of our weekend cookouts since everything went down about six weeks ago, and I am not looking forward to this one.

My brothers and I have all talked to the police. I haven't told them anything that wasn't said the night we were at Reid's. Everyone knows that I'm keeping stuff to myself, and they keep trying to get me to talk. It's getting old, but Riley has me scared. Even though he's playing nice, I don't trust him. I'm no longer afraid that he'll hurt me, I am worthless. It wouldn't matter if he hurt me. I'm afraid he'll hurt one of my brothers. I don't want to see anyone else I care about get hurt because of me. I decided last night that it might be time to come clean. I'm worried about my family, but I can't keep quiet any longer. It's time for the truth to come out.

When I get to the kitchen, Ryan is sitting at the table reading the paper and drinking coffee.

"Who reads the paper anymore? I thought every-one got their news online."

"Most people start with good morning," he says as I pour myself some coffee.

"Morning," I mutter.

"You're up early," he states.

"I couldn't sleep," I confide as I sit down.

"Want to tell me what has you so bothered?" Ryan asks as he folds the paper.

"Remember when I you told you that my mom was scared of Riley?"

"Yes. You said that he threatened her and told her not to tell anyone about the affair or that you might be his son."

"Well, there are some things that I want to tell you, but I've been too afraid."

"You can tell me anything, Kid. I'll keep you safe." Concern is evident in his voice. I take a few deep breaths to calm my nerves and hide my shaking hands in my lap.

"Even though Mom told me to stay away, I didn't listen. I was worried about her. I went to her apart-ment the night she died. I saw someone leaving as I was walking up the sidewalk. It was a man, but I couldn't see his face. All I could see was this weird glowing sailboat on the guy's t-shirt. I hid in the bushes until he drove away. When he was out of sight, I knocked on the door, but she didn't answer. The door was locked, so I checked a few of the windows. One was unlocked, and I climbed inside.

I found her in the bedroom. She was lying on the floor, not moving. There was a syringe in her arm and a pillow next to her head. I didn't really put it all together then, but I can't get that image out of my head. I think whoever was in there might have drugged her and then suffocated her," I stare at the floor. I can't look Ryan in the face while I confide all this darkness. This next part will have him so disappointed in me.

"Did you say the man had a glowing sailboat on his shirt?"

"Yeah," I wave him off because I need to get this out. "Anyway, I climbed back out of the window and ran as fast as I could. I was terrified. I should have called an ambulance. I should have screamed for help. I was scared she was dead, but I didn't want to believe it. What if they could have brought her back? She is gone, and it's my fault." I sigh deeply.

"What did you do, Carey?" Ryan asks.

"I hid in the dunes near my house for hours. The police came and went. When I showed up at home, my dad, I mean Reid, broke the news to all of us. That night was the first time I took drugs and drank. After everyone else was in bed, I took a couple of pills and washed them down with a beer. I've been barely hanging on for years."

"That's not a burden any child should carry. I am so sorry you had to deal with all of this alone," Ryan tells me.

"What if my silence allowed a murderer to be free for years? Things might be different if I'd told someone that I was there the night she died. But I didn't and now it's my fault that my family is living this nightmare."

"This isn't your fault."

"It might not have been my hands that took her life, but it was my silence that made her death look like just another junkie overdosing."

"You have to stop blaming yourself, Carey. We'll get to the bottom of this," Ryan says as he stands. He has a strange look on his face, but he stays focused on me. "What else?" Ryan asks.

"What do you mean what else? Isn't that enough?"

"I admit that you just dropped a caseload of information, but 'some things' is plural which indicates there is more than one thing to tell." I was hoping he wouldn't catch on to that.

"Riley showed up," I blurt out.

"What? Where? When?" Ryan looks around as if he expects Riley to appear.

"Here. The day you worked late on that breakthrough with the case. He said and did things that night that I didn't think much of at the time, but the more I think about it, the more I feel my suspicions are warranted."

"What are you talking about, Carey? What did Riley do?"

"He brought me a six pack. He said he wanted to have a few drinks with me and talk. I realized later that I did most of the talking *and* most of the drinking. I know it was stupid, but I was sick of being sober."

"Keep going," Ryan insists through gritted teeth.

"After several beers, I told him my thoughts on my mom's death. He acted concerned and then...um...well...he gave me a bag of medical grade marijuana."

"He did what?" Ryan yells.

"I'm sorry," I whisper.

"We'll deal with that later. Go on." Ryan is clearly upset but keeps us on track.

"He told me not to tell anyone about what I saw because no one will believe a junkie. The last thing he said was that it will all be over soon. That statement really stuck with me. I can't get the visit out of my head. Ryan, do you think Riley could know something about my mom's death?"

"Why didn't you tell me sooner?"

"I don't know. Riley made me think you wouldn't believe me, and I was afraid you'd be angry at me."

"I'm not angry with you. Detective Pearson will be back from vacation Monday. We'll be at the station when he arrives. You'll need to tell him everything you just told me," He tells me. "Hang in there," Ryan pats me on the shoulder, "We are going to take care of this."

"You believe me?" I question.

"I believe you know what you saw."

"Do *you* think Riley is involved?" I've had my suspicions, especially since Riley's overly friendly visit.

"Try not to worry about Riley over the weekend. Just be honest with the detective on Monday, and we will get to the bottom of this," I nod my agreement and Ryan continues. "I'm going to jump in the shower then we can hang out for the day. Anything you want to do. Let's get your mind off all this stuff with Riley," I agree, but have no intention of spending the day with Ryan.

Ryan is almost to his room when he turns around. "Hey, Kid."

"Yeah?"

"Why don't you go get that baggie Riley gave you so I can get rid of it." Ryan looks at me knowingly.

Shit! "Um...I..."

"Carey, where is it?"

"I smoked it?" It comes out more like a question. Ryan shakes his head, disappointment clear in his eyes.

"Guess I won't be passing that drug test on Monday," I bite out sarcastically.

"Go get dressed. I'll be ready in fifteen minutes. We'll discuss it then," Ryan tells me then heads into his room.

"Another fuck up. *Shocker.*" I mumble under my breath.

After the conversation, I felt like a burden had been lifted. Now I feel like shit. Ryan is mad at me about the pot, and I wonder what will happen if Riley finds out I told Ryan he was here? I can only hope that he comes after me and not a family member.

When Ryan turns on the water, I sneak out and head toward the beach. I know he'll be pissed, but it relaxes me to be there. The beach and the bookstore are the only places where I feel like I can escape for a while. The beach is empty this morning. It's early in the day and mid-October. I'm sure there will be plenty of people out here as the day warms, but it's still cool right now.

After I walk on the beach for a few minutes, I head up to The Reading Corner. The bookstore is actually an old house. It was one of the first structures on the island and was built in the early 1800's. The house has been in Mr. Watson's family for generations. Not long after he married Mrs. Watson, he inherited it, and they decided to turn it into a bookstore. The various rooms house different genres. They sell all of the new releases and classics like most bookstores, but my favorite part is the small room at the back that was once a bathroom. It's barely big enough for one person and holds old books. A few even date back to the sixteen and seventeen hundreds. They're worn and fragile. I have spent hours just staring at the spines, reading the titles.

"Good morning, Mrs. Watson," I greet her as I make my way inside.

"Let the words help you find your way, son." She smiles and greets me the way she does every time I arrive. She probably says it to other people, but I've never heard her. I like to pretend it's my own personal greeting.

I head to the special, small room that I'm so fond of and immediately find a book that I started over the summer. Then, I take it to the oversized green chair in the northern corner of the store. This area is hidden behind some shelves, and it's an easy place to remain unnoticed. I've been hiding out here for years. It's quiet and secluded, and the Watson's are the only ones who can find me in this chair. Once, when I was ten, I stayed here for hours after a fight with Nick. Jason even came by looking for me. I guess they were looking everywhere. The Watson's told my brother that they hadn't seen me.

Everyone should know how much I love to read. My dad read to us often when we were young. Long before I learned how to read, I would spend countless hours looking at the pictures. In almost every picture taken of me as a child, I'm holding a book. When I was four, Jason taught me how to read. Nick wouldn't sit still and listen, but I soaked up every word Jason said and was reading before Nick. He hated that his little brother was a better reader.

I get comfortable and continue reading where I left off months ago. This book isn't as old as some of the others, but it's my favorite. It's a firsthand account from a soldier during the Civil War. It's fascinating to read about how he lived and fought for his country at the age of sixteen.

I plan to stay in this spot until the light of day

begins to fade, then I'll make my way to Reid's before they send out a search party. Lost in a book is one of the few ways I can escape reality. After a particularly intense chapter, I look out the window to process what I have read. While admiring the ocean view, I drift into one of my first memories of my mother. I must have been about five.

Mommy is here visiting! I told Nick she'd come back for us. I rush downstairs to see her, but freeze when I hit the bottom step. She's in the kitchen with Daddy, and they both look really mad.

"Let me see my boys, Reid. You can't keep them from me," Mommy screams.

"Stop yelling. I don't want the boys to hear you. "

"Don't tell me what to do."

"Sarah, this isn't the right time. You aren't in any condition to see the boys. You need to leave, and I'll let you come back and visit when you're better."

"I'm not leaving here without my babies. I can take care of them."

"You can't even take care of yourself."

"This isn't fair. Why are you doing this to me?" Mommy throws a spoon at Daddy.

"Stop, Sarah."

"I miss my boys. I love them, Reid. I'm going to see them." Mommy yells and walks towards the stairs. I don't think she sees me.

"No!" Daddy says in his 'I am mad' voice. Mommy turns back to look at Daddy.

"Sarah, you are not doing this to them. Go home."

"Not until I see my boys."

"I'm not saying you can't see them. You just need to be sober when you do. Do you really want the boys to see you stumbling around like this?"

"I'm not stumbling. Just let me see them!" Mommy is getting loud again, and her words sound funny.

"You need to leave. NOW!" Daddy sounds serious, but she doesn't listen to him. She turns around and starts throwing things at him again. She just keeps shouting and crying and throwing stuff. I'm scared she'll throw something at me, too, so I run out of the house before she can hurt me. What's wrong with Mommy? I keep running down the beach as thoughts flood my head.

When I finally stop to catch my breath, I'm standing in front of a building I've never seen. The sign says The Reading Corner. I love books! I walk into the bookstore and discover a whole new world. There are more books than I have ever seen in one place. The children's room is bright and colorful, but a little noisey. I quickly choose a book and look for a quiet place to sit. As I wander behind a long shelf of books in the back room, I find a huge green chair. Climbing into the chair, I get comfortable and begin reading a book about a family of gypsies who travel the world.

Maybe I will write books like this one day! That would be so fun. I like to make up stories in my head.

271

After reading the whole book, I get up and walk around a little more. This is the coolest place in the world. I find a door leading to a porch with chairs and couches. I curl up on one of the couches and begin to read the book again.

"Sweetheart," someone says, shaking me gently. I open my eyes and the lady from the bookstore is standing over me. I frantically look around and realize it's dark, and I'm still on the couch. I must have fallen asleep. I put the book down and take off running for home. That lady calls after me, but I don't stop. I'm going to be in so much trouble when Daddy finds out. I'll probably get a spanking.

I sneak into the garage and curl up under an old blanket.

Shaking my head, I force myself back to the present. Reid found me later that night asleep in garage. He'd been frantically looking for me in the house and on the beach.

I never mentioned the bookstore to anyone. We passed it hundreds of times over the years, but no one else seemed to notice. None of them were drawn to the tattered curtains or the peeling yellow paint on the front door. No one noticed the words "The Reading Corner" that needed to be re-stained and were missing the 'd' in reading and the last 'r' in corner. None of them have ever been inside for more than a few brief moments. They didn't see the shelves of old books, or the giant chair that a child could get lost in, or the old timey cash register. The Watson's aren't interested in a computer to update their store. They like it just the way it is.

I turn back to my book and read a few more chapters before I get distracted by more memories. I sit daydreaming about life before all of this mess started. The more I think about it, the more I realize that my life has never really been normal. Most kids don't grow up with a drug addict for a mother. For the most part, things were good when my mother wasn't around. Reid has always been good to us and does the best he can raising four boys alone. When I try to think back to my life before I found the paternity test, it's hard to remember. So much happened so quickly that forced me to keep the secret, and then it just became easier not to tell. I thought things were good the way they were, with my brothers and Reid not knowing the truth. It wasn't until I was in the hospital telling Sean that I realized I had been kidding myself all those years. I always felt different from them and this secret has only widened the gap between us.

I was twelve when I found the sealed envelope. Puberty was well into its onset, and I was turning into a real jerk. After a particularly nasty fight, I decided to give myself the right to look through Reid's desk. I knew he considered his desk private because he sometimes brought work home, but I didn't care.

I wanted to needle him. I found the sealed envelope and knew it had to be something important. I also knew it was none of my business, but I took it anyway. I hid it in my room for a week before getting up the nerve to open it. Several times, I thought about returning it to his desk. It wasn't until Reid and I had another huge argument that I finally read it. I said a lot of things that I didn't mean, and Reid said some things he probably regretted in the morning. I had no idea the information in that envelope would alter my life. My mind returns to that night.

I shove the envelope in my backpack with a towel and a flashlight. It's just after midnight, and I'm sure everyone is finally asleep. I sneak down the stairs and out of the back door. My heart races as I feel my way over the first set of dunes in the dark. When I'm a safe distance from the house, I turn on the flashlight and let it guide me to the water's edge. It's a cloudy night so there's no moon to light my way. I drop my backpack on the beach near the surf and take out the envelope. The tide is going out so I know that I'll gain beach as I sit here.

The moist ocean air has softened the glue, so I'm able to carefully peel open the envelope in case I need to reseal it later. I pull out the papers inside and read the one on top. There's information about Jason. His full name, birthday, some medical information, and then some test results.

I flip through the pages and find one for each of us with the same type of information. All of them state that Reid is their father. Mine is the only one that is different. This can't be true! He has to be my dad. Why would he lie to me?

I take off my shirt and run into the surf. I know how dangerous it is to swim at night, especially alone, but I don't care right now. I grew up in the ocean, and I've always been a strong swimmer and good surfer. Tonight, part of me hopes I'll be unable to fight the undertow, or will be violently carried away by a wave. I swim in and out of the waves to the point of exhaustion trying to understand what I just read. I finally tire out and barely have the strength and energy to get myself back onto shore. My mind is reeling as I lie down on the towel.

I don't know where the tears came from or why they took so long to get here, but once I start crying, I can't stop. Sleep is the only thing that stops the flow.

I wake up shivering as the sun begins to rise. I love watching the sunrise over the ocean. It's a sight I've seen hundreds of times, but it never gets old. Today, the sun seems different. I'm different. Everything has changed in the breaking of a seal, on the beach, in the middle of the night. Maybe it was all just a dream. I pull my shirt on and wrap the towel around me trying to get warm. I look to the right and find the stack of papers under my backpack where I shoved them last night.

It wasn't a dream. The truth I have believed my entire life is a lie. Reid isn't my father. I fold the paper with my name on it and put it in the front pocket of my backpack. I carefully put the others back in the envelope and put the envelope in my bag. I'll have to return it to Dad's desk later.

I gather my things and head for the house. I have to sneak back in before anyone wakes up. My dad is always an early riser and will be angry if he catches me sneaking in. He must hate me. I make it up the stairs but run smack into my dad as he is coming out of his bedroom.

"Where have you been?" he asks angrily.

"Here," I say.

"Try again."

"I went for an early swim." It isn't exactly a lie.

"You're not wet."

I forgot that I've been out of the water long enough to air dry. I don't say anything else. I just head for my room.

"Hey, I'm not done."

"Well, I am," As soon as the words are out of my mouth, I know I've made a mistake. Dad grabs my arm and pulls me into his room.

"Let go!" I yell, trying to pull away. He pulls harder and then shoves me into his bedroom, closing the door behind us. I've been in this situation before. He doesn't punish us often, but lying is one thing that always gets us in trouble.

"Are you ready to tell the truth?" he questions angrily. There's no way in hell I'm ready to tell the truth because it isn't going to get me out of trouble. I'm going to get punished for talking back, and for lying.

"I went down to the beach last night and fell asleep," I concede. He doesn't need to know that I went swimming or that I found and read those papers.

"You did what?" His face turns red with anger.

"I'm sorry," I say, blinking back tears.

"Do you know how dangerous that is? You're just a kid!" He has a point. I'm only twelve, and a kid my age was kidnapped and murdered a year ago. It turned out to be a domestic issue with a family on vacation, but it still scared all of the parents on the island.

"I'm sorry," I say again. "I was mad at you."

"Anger is no excuse for acting stupidly!" he yells. I hate when he calls me stupid. When we were younger, he would spank us. It was never hard enough to leave a mark, just hard enough to get our attention. Now our punishments are restrictions. I hate when he takes my phone, or worse, my books.

I come back to the present. I have a lot of memories like that one. It seems that I'm always the one in trouble. It's been that way my whole life. Jason is the golden boy who can do no wrong. If Nick gets into trouble, he can usually weasel his way out of it. Sean is the baby and on the rare occasion he does do something wrong, I take the blame. I can't stand to see Sean get in trouble.

After that night, I decided to keep the secret, but my actions and attitude changed drastically. Since Reid wasn't my father, I didn't see any reason to listen to him. I started skipping school, sneaking out, and arguing with him about everything. I'm surprised he didn't send me away. My mom died a few months later, and things got worse. I lost my shit and became a huge, sarcastic pain in the ass. Mostly, I ignored Reid and started spending time engaging in other activities with some new friends, friends who helped me cope, friends who helped me escape. I kept the secret from everyone.

I look at my phone and see that it's almost six. It'll take me about twenty minutes to walk to Reid's from here, so I return the book to the shelf and wave to Mrs. Watson on my way out. My family probably doesn't expect me to show up tonight. I'm sure by now Ryan has told them that I've been MIA all day. I send a text to Sean as I head for the beach and start walking toward Reid's house.

Be there in 20

He sends a text back, but I don't bother reading it. I only have a few more minutes of peace, and I want to enjoy the walk down the beach. The tourist crowds from the day have left, but the locals' bonfires and parties of the night haven't started. This is my favorite time of day on the beach. It's peaceful as the sun sets in the distance. By the time I approach the dunes near Reid's house, I'm a little more relaxed. I take a deep breath and head toward them.

As I start to cross the first set of dunes, movement to my left catches my eye.
An uneasy feeling washes over me. I pause, but don't see anything, so I assume it's just my imagination, but when I start for the second set of dunes, I see it again. I freeze on the spot.

"Who's there?" I call. Of course, no one answers. Idiot. The person who calls out "who's there" is always the first to die in a horror film. I stand frozen in place for a minute but then nothing else moves, so I continue across the dunes. I'm sure it was just my mind playing tricks on me.

"Hey. I figured you'd come in this way." I hear Sean before I see him.

"Um, yeah, hey," I'm not sure what to say to him as he approaches. Plus, I'm still a little spooked. Was it Sean's shadow I saw?

"How are you, Carey? I've been...well I...I'm glad you're here," Sean stumbles over his words. Guess he doesn't know what to say either.

"You're the only one," I snap at him, and his face falls. Dammit! I did it again.

"Sorry, Seany, I just doubt anyone else wants me here," I try to lessen the blow my big mouth gave him.

He looks up at me. "Every single one of us wants you here, Carey. We love you, and I miss you." He looks away like he's embarrassed to admit he misses me.

"I miss you, too." We do the brotherly half hug thing.

"You look like shit," he says, stepping away from the hug.

"Back at you, baby brother," I deadpan. He hates when I call him baby, but he playfully shoves my shoulder.

"Seriously, Care. Are you okay?" He's not wrong. I do look rough. I've been working my way through the stash Riley gave me, and I haven't been eating or sleeping well. I don't want to worry him more so I blow it off.

"Really, Sean. I'm doing better. I promise." It's a lie, but I need to protect Sean.

"Okay," he says, but I can tell by his tone that he doesn't believe me. I'm thankful when he doesn't press me for more.

"Come on." He puts an arm around my shoulder, and we head to the house to face the inescapable.

As I reach the back deck, I hear laughter inside. They actually sound like they're having a good time;

like they're a happy family. Am I ready for this? I haven't talked to Reid or Jason in weeks, and the only reason I have talked to Sean and Nick is because I see them at school everyday. I know from the endless updates from Ryan that Reid is "really worried" about me. I am so sick of hearing I haven't talked to Reid or Jason in weeks and the only reason I have talked to Sean and Nick is because I see them at school every day. I know from the endless updates from Ryan that Reid is "really worried" about me. I am so sick of hearing about how concerned everyone is and how much they care.

"Come on, Care." Sean breaks into my thoughts. I didn't realize that I had stopped moving toward the door.

"I'll be right there." I tell him, and he walks inside. The only reason I'm here tonight is so they can see that I'm fine and back off. I haven't been fine in years, but surely I can fake it for a few hours. I can do this. I take a deep breath and follow Sean inside.

"It's about time," Nick greets me. This may be harder than I imagined. "Where have you been?'

"Really, this is how tonight is going to go?" I retort.

"You've been gone for ten hours. What do you expect?" Ryan says heatedly. Great, busted right from the start. If he hadn't told them already, now everyone knows I went missing this morning.

"Did anyone look for me? I thought the big shot detective and town's top cop would have sent out a search party."

Okay, so maybe we aren't off to such a great start. I don't even try to be sarcastic, it just happens. For some reason, over the past few weeks I haven't been able to hold my tongue. Whatever pops into my head, falls out of my mouth.

"Can we not fight tonight?" Jason pipes up, surprising me. I thought he was still angry with me. No one answers, but Ryan and I back down. There's a long tense silence, so I try to break the ice.

"What's for dinner? I'm starving," I say. I haven't had anything today except a cup of coffee. I don't realize how hungry I am until I smell the food. Out of the corner of my eye, I see Sean smirk. Well, at least I have one of them on my side.

"Chicken and rice casserole," Reid answers. Awesome! I love me some chicken and rice.

"Nice of you to cook my favorite dish for the prodigal son's return," I say sarcastically because a simple thanks would be too easy.

"Did you just make a Biblical reference?" Jason asks, grabbing his chest as if he is having a heart attack.

"I'm not a heathen," I say.

"Riiight," he says, sarcastically dragging the word out. "The church would probably burst into flames if you set foot in it."

"Let's eat!" Reid interjects trying to stop Jason and me from a fight.

We aren't exactly on track for a happy family

reunion. I expect nothing less from these idiots. We all grab plates and fill them with food. Hopefully, there won't be much talking while we eat. That would be nice. Maybe I can suppress some of my anger and calm down. I want to get through this with as little confrontation as possible.

Dinner starts out smoothly with a lot of eating and a little small talk. Then, the topic of school comes up. Now, I'm in for it. Reid asks Sean about some school project he's been working on, and Sean brags about it eagerly. Nick rolls his eyes, and I can't help but to chuckle. Unfortunately, it's louder than intended, and it gets Reid's attention.

"How about you, Carey? How is school going?" he asks. I don't know if he's aware that I'm once again failing several classes, but this is not the time to discuss it. I don't need everyone on my case.

"Great," I say. "School is great," I try to sound convincing, but it comes out as sarcasm. Ryan clears his throat as I speak, so I kick him under the table.

"Ouch," he says, giving me a dirty look.

"What's going on?" Reid asks, looking with concern from Ryan to me and back to Ryan.

"Nothing, school is fine," I say, hoping Ryan will keep his mouth shut.

"Glad to hear it," Reid states. I can't believe he is actually falling for this.

"How was the history test you had on Wednesday?" Ryan asks. *Just great!* I know he checks my grades online, but couldn't he give me a break for one night?

"It was fine," I say pointedly, returning the dirty look he gave me a few minutes ago.

"Really?" he asks with surprise. I can't believe he is doing this in front of everyone.

"What did you make on it?" Ryan continues, and I want to kick him again, but instead I shrug and continue eating.

"Don't shrug your shoulders. Answer the question. I've been on your side through all of this. The least you can do is honestly answer my questions." Ryan says with frustration and exasperation evident in his voice.

"I haven't gotten it back yet," I say, feeling guilty as soon as the lie leaves my mouth.

"I can't help you if you aren't willing to help your-self. I checked your gra..."

"A 43, okay. I made a fucking 43!" I yell, cutting him off. "I'm flunking. Are you happy now? I am failing three classes, and I have D's and C's in the others. Just like always, I'm the family screw up. I don't give a shit about school. If I flunk out, I won't have to go back. Then, I won't have to deal with any more of this bullshit!"
I yell, standing up and knocking my chair over in the process. I head for the door.

"Where are you going?" Reid asks. I can't tell if it's anger or concern. Maybe both. Once again, I messed up his perfect family night.

"I'm done."

"Carey, wait," Nick says with concern as he grabs my arm to stop me.

"Don't, Nick," guilt breaks my voice as I speak. I want to get outside as soon as possible. I hate myself for the grades I'm making, the choices I've made, and the hell I've put my family through. Crying would just give them another reason to be disappointed in me. Nick lets go, and I continue out of the front door, but he follows me outside and into the yard.

"Please leave me alone, Nicky," I say as I sit against the tree in the front yard and light a cigarette. I inhale deeply hoping to calm myself down. This is not the way I wanted tonight to go.

"I'll come back if I can just have a minute to calm down," I say, quietly hanging my head in shame. Nick squeezes my shoulder.

"You know I'm here for you, Carey. I can help you with history. It's the one class I actually understand," he offers. He can't make me care about school. I don't really need to study to pass. I just don't give a damn anymore.

I realize this is just his way of trying to help, but I don't know how to respond to him. Nick isn't known for his affection.

"I'm sorry," is all I can manage as I take another drag from my cigarette.

"Are you sure you're going to be okay? You don't have to come back in tonight. I can drive you back to Ryan's."

"I'll be back in as soon as I finish this," I say, indicating the cigarette.

"Don't let Dad see you smoking," he smiles and winks.

"Your dad or mine?" I ask without thinking and immediately regret it when I see the hurt in Nick's eyes. I look away because I can't stand to see him like that. Why am I such an asshole? Nick pats me on the shoulder and walks back to the house without another word.

I smoke the rest of the cigarette, but I'm still too upset to face anyone. I'm just lighting another one when I hear something rustle in the bushes that separate our driveway from the neighbor's. It startles me at first, but I compose myself before I let my imagination run away again. It's probably just an animal.

I take another drag off the cigarette before putting it out on the trunk of the tree so I can get back inside. I pocket the lighter and remaining cigarettes, then stand up brushing the dirt off of my jeans.

"You shouldn't smoke," a voice comes from the bushes. I jump and look up to see a figure standing in the shadows.

"What are you doing here?" I ask.

"You've been talking," Riley says angrily. "I told you to keep your mouth shut."

"You need to leave before someone sees you," I tell him. Does he know I talked to Ryan?

"I don't care if they see me. There's nothing any of them can do," Riley sounds different. It isn't anger exactly. I can't quite put my finger on it, but it creeps me out. I take a few steps back, ready to make a run for the house.

"Don't move!" he yells, pulling out a gun and pointing it at me. What the hell? My body freezes, but my mind is racing. I want to run, but if I do he'll shoot me. Of course, if I stay here he's still going to shoot me. I stumble back a little. Why doesn't anyone see us? Why did I send Nick away? We have huge windows lining the front of the house. Surely, someone will see us.

"Stop!" he yells, cocking the gun.

"Okay," I cry, putting my arms up in surrender, hoping to show that I'm listening. I can feel my body shaking with fear. "Don't do this, Riley. There has to be another way."

"You're right, son. There is another way." Riley sneers as he turns the gun on himself. "Maybe it would be best if I just took myself out of this cluster fuck you drug me into! You know this is all your fault."

"Go ahead. Blow your own brains out. It will definitely make my life easier if you aren't around." I shrug.

"You should have kept your damn mouth shut. You got yourself into this. I told you this wasn't over."

287

Riley turns the gun back on me. "Now shut the fuck up and do exactly what you're told for a change. I might spare the rest of your family." Has he gone completely mad?

"Come on. Please," I beg. I know he's going to kill me. It isn't the first time he's threatened me. I thought he was going to kill me the night he held the knife to my throat.

"Shut up!" he yells loud enough that someone has to hear him. He sounds manic.

I can feel myself shaking uncontrollably now and from the little I can see in the moonlight, he looks like he's shaking, too. Maybe I can appeal to his fear.

"Ri...Dad, please don't. I'll help you ge..."

"Shut the fuck up, you little prick! You can't help me! You can't even save yourself!" He's yelling at the top of his lungs now. I don't hear the door open, so Reid's voice startles me.

"What the hell is going on out here?" he calls from the steps. I start to turn toward him.

"Don't turn around. Send Reid back inside. This is just between us." Riley's voice drops to where only I can hear him, and he sounds maliciously evil.

"Everything is okay, Dad. I just needed some air." My voice quivers as I speak. "I'll be back inside in a second." I need Reid out of danger.

"Good boy." Riley purrs. "Now where were we? Oh, yeah. You were sticking your nose where it didn't belong. You must have gotten that from

Sarah. She might still be alive if she'd done what I told her to and kept her mouth shut and her nose clean." My eyes widen at his words.

Reid comes down the stairs even though I told him to go inside. "Shit!" He yells, seeing Riley standing in front of me.

"Riley's here," he calls over his shoulder.

"Don't come over here!" Riley calls, but Reid continues toward us until he notices the gun. Ryan comes running up behind Reid.

"Stop," Reid says, putting his arm up to stop Ryan. "He's got a gun."

"Put the gun down, Riley," Ryan says calmly, taking a step toward us.

"Don't be stupid, Ryan," Riley says. "I will fucking kill him." He waves the gun at me, and I'm about to lose my mind. I have never been this scared.

"It's okay," I say shakily. I force myself to act brave. "I've got this. Everyone go inside," I try to sound calm as I wave them both off. The last thing I want is to be responsible for getting one of them hurt or killed.

"Go tell the boys to stay inside no matter what happens," Reid tells Ryan, pushing him toward the house.

"I'm not leaving you two out here," he responds.

"No, you're going to protect the other boys." Reid yells.

"What's happening?" Nick calls from the porch.

"Dammit, Nick, stay out of this," Reid bites out.

"Dad? What's going on?" he asks, walking down the steps.

"Get in the house, now!" Reid yells. "Ryan, get him inside and take care of the boys." This time Ryan listens, but I can tell by his face that he doesn't want to leave us. Ryan meets Nick at the top of the steps, grabs his arm, and pushes him towards the house. Reid takes a step toward us and speaks calmly. One of his jobs as a detective is hostage negotiation. If anyone can get me out of this alive, it's Reid.

"Riley, put the gun down. You don't want to do this. Carey is your son. Think about that, Riley. You have a son. Lower...the...gun...," Reid continues to walk slowly toward us as he speaks. I can hear sirens in the distance. Shockingly, Riley lowers the gun.

"Good. Now, let me have the gun," Reid continues reaching his hand out. I breath a small sigh of relief as I begin to believe that this might be over, but I relax too soon. Suddenly, Riley points the gun back at me. Reid lunges forward at the same time I dive for the ground. Reid's body makes contact, adding to my momentum. My left side and shoulder slam into the ground, and my head bounces off of something hard. Shots ring out into the night; four, five, maybe more. Reid is heavy on top of me. I hear tires screech as the yard fills with police cars.

I'm disoriented, my head feels foggy, and I'm having trouble focusing. Someone yells "freeze." In my limited point of view, I see Riley's feet turn toward the voice and more shots pierce the night.

Riley falls to the ground next to me. There is mass confusion as my brothers fill the yard. Ryan pulls Reid off of me. Pain radiates through my body when I try to move. As I look down, I can't tell if the blood covering our bodies belongs to Reid or me. It's hard to see through the haze taking over my brain, and the blood running down my face. Nick is by my side almost instantly. I look at him and start to speak. He shakes his head.

"Don't talk. Help is coming. Just be still." He holds my hand and uses the end of his shirt to wipe some of the blood off of my face. I think I've been shot, but it's hard to tell where or how many times. Man, I am so sleepy.

"Love you," I manage before the world goes dark.

Nick

"Carey, CAREY!" I cry out, "Talk to me Carey. No, you can't go to sleep." I try to keep him awake, but it's no use. He whispers something that sounds like "Love you," but I can't be sure.

"I love you, too," I close my eyes and respond, not knowing if he can hear me. When I look at him again, he's unconscious. I completely panic. I start yelling his name and crying. He can't die! This isn't fair. I'm not ready to lose my brother. I wipe more blood from his face, but his head wound keeps bleeding. I can't be sure if he hit it on the ground or took a bullet or what.

"Where the fuck is the ambulance?" I yell. I know it's only been two or three minutes since I made the call, but it feels like a lifetime. I take my shirt off and hold it to the gash on his head. His arm is bleeding, too, but not nearly as much as his head. Jason kneels on the other side of Carey.

"What can I do?" he asks.

"I don't know," I say through my tears. "He won't wake up. Is Dad okay? Where's Sean?" I ask, looking around. I see Ryan with Dad, but he isn't giving him CPR or anything so he must be okay. I don't see Sean, and I start to panic again.

"Jason, where in the hell is Sean?" I yell.

"He's with the police. He isn't doing good. I didn't want to leave him, but I needed to check on you and Carey." As Jason talks, two ambulances pull up. Jason pulls me away when the paramedics start to take over care of Carey. Riley's body has already been covered. As much as I hate him for what he has done to my family, a part of me is sad to see my uncle lying dead in our yard. An officer guides Jason and me to a police car, and we climb in the back with Sean.

"Seany, are you okay?" I ask, pulling him into my arms. I know it's a dumb question. None of us are okay, but I don't know what else to say. He doesn't answer. In fact, he doesn't respond at all. He just stares straight ahead as if he didn't hear me. He doesn't even react to me touching him. His eyes are distant, almost empty. This is scaring the crap out of me.

"He's in shock, Nicky," Jason says as if reading my thoughts.

"Is he going to be okay?" I ask.

"Are any of us?" Jason responds.

We don't say anything else. We just wait silently while the police and paramedics deal with the chaos in our yard. I notice some of the neighbors standing across the street watching. I guess we'll be the talk of the town.

Mr. and Mrs. Kelley are talking to one of the officers. They're like second parents to us. Mrs. Kelley babysat us a lot growing up, and we eat at Miss Mel's, the diner she owns, almost as much as we eat at home. Well, we used to anyway. After whatever happened between Carey and Seth a few months ago, we have all kept our distance. None of us are rude to Seth when our paths cross, but we don't hang out anymore either. The car door opens and an officer pokes his head in.

"Jason, can I speak to you for a minute?" he asks, "Nick, can you stay here in case Sean needs you?"

"Sure." I tell him as Jason climbs out.

Jason

"The paramedics just loaded Carey into an ambulance. We'll meet them at the hospital in a few minutes. Tomorrow, when things calm down, I'm going to need to get a statement from each of you boys," the officer informs me.

"Yes, sir," I respond absently. He turns to walk away, "Sir, is Carey going to be okay?"

"Son, I don't know the extent of his injuries. I do know that the paramedics are concerned about his head injury. You'll get answers after you get to the hospital."

"Did he get shot in the head?" I ask.

"The head wound doesn't appear to be from a bullet," he tells me, and I relax a little. There was a lot of gun fire. I had gone up to my room before it started. I rushed downstairs when I heard the first shot, but lost count as I made my way outside.

"Thank you, Dave," Ryan says to the officer as he joins us. "Can I talk to Jason alone for a few minutes? Will you take this shirt to Nick?" Ryan asks.

"Sure. Let me know if you need anything else," the officer takes the shirt, and Ryan nods to him as he leaves.

"Jason, I need to tell you something."

"I know Riley's dead. I saw them cover his body. How's my dad? I didn't get a chance to ask..."

"Jason," Ryan cuts me off. Something in his tone tells me what I don't want to hear.

"No, Ryan. Don't say it...," I start to cry before I can finish the sentence. I fall into Ryan's arms and sob like a baby. "No. No. No. Please tell me Dad isn't dead," I beg through my sobs.

"I'm sorry, Jason. He was gone when I got to him."

"Riley killed him," I don't know why I state the obvious.

"Reid saved Carey's life," Ryan tells me as I break the hug and try to pull myself together. He's being strong for me, but I can see that he's been crying. He just lost both of his brothers. I can't imagine what he's feeling. I would be devastated if I was in his shoes.

"How am I going to tell my brothers, Ryan?"

"I can tell them. I told you first because you're the oldest, and they're going to need you. You can tell them if you want, but I can do it if that's what you need." Ryan offers.

I hear a car door close before I have a chance to make a decision. Why didn't Nick listen and stay in the car?

"Get back in the car, Nick. You were told to stay with Sean." I tell him.

"Sean doesn't know if I'm there or not," Ryan and I share a look as Nick joins us.

"Are you two just going to stare at each other all night, or are you going to tell me that my father is dead?" Nick doesn't even sound angry or upset. That seems a little odd.

"I was coming to tell you. How did you know?" I ask. I saw them loading my dad in an ambulance, his body not covered. I guess they waited for our sake.

"Ryan was just sitting next to him. Not doing anything to help him. Then, the paramedics put him on a stretcher and loaded him in an ambulance. They spent a lot of time working on Carey before they loaded him. I put it all together when I saw you crying." Nick is talking like he's telling me what he ate for lunch. Why isn't he freaking out or crying? This can't be normal.

"We need to tell Sean," Ryan says.

"Not right now," Nick retorts, "I don't even know if he can hear us. I was talking to him in the car, and he didn't respond at all. Like, no reaction. It's kind of scary."

"Let's go to the hospital and check on Carey. We can tell him when we get there," Ryan suggests.

"I'll ride in the car with Sean if you two want to go together," Nick tells us, heading back to the squad car. I'm not sure how to take his reaction. He doesn't seem affected by this news at all. Holy hell! Does this mean I have two brothers in shock?

"Nick will be okay, Jason." Ryan must read my thoughts. "I see people react strangely to tragedy all the time. It's okay for him to act this way. He just needs some time."

"Are you sure?" I ask.

"He's stronger than you think. You all are. We will get through this. Together."

Sean

We've been sitting in the emergency room waiting on some news for hours. I've been watching the clock. I've been watching the exit sign flicker. I've been watching the automatic door open and close. All I can do is watch. I can't talk to anyone or make eye contact. It's like part of me has shut down. I know I need them as much as they need me right now, but I can't make myself respond.

The Kelleys are here, too. I'm not surprised. They might as well be part of the family. Everyone has tried to talk to me at some point, even Seth's little sister, Rachel. She's close to my age. Part of me feels that if I just stay in my own little world, I won't have to face the truth.

I know my dad is dead. I was standing on the porch watching when Riley shot him. Ryan was dealing with Nick, who was trying to get outside to do whatever it is that Nick does when his hothead gets the best of him. Jason had gone upstairs when his phone rang. Probably some chick trying to get in his pants. No one saw me walk outside. I wish now someone would have stopped me. Dad pushed Carey out of the way, and Riley shot him twice. The image is on constant replay in my head. I keep seeing Dad's body jerk as the first bullet hit him in the back and the splatter of blood as the second one entered his head. I knew immediately he was dead.

Somehow, I felt it the moment the life left my father. If that wasn't proof enough, his eyes were unblinking and empty when Ryan pulled him off of Carey. I tried to run and almost made it out of the yard, but a cop caught me. I fought against him, yelling and screaming. I don't even remember everything I said. The officer just held onto me until I got it all out. When I went silent, he helped me into his car. I haven't spoken since.

They let us back to see Carey when we first arrived, but I didn't move or respond so Ryan and my brothers went in without me. I wasn't ready to face him. Not that he would know. From what I overheard, he's unconscious. We're waiting on the results of a CT scan to find out how bad his head injury is, and what will happen next. I can't face losing him, too. I feel like the walls are closing in on me. I feel like I am being eaten from the inside out.

Yet, my body is numb. All I want to do is scream. I stopped earlier because I was tired, not because I was done. I just need to get out of here.

"Sean, SEAN!" a voice calls, but I can't respond. "Sean, stop!"

Arms wrap around me from behind and I'm tackled to the ground. "Get the fuck off of me!" I yell. "Let go! Leave me alone!" I'm screaming and struggling to get away, but the arms hold me tighter.

"You need to calm down. I can't let go until I'm sure you won't run." Someone speaks calmly in my ear.

"Fucking let me go!" I yell again. I fight against his hold, but I can't get away. I scream as loud as I can, realizing tears are running down my face. My whole body is shaking. I don't know how long I cry and scream. When, I finally calm down, I'm completely exhausted. My eyes are heavy, my voice is hoarse, and my head is killing me.

"I'm going to let go now. Do not run," I finally recognize Seth's voice.

"Okay," I whisper. He let's go, and we just lay there. For the first time, I really look around.

"How did I get outside, Seth?" I ask, noticing my surroundings.

"One minute you were sitting all quiet and in your own head. The next minute you were making a run for it. Ryan, Nick, and Jason followed, but you were yelling at them to leave you alone. I think your exact words were 'Go the fuck away. I hate all of you.' Ryan tried to stop you, but you took a swing at him. The way I grabbed you, you couldn't get away. They stayed until you started to calm down. Then, I told them to go back inside, and I promised to stay with you."

"I don't remember any of that. I can't believe I told them that I hate them. I can't believe I tried to hit Ryan. What is wrong with me?"

"Nothing is wrong with you. They know you don't hate them. You've been through hell tonight. It's going to be okay."

"No one else is freaking out."

"You clearly haven't been paying attention," Seth snorts, "Jason got in a nurse's face, and she called security. They wanted to kick him out of the hospital, but Ryan convinced them to let him stay."

"Really?" I ask.

"You know Jason doesn't handle stress well." Seth says with a knowing glance. I nod in response.

"Nick is taking this hard, too. He keeps snapping at everyone. He even cussed at my little sister. If my dad hadn't stepped in, I would have punched him."

"Wow."

"We all handle tragedy differently. You haven't done anything wrong."

"I'm scared, Seth. What if Carey dies? We've almost lost him once this year. He's got problems. I worry about him all the time."

"Me too, Sean. He hasn't been himself in a while, and then things with us got out of hand. I don't know what's going on with him, but he's different at school. Even with the friends he still speaks to."

"What if he doesn't die?" I whisper.

"What?" Seth asked with confusion.

"You're right. Carey has been in a bad place for a long time. What if he makes it, but can't handle everything that happened with Dad and Riley?"

"I don't know, Sean. But I do promise you that if he comes out of this, I will do everything I can to make things right between us. I will be there to help you and Carey. No matter what it takes. You have my word."

Seth and I sit outside of the emergency room for hours, just talking to each other. He's a good friend. I don't understand why Carey turned his back on Seth. Will there ever come a day when all this makes sense?

It's been five days since my dad was murdered. Riley was buried yesterday, but Ryan is the only one who went to the funeral. I'm sure there were other people there; friends from work and other family members. I don't really care. We're burying my dad today, and I'm having trouble making myself get up. I don't think I can face this day. Maybe if I stay in bed long enough, it won't be true. I know that isn't how death works, but my new reality scares me.

"Carey," I say, trying to get my brother's attention. He's been in a bad place since he woke up in the hospital and found out that Dad is dead. He's angry, and hurt. I know he feels responsible. The guilt must be eating away at him. He hasn't told me, but I know. Actually, he hasn't said anything to any of us for days that wasn't full of anger and bitterness. He doesn't respond so I try again.

"Carey," I call a little louder. We're sharing the extra room in Ryan's small house. Jason and Nick have been sleeping in the living room. At some point, the five of us aren't going to be able to live in this two bedroom house. I sit up and find that his sleeping bag isn't on the floor. That's odd, Carey never picks up after himself. I get up and throw on a pair of shorts. When I lean down to grab a shirt out of my bag, there's a folded piece of paper on top with my name on it. What is this? I wonder as I open it.

Sean,
   I love you more than you can possibly imagine. I am so sorry for everything that I have done to you and our family. I don't expect you to understand my decision, but I can't be here right now. I don't know what's going to happen because honestly I don't understand anything anymore. Please don't look for me.
   Open the box inside your bag. I want you to have them. Keep them close to you, so I know that no matter what, we will always be part of each other. Goodbye, Seany. I love you.
Carey

   I'm shaking by the time I finish reading the note. Carey left me. He's gone, and there isn't anything I can do about it. I open my bag, and find a small white box sitting on top of my clothes. I open it, and fall backwards. The bed keeps me from hitting the floor. My chest tightens, and it's impossible to breathe. He left me his dog tags. Our mom gave them to him not long before she died. One has a picture of a book, a scroll, and quill. The other has a surfer with his name and date of birth. I don't understand why she chose those pictures. She clearly didn't know anything about Carey or the things he loves. These pictures certainly don't represent him. Well, maybe the surfer, but not the others. It didn't matter to Carey, though. He hasn't taken them off in over three years. They are his most prized possession. Now, he left them for me. This is a sign. He's never coming back.

"Goodbye," I say quietly, putting the dog tags around my neck, and pulling on my shirt. I walk aimlessly into the other room.

"Sean?" Ryan asks, his voice full of concern, "Are you okay?" I don't respond as I sink onto the couch. I have Carey's note in my hand, but I don't want to share it with them. It's too personal. His dog tags are hidden under my shirt.

"He's gone," I whisper. I'm not even sure I said it out loud.

"Your dad?" Ryan asks not understanding.

"No," I shake my head.

"Who?" Ryan asks, taking the seat next to me.

"Carey. He's gone," I tell them.

"I'm sure he's just in the bathr..."

"He's fucking gone!" I yell, cutting Jason off, "He isn't in the bathroom. He took his duffle bag and left. He left me a note."

"Let me see that," Nick says, reaching for the paper.

"NO! It's mine! You can't read it! Carey left it for me!"

"Um...okaaay," Nick says, taking a step back and looking at me like I have lost my mind. Maybe I have.

"Can you tell us what he said in the note?" Ryan asks cautiously.

"Yeah, he said he's gone!" I yell.

"Sean, you're really not making any sense," Jason ventures.

"I don't care if I'm making sense. Maybe you don't care that we lost our brother on the same day we have to bury our father, but I do. I can't take this. I can't do this anymore. I just want it all to end!" I scream. I don't even know what I'm talking about. I fall into Ryan's arms and just cry. I hear him tell Nick and Jason to go get showered and dressed. He just holds me without a word until I'm done getting it all out. It feels like I have been crying for hours when I finally gain some control. I sit up, wiping my face with my shirt.

"I'm sorry, Ryan."

"You didn't do anything wrong, Sean. You have every right to be angry, scared, and hurt. You've lost more than any kid should lose. I'm sorry that Carey left, but I'm not surprised. I thought he was doing better over the last few weeks, and he was finally starting to heal. When Reid was killed...well, you've seen him over the past few days. He's been out of it. I think he's been using again."

"I *know* he's been using again. I'm afraid it's more than just pills and pot this time. I haven't seen him use, but he's snuck out twice since Dad died, and both times came back out of his mind," I confide.

"Why didn't you tell me, Sean?" Ryan asks quietly. He doesn't even sound angry at me. Just worried.

"You've been so busy with the funerals. I thought it could wait until after today. I didn't think he would leave us. Especially, not before the funeral."

"Of course, he left us!" Nick yells, walking back into the room, his hair wet from the shower, "Carey always runs. That's what he does."

"Nick," Ryan warns.

"He gets high, and he runs. I'm surprised he waited this long to leave," Nick continues.

"Enough, Nick," Ryan tries to stop him.

"Truth be told, I'm glad he's gone..."

"NICK!" Jason yells, walking back into the room, buttoning his shirt.

"Maybe now we can have some peace. Good fucking riddance."

"Nicholas Sledge!" Ryan uses his full name in an effort to shut him up. It's too late. Nick's words unhinge something in me, and I'm on my feet without thinking. I hurdle over the back of the couch and catch Nick off guard. I have enough momentum to tackle him, getting in one solid hit to his jaw as we hit the ground. When I take another swing, Jason pulls me up before I can make contact.

"Damn, Rocky! Take it easy," Jason says, trying to stifle a laugh.

"I'm glad you find this funny," I pull out of his grip and head to the bedroom to get dressed.

"Stay the hell away from me." I bump Nick's shoulder as I pass.

Ryan

What a nightmare this morning turned into. As I drive Sean and myself from the church to the gravesite, my mind is a tilt-a-whirl. I knew this would be hard. Grief always is, but I had high hopes that we were going to be okay, that we could do this. I had envisioned the five of us riding to the funeral together. Leaning on each other for support. Being pillars for whomever was weakest at that moment and having the security to be able to be the weak one when needed. It's been my observation that trage- dy does one of two things to people. It either brings them closer together and forms a bond so strong it can never be broken, or it drives even the closest of families apart with greed, sadness, blame, or hate. After this morning's fiasco, I'm no longer certain any of us will survive.

It shouldn't surprise me Carey ran. Reid warned me that he always runs. I had so much faith in Car- ey, and my bond with him, I wouldn't believe Reid. I thought he was being close minded. I should have listened to him. He really did have an amazing un- derstanding of all of his boys. I was naive enough to think Carey wouldn't leave without first talking to me. Did I underestimate him? Myself? Our bond? The hold drugs have on him? I fear it could be any combination of these. I will find him. No matter what it takes, I will save Carey and get him the help he needs.

This morning's fight forced me to acknowledge how different these boys are from one another. I've been having the same internal conversation with myself for the past few days. What was I thinking taking on four half grown boys with zero parenting skills? I was thinking I had no choice. There's no way I would walk out on these boys. I love them. As bad as I'm hurting from losing my brothers, I know it's harder on them. They've lost their parents. I know what that's like, but at least I wasn't still a kid. As alone as I feel, they have to feel completely abandoned. I knew I had to take them in and do the best I could for them. Reid did so much for me when I was a kid. He saved me from going down the wrong path. I would raise them for him even if I didn't love them so much. I may not know what I'm doing, but I will do my best! Dammit! What if I can't do this? No, I have to do this. I want to do this, even though I don't know what I am doing. I didn't know how to properly handle a conflict like the fight this morning, but I will learn. I am determined to be what Reid would want me to be. This morning, I took a lesson from my parents play book and diffused the situation. We'll talk it out after the funeral when we are all calmer and hopefully in a better frame of mind. I asked Jason to drive Nick, and I took Sean with me to avoid further conflict. Sean hasn't spoken since the fight.

"You hanging in there, Sean?" I glance at him in the rear view mirror. I don't know why he got into the back seat. I guess he just needed space. He doesn't even look up. I think he's gone into some kind of shock again. Who can blame him? He's lost his dad, his uncle, and now his brother. I pray he doesn't get as bad as he did the night Reid was shot. Poor kid. My heart is just as broken, but I have to keep it together for these boys.

"Sean, we're here," I try again as I park the car. He still doesn't respond. I take a gentler tone, "Come on, son. We need to get to our seats." Sean gives a slight shake of his head.

"If you can't do this, it's okay. No one will fault you if you need to stay in the car. Just promise me you won't run. Promise you will stay here in the car if you don't want to or can't come to the gravesite." The nod is very small, but Sean isn't one to lie. I know he'll keep his word. I leave the car to give him the space he needs and walk toward the gravesite a wrecked man. Last week, I was a carefree bachelor with a loving family, my dream job, and a budding relationship with a hot nurse. I had everything under control.

Today, I am an instant father to four, orphan, teenage boys. And one has already run away. Father of the year, and I've only been on the job for a few days!

"Hey there!" calls the voice of an angel sent straight from heaven to comfort me at the perfect time. I look up into the most beautiful face I have ever seen.

"Claire! Wow! You came!" I grab her and pull her into a hug. It's very forward considering how conservative our relationship has been so far. I'm relieved when she returns the show of affection and holds me tight.

"I found someone to switch shifts with at the last minute, so I was running late and had to stand in the back," Claire tells me.

"Thank you for coming," I stammer as I release the long hug.

"I'm glad I can be here for you, Ry. I know this is probably the most difficult thing you've ever been through, and I couldn't imagine not being here to support my friend!" She's the only girl I've ever let shorten my name. To me four letters is short enough, but when Claire shortens it to Ry, I melt. I'm such a sap with her.

"So, I AM your friend," I love joking with her. On the other hand, I feel like a total hypocrite. I shouldn't be enjoying myself at a funeral while my life is a tornadic mess. I can't help it. She always puts a smile on my face.

"You are definitely my friend...maybe one day more," she winks, "but today, a friend here to support another friend. I want to be here for you, Ry. You're in a tight spot, and I want to help."

"Wow, Claire. You are...."

"Save the sweet talk for later. Let me help you and those boys through this right now." Claire cuts me off mid sentence, but for once I don't mind. She's right, we all need friends at a time like this. I glance at the gravesite and notice several empty chairs next to Nick and Jason.

"Sit with me?" I ask her. I really do need some support. I'm holding it together on the outside, but I'm an overwhelmed, shattered mess on the inside. I love that she knows me that well.

"Absolutely, Ryan," she smiles, and I realize that even during the storms of life, the sun is still shining. I take Claire's hand and lead her to our seats.

Claire is gorgeous, but I was more drawn to her gentle, honest demeanor towards her patients. I will forever be grateful for the care she gave Carey. Reid gave her my number in case she couldn't reach him regarding questions about Carey's care. She texted me everyday for almost two weeks to check on him after he was discharged. She would also ask about Sean even though he wasn't her patient. The first day she didn't text, I made it all the way until five in the afternoon before I sent her a playful text asking if she was tired of talking to me. We've texted and talked every day since. We have been on several amazing dates, but between her job as a nurse and mine as a cop, our free time rarely overlaps.

Even if things never go beyond short term friendship with Claire, she is a ray of light in this darkest hour. I will forever be grateful for her in this moment. As we take our seats, I scan the crowd hoping to find Sean and Carey. I am so worried about those boys. How am I going to get us through this?

Sean

There are so many emotions and thoughts running through me right now. I can't believe we're about to bury my father. I know Carey blames himself and that's why he ran, but no one else blames him. He thinks we hate him, but that couldn't be further from the truth. I wish he believed us. Dad loved all of us unconditionally. We *all* desperately love Carey. It's just that none of us knew how to help him. We waited too long to step up, and now it's too late. I rub Carey's dog tags as they lay heavy against my chest. It's all I have left of him. What if he never returns? How will I deal with losing Dad and Carey?

I hate funerals. I've been to more than my share. I buried my mom, then my grandparents, and now my dad. How is that even fair? I fear that one day soon I'll have to bury Carey.

The visitation last night was hard. I don't know why we had a church service for my dad. I can't remember the last time any of us set foot in a church. I hate all of the fake, sympathetic people offering condolences as if they know me, or my family. As if any of them can understand what I feel right now. We arrived at the cemetery a few minutes ago, and Ryan reluctantly left me in the car. Jason and Nick are already at the gravesite and most of our friends and family have arrived. They'll expect me to join them, but I can't seem to make my body move. I don't hear the door open, so the sound of her voice startles me.

"Hey. Can I sit here?"

"Shit!" I yell, grabbing my chest.

"Sorry. I didn't mean to scare you" she laughs a little at my expense, then smiles shyly, slipping into the seat next to me and closing the door.

"Um...it's okay?" I say, but it sounds more like a question. We sit in awkward silence for a few minutes. I have no idea what she wants or why she's even in the car. I've known Rachel my whole life, but we've never really talked. I mean, sure, we hung out as kids when her mom babysat us, but she was just the annoying girl in the mix; Seth's bratty, little sister. I guess that was before any of us boys noticed girls.

"So, I don't really know what to say, but you look like you could use a friend." Straight to the point with this girl.

"I don't need a fr...," I stop myself from being a complete asshole. She's just trying to be nice.

"Sorry. I'm fine."

"For what it's worth, I am sorry you're having to go through all of this. It isn't right. It isn't even fair. I've never lost anyone, so I won't pretend to understand." She says without looking at me.

"Wow...um...Thank you," I stammer.

"What?" She jerks her head toward me.

"You're the only person I've talked to in a week with a brain. I'm so sick of everyone's bullshit. 'I know this is hard.' 'You have to be strong.' 'He's in a better place.' I can't take it anymore. No one knows how I feel. No one gets to tell me that it will be okay or that my father is in a better place. He's fucking dead! That's not better. He would want to be here with his children. Not...not...DEAD!" I stop when I realize how loud I've been yelling. Rachel just sits there like it's all perfectly normal for me to have a mental breakdown in a car in a cemetery. She didn't even flinch. This girl is kind of amazing.

"Sorry," I mumble, "I shouldn't talk this way in front of a girl. My dad taught me better than this. He would be disappointed in me. I'm so sorry I ..."

"You have nothing to apologize for, Sean," she cuts off my apology, "You're right. People shouldn't be telling you any of those things. No one should assume they know how you feel."

"Don't take this the wrong way, but you shouldn't be the wisest person here."

"I'm wise beyond my years," she winks. I chuckle softly. Who is this girl and what happened to annoying little Rachel?

"You're funny. I like those blue highlights in your hair. They're cool." Wow, Sean, way to sound like a complete loser. She's going to think I am trying to pick her up or something.

"Don't look so freaked out. I like your green bangs." We share an awkward smile.

"Can I ask you something?" she almost whispers. I am afraid to say yes, but what else do you say when someone says that?

"Sure," I respond hesitantly.

"Do you know what happened between Seth and Carey? I know this isn't really the place to ask. It's just that I worry about Seth and he has..."

"I don't know what happened," I cut her off. "I don't care that you asked. I need to get my mind off of that," I say, pointing to the burial site.

"Seth has been a mess since our grandfather had his heart attack last May. When that stuff went down with Carey, he kind of turned into a jerk. Seth has never been mean to anyone, but lately none of us really want to be around him. He's just angry all the time," she says, sounding as sad as I feel.

"I've tried to get Carey to tell me something, but he's a closed book. I guess it's too late now," I shake my head.

"What do you mean?" Why can't I keep my stupid mouth shut? I did NOT mean to say that.

"Nothing," I clip.

"Sean, what is it?" The worry in her voice is evident.

"Nothing," I say again.

"You can tell me," she gently touches my arm. "I won't tell anyone. I realize you have no reason to

318

trust me, but I swear I will keep your secret," she vows.

"Carey left this morning. I don't know where he is or if he's coming back," I relent because for some reason, I trust Rachel.

"Wow, you lost your dad and your brother. Even with all these people hovering, you must feel completely alone."

"You're the only one who understands," I whisper. We sit in comfortable silence for a few minutes.

"Sean, I think we need to find our seats before the service starts."

"I don't know if..."

"You'll regret it if you stay here." I know she's right. I don't know what to make of this girl's raw honesty.

"Okay, let's go," I finally relent. We get out of the car and head toward the gathered crowd.

"Rachel?"

"Yeah, Sean."

"Would you mind sitting next to me?"

"Will there be room?"

"Yeah. The funeral home sat a chair for Carey, and he obviously can't handle it. You can have his seat." I know I sound bitter because, honestly, I am.

"If you're sure, I would love to be there for you." She actually sounds like she means her words. She takes my hand.

"Thank you," I stammer.

"That's what friends are for, Sean." Are we friends? I don't know if we are yet, but I think we will be. I can use another friend.

Carey

My life has been ripped apart over the past several months. And I did it to myself. I chose to reveal truths to my family that I should have kept secret. Reid is dead. Riley is dead. I spent two days in the hospital after Riley tried to kill me. My entire left side is bruised, and I have a concussion and eighteen stitches from hitting my head when Reid tackled me. There are twelve stitches in my right arm where a bullet grazed me. Reid took two bullets meant for me. I should be the one lying in the ground, not him. At least, his life was worth something.

We buried Reid this morning, but I didn't go with my family. It isn't right that he is dead, and I'm not. I can't face my family and their friends knowing this is all my fault. I sat under a willow tree on the hill on the far side of the cemetery and watched them put Reid in the ground. Everyone has been gone for hours, but I'm still glued to this spot. I can't take my eyes off of the mound of dirt covering the only father I have ever known. He did everything to save me from myself and my choices. Look where that got us.

"Carey," I jump when a voice startles me. I didn't think anyone knew I was here. I don't acknowledge his presence. "Look, I'm sorry. My intention was never to hurt you or push you away. I was in a bad place this summer and made some mistakes, but I'm getting better. You're in a bad place now."

"What do you want from me, Seth?" I ask angrily. What is he doing here? I bet Sean sent him. I saw them talking at the funeral.

"I just want to help you. Talk to me. You don't have to do this."

"Do what?" I question, mocking the concern in his voice.

"Run," he says, indicating the duffle bag and backpack beside me.

"Yes, I do. You can't save me, Seth. Stop trying," I get up, and put the backpack on my shoulders.

"Carey, please don't do this. You're my best friend. Your brothers need you. Sean needs you."

"No, they don't. I've caused too much damage," I ignore the friend comment on purpose. I believe him, but I'm still too angry to forgive him.

"Dammit, Carey! Listen to me," he says, grabbing my arm.

"Keep your fucking hands off of me unless you want another broken nose," I shove Seth into the tree behind him. His back hits hard, and it had to have knocked the breath out of him.

"I'm not ready to make nice." I mumble as I pick up the duffle bag and walk away without looking back. He doesn't try to stop me again.

It's getting late, and the sun is starting to set as I make my way through town, walking past all of the places I grew up calling home; Miss Mel's Diner where they make the best cherry pie in the world, the playground where I broke my first bone, and the high school that I will never graduate from. I pull the hoodie down over my eyes a little as I pass a few people. The last thing I need is to be recognized. I'll never be able to face my family or the people in this small town again. There have only been three murders in the past ten years. Two were all my fault: my mom because I didn't say anything and Reid because I did. Not exactly a brand I want on my family, but one I brought to their doorstep.

I took the long way, walking all the way around the island. Continuing on to the beach, I slowly pass The Reading Corner, my favorite place in the world. Even getting lost in all of those books couldn't save me.

Without realizing it, I find myself standing on the dunes behind my childhood home. The last place we were together as a family. The last place Reid was alive.

The house is dark, empty. How can it look so cold and desolate when it's only been a few days?

I walk through the house gathering a few personal items. Realizing this will be the last time I ever set foot in this house is proving to be more difficult than I could have ever imagined. When I step into the bedroom Sean and I shared, unexpected emotions almost knock me down. Knowing I'm leaving Sean here alone makes it hard to walk away, but I have to get out of this town before I cause anymore damage.

Police tape still surrounds the yard. I look down the palm tree lined street. Sea Turtle Way was once a happy place. A place I felt safe. A place where I had friends, brothers, and family. All of that is gone now. I've lost everyone and everything that was good in my life. I adjust the backpack on my shoulder and follow Ocean Boulevard to where it meets Shore Drive. It's several miles to Route 1. I take my time because time is all I have now. My legs are tired when I pass the sign thanking me for visiting Paradise Cove. I don't look back as I walk away from this life. Maybe now I can finally escape.

Coming Soon

In The Light in the Darkest Hour Series

Book Two: The Fighter's Stance

Book Three: Beyond the Blackboard

Acknowledgements

We would like to thank the following people for their support during this adventure.

First and foremost we need to humbly thank each other for resisting the urges to strangle one another in the process of creating this book.

Our husbands, Rick and Nathan, for their constant support and love. We know it hasn't been an easy road, but we are grateful for everything you have done for us.

Our children, Coleman, Anders, Morgan, Grady, and Owen for your love and understanding. It has been a two-year rollercoaster, and we are blessed to have each of you in our lives.

Our beta readers, Rick and Shirley for the feedback and advice. We appreciate you helping us from the beginning.

Our editor, Kim Morgan, for your feedback, advice, criticism, and support. You were our cheerleader from the moment you knew we were writing a book. You were our friend long before our editor, and we appreciate all the hours and long nights you put into helping make our book a success.

Our friends and family for their love and support even when we kept the book a secret. Thank you for understanding all of those nights we were "busy" and couldn't go out to dinner, return a text, or talk on the phone. Thank you for still loving us!

CPSIA information can be obtained
at www.ICGtesting.com
Printed in the USA
LVHW041024180319
611004LV00009B/624